W9-BIW-570

# THE SMILER
# WITH THE KNIFE

Also available in Perennial Mystery Library
by Nicholas Blake:

THE DREADFUL HOLLOW
END OF CHAPTER
THE WHISPER IN THE GLOOM

# THE SMILER
# WITH THE KNIFE

## Nicholas Blake

PERENNIAL LIBRARY

Harper & Row, Publishers, New York
Cambridge, Philadelphia, San Francisco, Washington
London, Mexico City, São Paulo, Singapore, Sydney

A hardcover edition of this book was originally published in 1939 by Harper & Brothers.

THE SMILER WITH THE KNIFE. Copyright 1939 by C. Day Lewis. All rights reserved. Printed in the United States of America. No part of this book may be used or reproduced in any manner whatsoever without written permission except in the case of brief quotations embodied in critical articles and reviews. For information address Harper & Row, Publishers, Inc., 10 East 53rd Street, New York, N.Y. 10022. Published simultaneously in Canada by Fitzhenry & Whiteside Limited, Toronto.

First PERENNIAL LIBRARY edition published 1978. Reissued in 1988.

LIBRARY OF CONGRESS CATALOG CARD NUMBER: 87-46120

ISBN: 0-06-080457-2 (pbk.).

88 89 90 91 92 OPM 10 9 8 7 6 5 4 3 2 1

"Ther saugh I first the derke imagining
Of felonye, and al the compassing;
The smyler with the knyf under the cloke;
The shepne brenning with the blake smoke;
The treson of the mordring in the bedde;
The open werre, with woundes al bibledde."

CHAUCER: *The Knight's Tale*

# Contents

# THE SMILER
# WITH THE KNIFE

# 1.  The Episode of the Major's Mother

A morning in January. Sunlight welled in through the low windows of the cottage, giving the beams, the great stone fireplace, the Dutch rushmats on the flagged floor a look of freshness as if they had been spring-cleaned. After the constant rain of the last few months, this sunshine was more than a blessing—it was a miracle. Living in the country, thought Georgia, you really are a part of the seasons: in the dark months you hibernate, the blood slows down, the mind goes sluggish; and then one morning something stirs in the air, the sun comes through, and life begins to move at a different tempo. I must be getting domesticated, though, she thought, because I don't want to leave here at all, ever, and I believe I never shall. The idea was so odd that she stopped in the middle of stirring her tea, her hand remaining poised over the cup. Always, until now, when the first whisper of spring made itself heard, Georgia had felt restless: something in the distance seemed to tug at her imagination and her body, and as often as not she would yield to it and go traipsing off on one of those journeys that had made her the most famous woman traveller of her day.

Today, she did not know whether to be glad or sorry that this influence was not felt. Perhaps it's just that I'm getting old, she said to herself; after all, I'm thirty-seven, and at that age a female ought to be sobering up.

She was roused from her day-dream by Nigel, who put his hand over hers and made her swish the spoon round in the tea-cup.

"Shall I draw the curtains?" he asked politely.

"Draw the curtains?"

"Yes. You looked as if you'd had a touch of the sun."

Georgia laughed. Dear Nigel—he always knows what's in my mind. She said, "You're not quite right this time, though. I was thinking that I'm getting domesticated. Are *you* still glad we came here?"

"Mm. I must say I had my doubts these last few months. Living in the country is one thing, and living on a half-submerged derelict is another."

"Oh, it wasn't quite as bad as that."

"My dear, the house was positively awash. Gales beating up the valley, all our timbers shivering, windows streaming with rain. When *did* you last manage to see out of those windows?

"You look all the better for it," said Georgia, glancing affectionately at her husband.

"The sedentary life has always suited me. And of course there's a certain moral dignity attached to living in these outposts of empire."

"What I can't understand is how you manage to thrive on doing nothing."

"I'm not doing nothing. I'm translating Hesiod."

"I mean never taking any exercise or—"

2

"What d'you mean—never taking exercise? Don't I walk down to the pub every evening? If you expect me to come splodging through the mud with you every afternoon as well—"

"I like this place, mud or no mud," Georgia said dreamily. "I shall settle down here. Deeper and deeper. Like a turnip."

"Knowing you, I should say that was improbable. And now let's see what news there is from civilization."

He began to open his letters. The post had brought nothing for Georgia but a seed-catalogue, in which she was soon immersed. Presently she giggled. "Listen to this. 'The Duchesse de Parma is very showy, a splendid bedder, orange-red edged with yellow.' Shall we have the Duchesse in the garden? She sounds just your type."

"Here's an extraordinary communication," said Nigel a few minutes later.

"Oh, dear," Georgia sighed. That was the worst of being married to a private investigator. You never knew when a letter would come out of the blue, and Nigel be dragged into some queer criminal tangle. Not that they really needed the substantial fees he charged, either. It was just his insatiable curiosity that led him into one case after another. "What is it this time? Murder? Or a bit of blackmail?"

"Oh, neither. It's our hedge."

"Hedge? What—?"

"Listen, and I'll tell you." Holding up the printed form, Nigel Strangeways began to read out, " 'Pursuant to the provisions of an act of Parliament—pom pom pom—I, the undersigned, the Surveyor of Highways—pom pom—do hereby give you notice, and require you forthwith to cut, prune and trim your hedges next adjoining the County Roads—pom pom—and also to pare

3

the sides of such hedges close to the bank, and the growth on the top of such hedges at least perpendicular from the Comb, and to cut down, prune or lop the branches of trees, bushes and shrubs—pom pom pom *pom*—in such manner that the said Roads shall not be prejudiced by the shade thereof, and that the Sun and Wind may not be excluded therefrom to the damage thereof, and to remove the material cut therefrom.' Pom. Isn't that superb? The tongue that Milton spoke. Who'd have thought there was such poetry in the soul of a Surveyor of Highways? 'that the said Roads shall not be prejudiced by the shade thereof, and that the Sun and Wind may not be excluded therefrom.' "

Nigel began singing the phrases to the tune of Purcell's Chant.

"What happens if we disobey the S. of H.?"

"We get complained of to a Justice of the Peace."

"Well, thank goodness," said Georgia. "I thought at first it was another bit of trouble on the way."

And indeed it was, though neither of them could possibly have foreseen it. It was not, after all, reasonable to suppose that a notice from a Rural District Council could cause any one much trouble—let alone alter the course of history, or that England might be saved by the cutting of a hedge. Yet so it turned out. Looking back on it all afterwards, Georgia seemed to see those enormous events, like the angels of the Schoolmen standing on pin-points, balanced upon a few tiny and precarious ifs. If we had taken a cottage in any other county in England, we shouldn't have had to pare the hedge ourselves, for Devonshire is the only county where landowners still have to cut their own hedges on the road side. If the sun had not come out that morning, I'd probably have left the hedge for the gardener to do.

If any one else had cut it, he'd probably not have noticed the locket—Nigel always said I have eyes like a hawk—poor darling, he's so short-sighted himself: and, even if it had been found, only a person of Nigel's inquisitiveness would have bothered to give it more than one glance. And, talking of inquisitiveness, what about the magpie?—it must surely have been a magpie that started the whole thing. Yes, if that anonymous magpie hadn't had an attack of kleptomania, the locket would never have got into the hedge. Which only goes to show that crime does sometimes pay. . . .

The sun poured in through the cottage window, increasing the pallor of Nigel's face. Like many other things about him—his untidy, tow-coloured hair, for instance, or the childish pout of his underlip—this pallor was deceptive. His health was far from delicate, his character not in the very least childish: you realized the latter as soon as you looked at his eyes, which were sane, kindly, a little detached, but liable at any moment to narrow and spark into the most concentrated attention. Georgia knew well enough what a self-sufficient creature he was; yet she liked sometimes to pretend that he needed looking after, and he played up to her pretence with the same subdued, affectionate amusement.

She was thinking now, how could I ever leave Nigel? He does need me. But supposing I get the itch to travel again? On a day like this, it might come over me any minute. I must be forearmed against it.

"I think I'll have a go at the hedge myself," she said. "This morning."

"Mm." Nigel's face was buried in the newspaper. Georgia felt a sudden impulse to make him acknowledge her mood, to shake him out of his gentle security.

"Would you mind very much if I left you, Nigel?"

5

He took off his horn-rimmed glasses and gazed at her with interest. "For another man, do you mean? I should say I'd be very cross indeed."

"Don't be silly. Went on my travels again, I mean."

"Have any particular expedition in mind?"

"Not exactly. But—"

"I suppose I'd get on all right," said Nigel. "It'd seem a long time, though, till you came back."

Georgia leant over him, kissed the top of his head. "Oh, I'm glad I married you and no one else," she whispered.

Yes, she thought a few minutes later, as she put on her old gardening coat and loose leather gloves, I *am* lucky. There's no other man in the world who could have resisted pointing out my inconsistency—first saying I wanted to be a turnip and a moment later raving about going off to the ends of the earth. What can it be that Nigel finds attractive about me, she wondered, happily studying in her mirror the small, irregular features of a face that could change so quickly from vivacity to a plaintive, appealing ugliness. "She looks like the ghost of an organ-grinder's monkey," one of their friends had once said. Pretty accurate, and not altogether unflattering, she thought, grimacing at herself. She was to find out before long how queerly prophetic that absurd conversation with Nigel had been.

For the present, though, there was nothing but the sunlight and the fields folding down from the hill above like the fall of a green dress. The lane ran from the village past their cottage over the brow of the hill; you could get to the sea that way, after five miles of rough going; but motorists usually gave one look at its fearful gradients and—if they succeeded in turning their car—scurried back to the main road. Where she stood, on the high bank above the lane, Georgia could see the thatched, whitewashed cottage that seemed to have dug itself out a niche in the hillside, the silver coils of the river in the valley below, and beyond it a tumble of green and brown hills ranging up towards the horizon. Everything was peaceful. There was no sound or movement but the distant rattle of an express that hurried westward on the far side of the valley, white smoke laid along its back like an ostrich feather. Georgia took up her bill-hook and attacked the hedge.

Nigel found her there when he strolled out of the house an hour later. He stood in the lane, looking up at her. Dark hair fell about her face; the exercise had brought a carnation flush to her pale brown skin; she attacked the hedge with a kind of savage grace, unaware for a moment that he was watching her.

"Still hacking our way through the primeval undergrowth?" he commented politely.

She turned quickly, involuntarily smoothing back the hair from her face. "Goodness! It's hard work. I must look like Medusa."

"If ivory could blush, it would look like you."

Georgia jumped down from the bank into the lane. One foot, slipping back, displaced the olive and coppery sediment of leaves that lay in the ditch. As she recovered herself, Georgia's eye caught a dull gleam among the leaves. She bent down and picked up a small, round metal object, tarnished by the weather to the colour of a decaying leaf.

"Look what I've found. Buried treasure."

Nigel took it, examined it curiously. "Some sort of a locket, isn't it? A very cheap one, I should think Woolworth's. I wonder how it got there."

"Folk courting under the hedge. What a pity—I

7

thought it was real gold at first. Chuck it away."

"No," said Nigel, "I'd like to see what there is inside."

"Darling, you're incorrigible, you really are. All you'll find is a piece of greasy hair or a photo of some pop-eyed peasant."

"It's going to be quite a job to get it opened," said Nigel absent-mindedly, feeling in his pockets. "My penknife's indoors somewhere."

"Don't cut yourself," she called out after him, half-seriously. Nigel was not too clever with his hands.

When she came in to prepare lunch, Nigel was sitting at his desk.

"I say, what do you suppose 'E.B.' stands for?" he said over his shoulder.

"Early bird," Georgia suggested.

He handed her a small paper disk, a little discoloured, but showing plainly a Union Jack and the letters E.B. stamped on it.

"No, it must be Eat British," she said. "Where did you find it?"

"It was in the locket. And this too."

Georgia looked down at the thing he put in her hand—a round piece of cardboard, a daguerreotype depicting the face of a young woman with heavily marked eyebrows, and gleaming black hair parted in the middle and falling to her bare shoulders in thick corkscrew curls. The head, tilted a little to one side, gave a touch of coquetry to her expression, softening the brooding intelligence of mouth and eyes. In line, the face was an oval of singular purity.

"She's a beauty, isn't she? What's she doing with a Union Jack in this trashy locket?"

"That's just what I was wondering," said Nigel. "You see, the odd thing is that the flag was sandwiched

8

between the picture and a cardboard back. If the whole thing hadn't been a bit damp, I'd never have noticed the join. Why should the owner want to conceal the Union Jack inside his beautiful relative?"

"What a snooper you are! Well, I expect there's some quite simple explanation. Come and have lunch."

"I'll just stick the whole dingus together again." Nigel pasted the rims of the two disks, put the paper flag between them, fitted them inside the locket and tossed it down on his desk. There it lay for a couple of days, and might have lain for months if Fate, in the improbable guise of the Folyton Bell-Ringers, had not once again taken a hand.

The Strangeways had passed the time of day quite often with Major Keston as he passed their cottage to and from his house over the hill. They knew that he had built this house two years before, and although a comparative new-comer to the village was already a power in it. But he had shown no sign yet of extending hospitality to them, and they for their part did not suppose he would be at all their sort. It was therefore a surprise when he landed up at the door with his bull-terrier that evening—a small, hard-bitten figure of a man with a slightly aggressive manner and the kind of eyes that meant, in Nigel's experience, either a bad liver or a permanent grievance.

"See you've settled in all right," he remarked, glancing round the room with a curiosity that contrived to be both furtive and faintly impudent. "Snug little billet, this. How does the Mem like country life?"

Nigel gathered he was referring to Georgia. "Oh, very well, thanks. She'll be down in a minute. Will you have a drink?"

"Thanks, no. Don't touch it."

It must be a grievance then, thought Nigel, not a bad

liver. Major Keston went on hurriedly, as if apologetic for his curtness:

"Ought to have called before. Tell you the truth I was a bit scared. Your Mem's a celebrated woman, I mean. Wouldn't expect her to have much time for simple folk like us."

So that's it, thought Nigel: he resents our coming to his village—he's afraid the limelight will be diverted from him to Georgia.

"I don't think you'll find her very terrifying," he said equably.

They discussed the weather for a little. Then Major Keston intimated that one object of his visit was to touch them for a subscription to the village bell-ringers' fund. Nigel went over to his desk, switching on the light above it to look for the treasury notes that were generally kept loose in a pigeon-hole there. The pigeon-hole, however, was empty this evening, and Nigel started to go upstairs for the notecase he had left on his chest-of-drawers.

On the wall under the staircase hung a convex mirror. As he neared it, Nigel noticed the major's reflection. Major Keston was certainly a quick mover: already he was standing, though Nigel had not heard a sound behind him, close to the desk. The manikin in the mirror, as Nigel passed, half-raised its miniature, brilliant hand; then, as if thinking better of it, turned away and flashed silently back to the fireplace.

He might at least wait till I'm out of the room before he starts rifling my desk, thought Nigel, who was very, very seldom surprised by the vagaries of human nature. And I don't see why I should give him another opportunity.

Instead of going upstairs, he called out to Georgia to bring the notecase down with her. Presently she appeared, and Nigel introduced Major Keston. It always amused him to see her greeting strangers. She possessed an instinct, sharpened by her experience in strange places among strange peoples, for instantly reacting to the real nature of those she was meeting for the first time. It was not often that she took an immediate dislike to someone; but, when she did, it was always proved to be justified in the long run. On such occasions her physical sense of distaste, of repulsion, was so strong that she felt it must be written up in neon lights all over her face, and to conceal this she would assume a gushing, hostessy manner entirely foreign to her.

She was gushing now, as Nigel observed with secret amusement. And the leathery little man seemed to like it.

"I'm *so* glad you looked in, Major Keston. We've both been wanting to meet you properly, get to know you. We've heard so much about you in the village."

Georgia chattered away. The major visibly thawed. Presently he said:

"Hope you don't mind my mentioning it, Strangeways. I noticed you went to that desk over there for money. If I may say so, I shouldn't keep money there, not just at present. Desk too easily opened. Been a lot of burglaries around here lately—amateurish affairs, rather. That desk just the sort of thing the fella would make for."

"Thanks for the tip. I don't think it would pay any burglar to have a stab at us, though. My wife's a very light sleeper, and a first-class revolver-shot."

Georgia giggled nervously. "Yes, I have shot one or two people. In self-defence, of course." Which was in fact quite true.

Major Keston's pebbly little eyes flickered. He seemed momentarily at a loss. Then he said:

11

"I suppose you're quite handy with a gun, too, Strangeways? Have to be, in your job."

"My job?" Nigel stared at him blankly: he did not like it to be common property that he was a private detective; his name never appeared in the papers in connection with any case he undertook, and he did not see how the major could have got on to it.

"Well, dash it, arresting murderers and so forth."

"Oh, I don't do any of that. I leave arrests to the police. I'm terrified of firearms," replied Nigel in his mimsiest voice.

Major Keston's glance was eloquent of contempt. The subject, however, seemed to have given him his cue. He proceeded to question them, with an effrontery that Nigel found unpleasantly dictatorial, as to why they had come to live in such a remote part of the country. Georgia chattered away enthusiastically about the beauties of Devonshire, the rewards of the simple life, her desire to get away from their rackety existence in London, and the rest of it. After a while, their visitor appeared to be satisfied, though Nigel could scarcely restrain himself from asking why they should need a permit before settling down in the major's village.

At last Major Keston rose to take his leave. As he did so, his eye lighted upon the desk. He exclaimed:

"God bless my soul! What's that there? I believe it's my locket. Yes, it is. Where ever did you find it? It's been missing since last spring."

Georgia explained. "I'm afraid we opened it. We thought it might give some clue to the owner. But there was nothing inside except an old photograph."

"Yes," said the major. His voice sounded subtly different to Nigel. "My mother, as a matter of fact."

12

Georgia's eyes opened wide. She paused a moment, then said quickly:

"Your mother? What a beautiful woman! We were immensely taken with her—weren't we, Nigel? I suppose she was quite young when this was done?"

"Yes. I believe so." The major went on gruffly, "Must've been. Remember her looking like that when I was a boy, coming to say good-night to me before she went out to parties. All togged up, y'know. Hrr'm. Poor soul, she died when I was quite young. Consumption."

"Do you mind if I have just one more little look at her?" asked Georgia. Now why, Nigel wondered, has she gone all kittenish? Georgia opened the locket, took out the daguerreotype and strolled over to the fireplace to see it in a better light. The next moment she exclaimed, "Oh, how clumsy I am!" She had let the picture fall into the coal-scuttle. The major bent down politely to pick it up, but she was before him. She rescued it, and began rubbing it briskly with her handkerchief.

"I'm *so* sorry. There. I think she's all right now. I'm afraid the locket's been spoilt by lying in that ditch. Poor darling," Georgia burbled, "covered up with leaves like the Babes in the Wood. How glad you must be to get her back!"

The major's hand was indeed trembling with emotion as she put the locket into it. "Very grateful," he muttered. His eyes, shamefast yet still touched with suspicions, swivelled uneasily from Georgia to Nigel. All at once he barked, "A bird! That's what it must have been. A damned magpie."

"Stole it, you mean?" asked Nigel.

"That's right. A lot of the brutes up my way. Notice an old nest anywhere above the place you found it?"

13

Georgia shook her head. "There are a couple of trees there, though."

"Ah, that's it, depend upon it." The major seemed extraordinarily relieved to have got to the root of the matter.

When the sound of his footsteps, stumping up the lane, had died away, Nigel took Georgia by her two wrists and shook her.

"Now why did you give that sickening display of ingenuousness, my sweet? And why did the helpless little woman deliberately drop the major's mother into the coal-scuttle?"

"Oh, Nigel, didn't you see? Whoever that beautiful lady may have been, *one person she couldn't possibly be is the major's mother.* That's why I dropped her, I didn't want the major to find out we'd opened her up, the paste you put on might look too fresh, that's why I rubbed in coal-dust well around the rim, he's an abominable creature and gave me gooseflesh, but not such a fool as he'd like us to think, so—"

"Here, one thing at a time," Nigel interrupted his wife's outburst. "Why couldn't she be the major's mother?"

"The corkscrew curls. That style of coiffure went out about 1850. Our mendacious major claims to have seen her like that as a child. Which would make him anything from eighty to a hundred years old today. It won't add up."

"Fancy-dress, perhaps?" Nigel suggested. "No, of course not; he gave the impression it was her normal appearance in the evening, going out to parties. Well, if she wasn't his mother, why was he so darned keen to get the locket back? Presumably the Union Jack with E.B. on it is the important thing. Yes, and at first he didn't want us to connect him with the locket at all. Hence the burglary scare."

"Don't talk in shorthand, darling."

Nigel told her what he had seen in the convex mirror. "When he noticed the locket lying on my desk, his first impulse was to grab it. He realized at once, however, that we might connect him with its disappearance. His next move was to hand us a local burglar—'amateurish' was a good touch: he meant to prepare our minds for a burglary. No doubt he intended to break in himself one of these dark nights, take the locket, and a few other things to cover up its loss—"

"Goodness! Time must hang heavily on their hands here if that's his idea of winter sports!"

"—but when I said you were a light sleeper, and you weighed in with that airy reminiscence about the people you'd bumped off—well, he thought better of it. So he invented his mother."

Georgia stared at him, her brow wrinkled. "But, Nigel, it's fantastic. I admit I didn't *like* Major Keston, but—"

"I noticed that." Nigel smiled absently. "You know, if it was his locket, and there's some secret attached to it, he'd surely not have slipped up over the daguerreotype. Therefore the locket must belong to someone else, someone he knows, and the major is desperately keen to lay his hands on it. What does that suggest?"

"Search me."

"Blackmail, my love. I really think I shall have to inquire a little further into these goings-on."

"Oh, Nigel," Georgia wailed. "*Must* you? Just when we're settling down, and—"

"Well, it won't affect you. Your job was over when you'd spotted the ringlets."

But, for once, Nigel was wildly, abysmally wrong.

# 2. The Episode of the Misguided Tramps

"I think I'll pop down to the Green Lion and tap the fountain head," said Nigel the next evening. "If we go now, we'll probably find Harry alone: the boys don't start trooping in till seven o'clock generally."

" 'We'? Last night you said I'd done my part of the job."

"Oh, but you're dying to find out more about the mysterious major, now aren't you? You can just sit and wag your ears while I do the talking."

Five minutes later they were sitting in the bar of the Green Lion, toasting their feet at a blazing fire. Georgia, who had acquired a taste for the rough, West-country cider, together with a healthy respect for its potency, held a mug of it between her hands.

"Good luck, Harry," she said, taking a sip. The Green Lion was none of your fancy town pubs, all chromium and quick ones: here, you settled down on a hard bench for the evening, spinning out your modest pint or two to last three hours of deliberate drinking and even more

16

deliberate conversation. Silence itself was sociable here. It reminded Georgia of a council of war she had once attended among the Melanesian islanders. After squatting completely mum for half an hour or so in the hut, the warriors had dispersed. Georgia had asked their chief when the council of war was to be held. "We've just finished," he replied.

Telepathy seemed to be the mode in the Green Lion, too, for Harry Luce suddenly broke the companionable silence with:

"I hear you've had a visit from Major Keston."

"News travels fast in Folyton."

"Oh, he were in here day before yesterday, wasting my time with a lot of daft questions about you. 'Why, damn *me*,' I says to en, 'if thee wants to know so much about them, why don't thee go and ask them theself? 'Tis no concern of I,' I says. So he said he would."

"And you put two and two together? But I'm surprised at his coming in here. He told me he didn't drink."

An expression of righteous indignation came over Harry's thin, ferrety face. He flicked cigarette-ash off his waistcoat and spat volubly into the fire.

"No more he does. Stands at my bar twenty minutes by the clock and don't buy even a packet of Woodbines. 'Tis not right—not to my way of thinking."

"Pretty popular in the district, isn't he?"

"He is, and he isn't. He's in with the farmers, and the gentry calls up to Yarnold Farm quite a bit, so they do say. But he wants to rule the roost—he's too bossy for we down here. Mind *you*, when he comes first, us rings the joybells for en—as you might say—seeing his family used to be squires in Folyton—"

"I never realized that," Nigel interrupted. "I thought he was a new-comer."

"He was, and he wasn't," Harry replied deliberately. "The Kestons haven't lived here for two generations now, and Folyton House has been empty of late. Now what I wants to know, Mr. Strangeways and Madam, is this—why didn't he take Folyton House, if he wanted to set himself up as squire?"

"Couldn't afford it, perhaps."

"Why, damn *me*, he must have spent thousands rebuilding Yarnold Farm. He has the money, for certain. There's another thing, now. He used local labour for that job, but last year, when he wanted to add on another bit, he brought in a lot of foreigners to do it."

"Foreigners?"

"From London, or some such. Us didn't have no truck with they. 'Tweren't right, not to my way of thinking. Wonderful workshop he's built himself up there, so they do say. Wonderful man with his hands."

"We must walk over and have a look at it."

"Don't thee go by night then," said Harry, winking slyly at Georgia.

"Why ever not?"

"Has thee never heard of the ghoost up to Yarnold Cross? Thee'd best ask Joe here. None of us likes to go past the cross at night, do us, Joe?"

Joe Sweetbred, who during this conversation had taken his usual place by the fireside, poked the fire with his stick and poured out his cider, which had been warming in a saucepan there. He was a very old man and—to Georgia's eye—indistinguishable from one of those extras, dressed up to look like rustic ancients for a British quota film, who enliven the proceedings by bursting out every now and then into Somerset folksongs in perfect harmony and Portland Place accents. Joe's voice, however, failed to preserve the illusion. It was thickened by age, an almost unintelligible dialect, and what seemed to Georgia an all-time high in adenoidal growth.

"Yis, maaster, yes, 'tes right," Joe Sweetbred whined vivaciously. "Ghoost up to Yaarnold Cross. I seen en. Heh-heh! Churning butter. Poor maid."

"Maybe she'm keeping herself warm," Harry suggested. "Her was dairymaid up to Yarnold Farm, see?—a hundred years ago, 'twould be. Her started making eyes at farmer, see? So farmer's wife—"

Joe chipped in—"Her took a stake, and her sharpened he, and her stuck he in maid's eyes. Maid rushes out of house, yowling fit to bust, and falls down girt well, poor soul, heh-heh. Now she'm walking up along at cross-roads. I seen en."

"They bricked up the well," Harry added, "but naught went right for they after that. They left the farm and it fell down in ruins. So 'twas."

"Has any one seen this ghost lately?" Georgia inquired.

"Young Henry Tule, he seen en. He was courting and he went up over the cross one night. That was after Major Keston came, weren't it, Joe? Came fair busting down the hill on his bike. 'I seen en,' he yells. So white as a sheet he was. Mind *you*, young Henry's a bit simple. Did you ever hear about the time he got into the tub?"

"No."

"Well, this young Tule, he was feeling poorly one day. So he goes to the doctor, and then he comes home and eats a hell of a great dinner. After dinner he goes out into the yard, and presently his mother hears him calling. Out she pops, and finds young Henry sitting stark naked in a tub of water. 'What's thee doing in tub?' says she. 'Hell,' says he, 'will thee fetch thic bottle! Doctor told I to take medicine three times a day, after meals, in water.' In water, see?—so he gets into tub. True as I'm standing here. Damn *me*, it was a laugh. Young Henry's a most simple chap, no doubt of it."

When Harry got launched on the local folklore, there was no holding him. After a little, since the subject of Major Keston seemed to be exhausted, Georgia and Nigel started home.

"I wish I could remember—I'm sure I've heard something about the major before," said Georgia. "Where did he come from? It's queer Harry not saying anything about that, considering he's a sort of walking Who's Who for the neighbourhood."

"Let's go up to Yarnold Farm tomorrow and ask him. He seems to have been inquisitive enough about us. About time we had a return match."

So the next afternoon saw them walking up the lane that led to Yarnold Cross. At the top of the hill, it veered to the right and stretched in front of them along the ridge. Already the sky beyond held that possessed and luminous look which tells the traveller he is nearing the sea. Instinctively, though they were breathing hard from the sharp climb, they quickened their pace—Nigel walking with his ungainly, ostrich stride, Georgia moving with the beauty and tireless swing of an athlete. A quarter of a mile brought them to the cross. Here they paused for a moment while Georgia took their bearings. Ahead, the lane dodged downhill in a series of steep, narrow turns to the main road which swung inland here from the coast. To their left, another lane wandered off towards the Exeter road, which farther west passed through their own village. The right-hand road, little better than a stony track, dropped down sharply into the combe where Yarnold Farm was situated. Yarnold

Cross was the end of this inland promontory, from which the brown and green hills fall away on three sides. Hardly aware that she was doing so, Georgia drew a sketch-map of the place in her mind's eye. Then they turned right, and in a couple of minutes, heralded by a loud barking of dogs, were standing outside Major Keston's door.

While they waited for their ring to be answered, they had ample leisure to look around them. Some derelict outbuildings were the only survival of the old Yarnold Farm that they could see. The new house, built of brick and roofed with green tiles, would have graced a high-class, residential suburb: in this desolate spot, however, it looked not so much pretentious as absurd—like a poster advertising a luxury hotel in some remote country station. The suburban illusion stretched as far as the front lawn, which was plotted out primly with flower-beds and concrete paths: beyond these it faded out into a wilderness of unkempt hedges and rank pasture. The house stood, like a wealthy urban parvenu in plus fours, staring both patronizingly and ignorantly at the combe that rolled away to the south, turning its back on the wooded slopes protecting it to the east and north.

"Do you think he's out?" asked Nigel.

"Ring again. I say, where d'you suppose the well is—the one the poor maid fell into, heh-heh?"

"Round at the back somewhere, I expect."

At this moment, the door was opened by a tall, bleak-faced woman, formidable enough—Georgia thought—to be a reincarnation of the farmer's wife who had sharpened a stake and given that pretty dairymaid one in the eye. Surveying them for a moment, with a faintly puzzled expression, she said:

21

"You're wanting Major Keston? Step this way. You're new here, aren't you?"

Involuntarily Georgia glanced down at her trim, green Harris-tweed suit. What was wrong with it? Why should the woman be eyeing it so curiously? And "you're new here" was surely a peculiar conversational gambit? She had no time to speculate on these questions, for they were shown into an unexpectedly attractive room, cheerful with brick fireplace, log fire and bright linen curtains. A strangely feminine room, thought Georgia, which it was difficult to connect with the major or his ramrod-backed housekeeper. Nigel was already on the prowl, poking his nose into the shelf of novels, the mantelpiece ornaments, the pile of Victorian ballads on the upright piano. "This," he muttered to himself, "is a remarkably noncommittal room. Not so much *rus in urbe* as *suburbia in rure*."

"Hallo, hallo!" Major Keston entered, briskly rubbing his hands. "Come to see my little grey home in the west? Had tea? No? Good, I'll see what Mrs. Raikes can rake up, what?"

Georgia and Nigel glanced at each other, stunned by this explosion of affability. What's come over the man? Georgia asked herself, as he popped up and down, pressing cakes on her, poking the fire, rearranging the screen at her back. Have I made a hit? Or are these preliminary moves in the blackmail game? No, that's just Nigel's professional suspiciousness. But there is something weaselly about Major Keston—and a weasel seeking to ingratiate itself is certainly a bit weird.

Nigel was saying, "You've been out east, haven't you, Major?"

"Oh, yes. Rather. Then I got a legacy, sent in my

22

papers, came back to England. My family used to live here, at the Manor, y'know."

Did it all come a little too pat? Georgia wondered. The major's reply had been on the surface quite open, yet it had given remarkably little away. Nigel threw her a significant glance: he wanted her to return his lead.

"Whereabouts were you stationed?" she asked. "I've knocked about in the east myself quite a bit."

Had she imagined it, or did a certain wariness come into his face—a suggestion of the weasel, nose quivering, snuffing danger? He said:

"India. I was in the police, actually. Well, what about having a look round my little place?"

"Oh, yes. I'd love to. You've made it awfully comfortable." Georgia smiled at him charmingly. Nothing in her attentive, brown face betrayed the fact that she had just remembered what it was she had heard about Major Keston.

He showed them round with the rather perfunctory air of a house-agent conducting a pair of unpromising clients. Dining-room, kitchen, study: four or five bedrooms upstairs. Major Keston flung open doors, switched on lights, allowed them a glance and then hustled them on to the next room. It was a large house for so small a household. When they were down in the hall again, Major Keston paused meaningly. He evidently was hinting that it was time for them to go, but Nigel somehow failed to take the hint.

"I hear you've a wonderful workshop," he said. "Harry Luce told us."

"Not so bad. Need it, y'know, living in a place like this. The locals are a pretty lazy, inefficient lot. Show you over some time, if you're interested. Bit dark now."

Nigel glanced at his wife again. The sympathy

between them was so perfect that she understood at once what he wanted. She drifted into the drawing-room, on the pretext of fetching her gloves, and began to chatter again. Their host became visibly more fidgety. At last he said:

"Well, don't want to speed the parting guest and all that. But I'm going out to dinner tonight. Black tie affair. Got to change."

"Oh, I'm *so* sorry. Look, Nigel, it's nearly six o'clock." Georgia indicated the clock on the mantelpiece with every appearance of horror and contrition. "How thoughtless of us. The time has gone so quickly. Now we really must be off. A charming house, Major Keston."

When they were out of earshot of the charming house, Nigel took her arm. "Your delaying tactics were magnificent, my sweet. I thought he was itching to be rid of us, and I wanted to make quite sure. Now why?"

"Perhaps, he's really got a dinner date. I say, I remembered—when he said he was in the Indian Police. There was some scandal: hushed up for reasons of policy, I believe. He ordered his men to fire on a crowd and several women were killed. They whitewashed him officially, but he was told privately that he'd better resign."

"That accounts for the permanent grievance stamped on his unlovely features."

There was a lot more Georgia wanted to ask. But at this moment they reached Yarnold Cross and were about to turn left when they heard footsteps approaching along the road opposite. Nigel drew her quickly into the shadow of the deep hedge. Presently two men appeared, shuffled over the cross-roads and went down the lane leading to Yarnold Farm. There was still enough light in the sky to see that they were tramps.

"I always thought tramps kept to the main roads," whispered Georgia.

"So they do. Unless—Let's wait a few minutes."

They waited a quarter of an hour. The tramps had not returned. "They can't have gone farther on. That lane peters out at Major Keston's house, doesn't it?" said Nigel. "And I shouldn't have thought the major was exactly a person who keeps open house for tramps. Look here, do you mind a bit of a walk?"

He took her arm again, and they went down the eastward lane along which the two men had come. Georgia knew better than to ask Nigel what he had in mind. There was a strain of secretiveness about him, which made him keep a theory to himself till he had proved it; and there was also his boyish love of springing a surprise on you.

A mile further on the lane joined the main road. "I stopped, and I looked, and I listened," quoted Nigel. "Hear any one coming? No? Then lend me your torch."

The round of light glanced about like a dancing jellyfish as Nigel moved up and down the road-junction. At last it came to rest on a gate in the hedge. "Look at this," he said.

There was a chalk sign on the gate-post. "That's a tramp's sign," Nigel said. "They leave them about— information as to what houses keep fierce dogs, or can be relied on for a square meal, and so on."

"Well, that explains why those two men turned off the main road here. Major Keston must have a soft spot in him for tramps."

"Oh, dear me, no. You see, I happen to know this particular sign means 'Don't come this way. Nothing for you.' So what?"

Georgia gasped. Her quick mind flashed the implications. Major Keston's was the only house along that road, so the sign must refer to it. But the tramps would never have left the main road unless they were sure of hospitality in that direction. And the sign told them plainly they would not get it. Therefore they were not bona-fide tramps. Then why on earth should—

Nigel broke into her thoughts with, "You see what it means. It's possible even that they chalked that sign themselves, to stop any real tramps coming up this way. It looks as if the major and his misguided friends wanted to be alone."

"Possibly the boys are celebrating the Black Mass tonight. But why go to all this trouble? Why not roll up in expensive cars?"

"I haven't the foggiest. What about another walk after dinner?"

Night keeps her old mysteries in the country. There are dark hints in the air: a chilling breath rises from the ancient earth and lifts the hair on your neck: owls shriek and flit as if the furtive darkness itself had grown wings and found its voice. The lighted window beckons you to hurry home, and once you are inside the night draws back baffled. Glancing at Nigel across the dinner table, Georgia could no longer believe in the little shudder of premonition that had passed over her spirit, like a cat's paw, when he suggested they should go up to Yarnold Farm tonight. How many nights have I slept out in the jungle, in deserts, in friendless and unchancy places, she reminded herself, and yet the idea of a starlit walk in the heart of England made me uneasy. It's absurd. The whole thing's fantastic. "What came ye out for to see?"—a retired major of Indian Police, a respectable, commonplace citizen, whom—on the strength of a locket and a couple of tramps—we are suspecting of some nameless villainy. Serve us right if we catch nothing but a chill.

The more she thought of it, the less rational their conduct appeared. Nigel was buried in a book, the image of a placid householder taking his ease. The electric light shone mildly down through its parchment shade on a scene of domesticity—on two harmless-looking people, she said to herself, who harbour the most verminous, noisome and unneighbourly thoughts. Nigel looked at his wrist watch. "Ten-thirty," he said. "We'd better be trotting along. I should wrap up well, if I were you."

"And bring my sub-machine-gun?" she replied.

"I'm afraid you're not taking this seriously." Nigel was smiling quizzically at her; but at last she realized, with mingled excitement and exasperation, that he himself was taking it very seriously indeed.

The sky, when they trudged up the lane once more, was pricked out with frosty stars. A sliver of new moon hung over their shoulders, and the earth gleamed faintly like an old mirror. Every now and then a breath of wind stirred the bare boughs, as though the earth, turning over in her sleep, had sighed. Their feet on the lane's rough surface seemed to shatter and grind the silence into a thousand harsh fragments. Now they had reached the summit. They moved quicker, more silently now. Beyond the next curve lay Yarnold Cross—and a thing that, though Georgia might have expected it, took her utterly by surprise. Rounding the bend, they saw, a bare fifty yards in front, the ghost of Yarnold Cross. It stood where the four roads met, a tall figure, light playing over the arms that moved in a weary effort, up and down, up and down. A sound came out of its mouth—a kind of howling shudder, which was answered at once by

27

Georgia's screams and the panic padding of their feet as they raced back along the lane.

At a safe distance they stopped. "Blast!" panted Nigel. "I should have thought of that. It's a perfect place for them to post a sentry—and that legend to back it up. Well, it shows they've got some fun and games going on. You showed great presence of mind screaming like that. Let's hope they think we're a pair of village swains and they've scared us off for good."

"Sh. Just listen a moment. Why aren't Major Keston's dogs barking? With all the shindy we kicked up—"

"They're being silenced. Yes. It must mean that people are moving about down there tonight, and he doesn't want any one to know it. We'd better make a detour. Could you find your way to that wood overlooking the house?"

Georgia's wonderful eye for country, and the map she had made in her head, now came in useful. Climbing a gate, they struck off across the dark upland, the turf silent beneath their feet. It was a difficult journey, because they dared not break through the hedges that stood in their path and had to find gates or gaps through which they could pass noiselessly. At last a deeper bulk of gloom showed up in the darkness before them—the wood that sloped down to Yarnold Farm from the north. When they reached its edge, Georgia gripped Nigel's wrist and drew him close beside her.

"I'd better go ahead by myself now," she whispered. "You wouldn't be able to see much in the dark, and it's going to be a job getting through this wood quietly."

It was typical, of both Nigel and the relationship between them, that he attempted no protest. He knew that she could find her way about in the dark like a cat, whereas he himself would probably resemble a squadron of tanks if he tried to penetrate this tangle of trees and bushes. "Very well. Take care of yourself," he said. "I'll expect you when I see you. I'll just sit here and think."

The next moment Georgia was gone, slipping like a shadow into the wood. A faint swishing of boughs was all that marked her progress, and soon that noise too faded out. Nigel set his mind to work on the strange problem which had brought them here. It was like trying to reconstruct the anatomy of some prehistoric monster, with only a few scattered bones to guide him. The original theory of blackmail could surely be counted out. Drawing upon his phenomenally accurate memory, Nigel set out the pieces of the puzzle: (i) the locket, (ii) Major Keston's inquisitiveness, (iii) the position of Yarnold Farm, its remoteness from other dwellings, its proximity to the coastal road and the sea, (iv) what Harry had told him about the major, and the scandal that had compelled him to resign from the Indian Police, (v) Major Keston's eagerness to get them out of the house this evening, taken in conjunction with the arrival of the bogus tramps. How many more "tramps" might have been making their anonymous way to Yarnold Farm today? (vi) the "ghost" at the cross, which had begun to appear again after the major's arrival in Folyton.

So absorbed was Nigel in his problem that only his subconscious mind noted, some time later, the hum of a lorry distantly carried over from the direction of the coast, approaching, stopping somewhere in the valley below. Minutes after the lorry's hum had ceased, Nigel remembered that he had heard it. "So that's it," he muttered. "No, it's grotesquely improbable. But what else could explain it all?" With increasing anxiety now, he awaited his wife's return.

Meanwhile Georgia had worked her way patiently through the wood, and looked down on the shadowy bulk of Yarnold Farm, where a light still burning in some downstairs room threw a patch of white, like frost, on to the front lawn. Presently a figure was standing in this patch, back turned to her, staring towards the downland that divided Yarnold Farm from the sea. The figure returned to the house, and for what seemed an age no sound or movement came. Her ear, trained to danger, could detect nothing which suggested that the alarm given by the ghost-sentry had been followed up. Excitement ebbing from her, the cold beginning to strike through the layers of thick clothes she had put on, she felt the whole thing must be a false alarm too. The ghost was some village lad playing the goat, the figure down below had been just the major taking a breath of fresh air before turning in for the night. At this moment, as if to clinch her disappointment, the light in Yarnold Farm went out.

Georgia was tenacious, though. Some unlikely event might still happen, and she was determined to wait on the off-chance. If she had known what to look for, she might have prowled down closer to the house, in spite of Nigel's insistence that she should not run any risk of being seen. For half an hour she stayed there, leaning her back against a fir. At last something broke the quiet innocence of the night—a sound innocent enough in itself, the distant hum of a lorry. Idly, Georgia listened to it. Then she stiffened. The lorry, surely, was not passing along the main road. Its sound came from straight ahead, from the direction of the sea. But that was only the road that led to Cathole Cove, she remembered. What was a lorry doing, travelling from the cove at this time of night?

A few minutes later Georgia slumped back disappointedly. She had expected the lorry, on reaching the main road, to cross over and attempt the corkscrew lane which led up to Yarnold Cross. Instead, she saw its lights flash out, and it had turned left along the main road, which, just beyond this point, curved in towards Major Keston's land. "Damn! All this for nothing. It'd just lost its way or something. I suppose there was some fold of the ground that prevented me seeing its lights," she thought. She was so annoyed with herself, Nigel, the whole set-up, it took her several seconds to realize that the whine of the lorry's engine had stopped.

In a moment, flitting like a tawny owl, she was off down the hillside. Making a wide sweep to keep away from the house, she gradually neared the main road. Still she could see nothing but a vague glow from the lorry's lamps. She must get nearer, she must. Here was a lofty, tangled hedge, a boundary of the major's property, that led down to the road. Keeping in its cover, she advanced step by step. At last the road gleamed palely before her. She wriggled down silently into the ditch that ran beside the hedge. She parted the hedge-growth.

There was the lorry, drawn in at the side of the road, the driver hunched up in his cabin as if asleep. Well, he might be asleep, but there were others who most certainly were not—ragged tramplike men, half a dozen or more of them, who were lifting wooden cases out of the back of the lorry, and carrying them through the gate into Major Keston's paddock. The cases seemed very heavy for their size: it took one man at each end to lift them. While she watched, the phantom glow of a car's headlights showed up in the distance. Someone must have been on the look-out. Instantly the backboard of the lorry was fastened up, the ragged men scattered away behind the road hedge, and the belated motorist when he passed saw nothing more noteworthy than a long-distance lorry drawn up at the roadside, its driver taking a nap. The next minute the men were at it again, working with a speed and orderly discipline that, contrasted with their ragged guise, gave the scene an incongruous and nightmare quality. It could not have been much more than ten minutes before the lorry, unloaded, ground off again into the night.

# 3. The Episode of the Detective's Uncle

". . . And you say these cases looked heavy?"

"Well, it took a couple of the ragged rascals to tote each of them," Georgia replied.

Sir John Strangeways raised one bushy eyebrow at his nephew. "That about settles it, I think," he said.

The three of them were sitting in the flat which Nigel and Georgia had kept as a *pied à terre* for their visits to London. It was three days after the night-manoeuvres at Yarnold Farm. On the following morning, Nigel had gone up to town, leaving Georgia to consume her own curiosity and impatience as best she could. Later he had rung up asking her to follow him, but had firmly rung off when Georgia began to ask questions. Even after her arrival he would say nothing, and the subdued excitement which she sensed beneath his calm had worked her up into a high fever of curiosity. Then, this evening, his uncle had turned up and made her repeat exactly what she had seen from behind that hedge; and, in the very act of repeating it, she saw light.

"And now," she said, grinning mischievously at Sir John, "perhaps the two clams will open up. Or shall we just see if there isn't a masked man outside with his ear clamped to the keyhole?"

She stalked with exaggerated stealth to the door and flung it dramatically open. A broad, mackintosh-clad back confronted her.

"Oh!" she cried, slamming the door, "there — there *is* a m-man there!"

"Yes," said Sir John. "He's one of my men, as a matter of fact."

Georgia sat down rather suddenly, and gaped at him in bewilderment. Sir John Strangeways looked less like an official personage than one could believe possible. Curled up in the deep arm-chair, he resembled an intelligent, shaggy-haired terrier. "Inoffensive" seemed the best word to sum him up. Whenever Georgia set eyes on that draggled, sandy moustache of his, the shapeless, drab overcoat, the corn-cob pipe that fumed like Gehenna, she received once again the illusion that here was a suburban householder — a retired grocer, say — who had just returned from pottering about in his garden, thrown off his gardening-gloves, and settled down to listen to a talk by Mr. Middleton. It needed a positive physical effort to remind herself that Sir John was in fact head of the C. Branch of Scotland Yard. Only when you noticed his eyes — a deeper blue than Nigel's, far-sighted, dreamy, suddenly focusing into alert interest or quizzing you with a humour that drew a network of wrinkles at their corners — did you begin to perceive his quality.

"Well, anyway," said Georgia, recovering herself, "I know what it's all about."

"Oh, you do, do you?" Sir John removed the pipe

from between his discoloured teeth and tickled his ear with its stem.

"Yes, I do. Smuggling."

There was a short pause.

"Smuggling? Smuggling what?"

"Oh, I don't know. What do people smuggle nowadays? Silk?—no, the cases were too heavy. Dope?—no, too big. Brandy perhaps; that must be it."

"Why not—er—machine-guns?"

Georgia giggled. "Why not? Or howitzers. Or tanks."

"No, machine-guns will do," said Sir John, so seriously that she half-believed he could not be pulling her leg after all.

"Well, I know we're going in for rearmament, but it does seem to me rather a roundabout way to do it," she said.

"Now, if you'll stop chattering, I'll tell you something," Sir John replied. He pointed his pipe stem at the door. "You'll realize that man is not outside there for fun. This has to be confidential. Do you remember the Cagoulards in France?"

"The Hooded Men? Yes, I remember vaguely—a few years ago—"

"It was a conspiracy to overthrow the Popular Front government and set up a Fascist dictatorship in France, aided, it was alleged, by arms and money from two European powers. Arms dumps were discovered in Paris and other big cities, plans for kidnapping ministers and occupying strategic points. It nearly came off. None of your comic-opera plots—that one was. I advise you to read it up."

"But—but you're not suggesting?—not in England?"

"That's what they all say," Sir John remarked drily. "I suppose you won't take my word for it, so I'll have to give you a short political lecture."

Georgia never forgot the scene, though the dramatic events that were to follow it might well have chased it out of her head: the distant surge of traffic, a newsboy crying like a seagull in the street below, Nigel standing by the mantelpiece with an air of polite inattention that did not for a moment deceive her, and Sir John mildly gesturing with his pipe stem—outlining in his most matter-of-fact voice a theory which, from any other mouth, would have seemed as incredible as one of Scheherazade's fantasies.

"So there it is," he concluded. "The gist of it is that this conspiracy is already under way, and we've got little to work on and very little time to work in."

Stumping over to the fireplace, he shook out his pipe.

Georgia set her bewildered mind to grasp the implications of what he had said. She had a queer feeling that they had just come through an earthquake which had shaken down the wall of the house, tumbled down all the houses around, left her staring out at a shattered, unfamiliar prospect. Like the footsteps of a rescue squad, his phrases echoed hollow and sombre in her head. Even now, it took an effort to make sense of them. A General Election before long. An all-party government coming into power which would reverse the policy of appeasement, stand up to the European dictators. The growing indignation among the British people against being bluffed and bullied into concessions. And, on the other hand, a conspiracy organized by the friends of Fascism in the country to discredit this government and overthrow it by armed force—the last, desperate throw of those who saw the future slipping out of their hands.

"But I don't see—" Georgia said weakly. "You mean, Major Keston is one of them?"

"I'll come to that in a minute. My department and the Secret Service have had wind of this underground movement for some time. But we're badly handicapped. In the first place, there's any amount of money behind it—just as the rich families in France were behind the Cagoulards: we don't know who they may have bought over, in the police, the army, the Civil Service. We don't know"—Sir John's sober voice set her nerves quivering —"*we don't know who we can trust*. The other thing is—we don't know who the leaders are: we've got on to some of the subordinates, they're being watched, but so far they've given us no lead to the people at the top. I'll tell you frankly, we've not even got a suspicion. A few months ago, for instance, we found an arms dump beneath an empty house in Maida Vale. At first we assumed it was a left-over from the I.R.A. bombings in 1939. That's what they intended us to think. Oh, yes, we even had the last tenant of the house—when we'd rounded him up—admitting it, producing evidence that he was a member of the I.R.A. We'd not have thought twice about it if we hadn't discovered that the bombs were of German manufacture, and if the chap hadn't been a touch too eager to confess his association with the I.R.A. There've been other things, too. They're a clever lot, wonderfully organized—their organization must be in watertight compartments. You break through into one, but you're still very far away from the centre."

After a long pause, Georgia asked him point-blank, "Why are you telling me all this?"

Sir John Strangeways glanced up from the bowl of the pipe he was lighting—one of those placid, homely glances which so endeared him to her and seemed to make dream-nonsense of everything he had been saying.

"Have you ever heard of the English Banner?" he inquired with apparent irrelevance.

"No. English Banner? What's—? Oh, E.B. The E.B. printed on the flag we found in that locket?"

"Holed out in one. The English Banner is a queer sort of semi-mystical society, which flourishes mainly in country districts. They believe in the natural aristocracy of the landowning class, and of course they let in a few selected hangers-on—gamekeepers and the like—to give the thing a more catholic appearance. The idea," Sir John added drily, "is that they are really the best people in the country and therefore ought to be its rulers. They're quite harmless."

"But if they're harmless—"

"The point is that they wrap themselves in mystery as well as in mysticism. They're a secret association—a freemasonry without aprons and lodges. Now just consider: if you wanted a good cover for a *dangerous* secret organization, what could you find better than a *harmless* ditto. Take smuggling; a false bottom to your suitcase which is fairly easily disclosed: nothing in it: let off with a caution: but, beneath that, another false bottom. Which of course brings us to your military friend."

"Has Major Keston a false bottom?" Georgia asked dazedly. "Or two false bottoms? You're getting me a bit groggy."

Sir John grinned at her. "Major Keston is a man with a grudge and considerable organizing talent. As you know, he was politely sacked from the Indian Police. He's just the kind of material the big people in this movement can use. Don't underestimate him and his like. They're probably quite sincere. Nothing easier than to turn a personal grievance the other way up and see it as patriotism." He glanced at Georgia a little guiltily: there were few things Sir John Strangeways more disliked than to be caught making generalizations. Georgia, however, was only concerned with the truth of what he had said.

"I quite see that," she replied. "But have you any evidence for connecting—?"

"Oh, yes." Like his nephew, Sir John had an uncanny gift of anticipating one's argument. "The really interesting thing is that the disk you found in the locket—the Union Jack with E.B. on it—is not one of the English Banner's properties. We've got one or two people inside the English Banner, just to see they're keeping out of mischief, and I asked about it when Nigel came along with his story. They report that there is no such membership token. You see the implication? It means that this token is only in use among an inner circle of the E.B. But, if the inner circle is as harmless as the rest of the organization, why don't the ordinary members know about it?"

"What are the disks for, then?"

"I suggest they are the means of identification by which the leaders of this conspiracy make themselves known, when necessary, to its subordinate officers. That's only a guess, of course. But if one of the disks was seen by the wrong person, its owner could always in the last resort explain it away by a reference to the English Banner. That's the advantage of working under cover of a semi-secret organization."

"It all sounds absurdly melodramatic to me."

"Conspiracies *are* melodramatic, my dear, especially when they're made by rich people with too much money and time on their hands. Look at the Cagoulards conferring together in white hoods. It doesn't necessarily stop them being efficient, though. Wish it did. I'm worried to death about this, and I don't mind saying so."

"Dear Uncle John! I'm sure they'd be much more worried if they knew you were sitting on their tail. . . . But honestly, I can't believe it yet. What proof on earth have you that Major Keston was smuggling arms, for instance?"

"Better ask Nigel. He worked it out. Here, boy, give me something to drink: I've talked myself dry."

Nigel poured out drinks for them. As he talked, he moved about the room, setting down his own glass precariously on the extreme edge of any piece of furniture that was handy. Georgia had never become quite used to this unnerving habit of his: this evening, however, what he had to say kept her mind off household breakages.

"The tramps gave me the clue," he began with unusual abruptness. "Obviously the major was smuggling something. Well, you don't smuggle any of the ordinary things—silk, drugs and so on—in heavy cases. It might conceivably have been liquor of some sort. But, if so, why drag a lot of bogus tramps into it? Why *tramps?*— that's what kept tapping on my bump of curiosity. As you remarked, Georgia, why shouldn't the major's assistants roll up in expensive cars—or plain vans at the least? Of course, there was only one explanation."

"Of *course*," said Georgia acidly. "Don't stand there leering at me as if I was a half-wit village maiden."

"The only reason why people should disguise themselves as tramps and plod all the way to Yarnold Farm is that they were local people who otherwise might easily be recognized and couldn't afford to be recognized. Now one can't imagine a set of local bigwigs engaged in running liquor on that scale: unfortunately, the political situation being what it is, one can only too easily imagine them running arms. No doubt they've been convinced that the next government will be bright Red, take all their possessions away and murder them in their beds. The tramp disguise safeguarded them in several ways. When you see a tramp, you think of milestones, don't you? — you naturally assume that he has no home and comes from a distance."

"But why couldn't the major have just invited them to a dinner-party that night, all apparently open and above board?"

"Because, if anything happened to the consignment of arms on the way, if any suspicion arose about the transactions of that night — and you know how rumours do fly in the country — they'd all be in the cart. Besides, disguise is second nature to those sort of people where anything touching their respectability is concerned. Their conscience, so to speak, allows them to betray their country in white hoods but not in dinner-jackets."

"If they were so terrified of being recognized, why didn't they get a gang of weight-lifters from somewhere else?"

"It's not easy to import a gang of strangers into a remote country place without rousing talk. In fact, it's next door to impossible. Major Keston had done it once, you remember, when he was building an 'addition to his house' as Harry called it. I bet that addition was his workshop and a cosy underground chamber — the workmen were probably told it was for a wine-cellar — where the arms could be stored. There is also the point that this conspiracy is decentralized — in watertight compartments, Uncle John called it. The Keston Regional, if I may so refer to the major's little set-up, does all its own work as far as possible; thus, if an accident should happen, the damage would be localized, and no lead given to other centres of the plot."

"They certainly must have packets of money behind them, building that house and everything."

"Yes. That's another significant point. There's not much doubt where Major Keston's 'legacy' came from. Yarnold Farm was chosen for its strategic position, near the sea, remote from other dwellings. Cathole Cove is a deserted place, like the downs above it. A cargo of arms could easily be landed there, loaded on to the lorry by the people who brought them, unloaded by the major's chaps. If any one came across the lorry-driver on the road to Cathole Cove, he could say he'd been half asleep and taken the wrong fork off the main road. But the chances were a thousand to one against it at that time of night. The lorry's numberplates were false ones, by the way, Georgia, so we've got no further in that direction. No doubt the locket belongs to one of the leaders of the conspiracy, who visited Yarnold Farm last year to make arrangements, and had it pinched somehow by a magpie. Maybe he was sunbathing. I wonder would that give us a clue," said Nigel dreamily.

"I should have thought the simplest thing would be to get a posse and burst into the major's cellarage."

"No, no," said Sir John briskly. "Don't want to put 'em on their guard yet. Just stop 'em landing any more arms for the present."

"And how do you propose to do that? Lay a minefield in Cathole Cove?"

Sir John's eyes twinkled. "No need for anything so drastic. I've tipped off Jimmie Blair — you know the fellow, he's doing that 'Some Spooks I Have Met' series for the *Daily Post*. He'll write up the Yarnold Cross ghost, and that'll bring a horde of sightseers and psychic researchers up to the farm. They'll have to withdraw their sentry till it blows over — and by that time — "

Sir John broke off. Georgia became aware of a certain tension in the air. Nigel and his uncle studiously refrained from looking at each other. They were like two children, she thought, who share a guilty secret: it was as if, about to spring some practical joke upon her, they were not sure how she would take it. When Sir John spoke again, however, his words seemed innocent enough.

"Our real problem is to find out who the leaders of this movement are. The smaller fry can take care of themselves for the present. Young Nigel has an idea." His voice trailed off.

"It's entirely theoretical, of course," said Nigel. "But here it is, for what it's worth. Granted this movement to set up some kind of dictatorship in Britain. Now, if there's one thing the British people wouldn't stand for, it's dictatorship by any of the ordinary politicians. No doubt the conspirators mean to work up a state of crisis, lawlessness, bloodshed and the rest, which will justify the Strong Hand at the Helm. Temporarily. We'd not submit to it once the trouble had been cleared up, *unless* the Strong Hand was someone of national popularity — not as a politician, but as, well, as a chap.

"There are a few people in the country who have caught the popular imagination — the Englishman still has a sneaking affection for the highly coloured, dynamic, adventurer-type — we're descendants of Drake, after all. If the conspirators are as clever as we believe them to be, they'll have chosen someone who can appeal to the ordinary Englishman's romanticism and hero-worship."

"Yes," murmured Georgia, "there's something in that. The inspired amateur. It's part of our national romanticism to trust the amateur rather than

43

the professional. But how do we find him?"

The tension grew again. The whole room seemed to be holding its breath. Nigel fidgeted with the black wooden horse that Georgia had brought back from Africa. Sir John was filling a pipe as meticulously as though he were filing official papers. At last he looked up and said briskly:

"We want you to take a hand, my dear."

"*Me*? But I don't—why not Nigel?"

Sir John went on as if she had not spoken. "You're the only one of us, except for Nigel, who has seen the picture in the locket, and that picture is our sole clue. You have the entrée into fashionable society, and it's somewhere among the rich families that we've got to look for the centre of the movement. Also—I'll be quite frank with you—you're a bit of a legend in the country yourself: therefore this movement would be glad to make use of you, and equally you'll be excellent propaganda *against* it when the time comes for a showdown."

" 'Conspiracy foiled by famous woman-explorer.' Boy, what a story!" exclaimed Nigel.

Sir John brushed it aside with an irritable gesture. "The reason Nigel has to keep out of this is obvious. He's my nephew, and his connection with the police is known. That's why Major Keston was so inquisitive. They'd never trust Nigel."

"But the same applies to me. I'm married to Nigel, aren't I?"

"The idea," said Sir John, calmly puffing away at his pipe, "is that you should not be married. Arrange a separation—not a legal one, of course—just drop a hint to the gossip-writers that you've decided to separate: they'll do the rest."

So that's it, thought Georgia, speechless with surprise and indignation. So that's what their little game was leading up to!

"Have I got this right?" she asked, when at last she had recovered her voice. "You have the almighty nerve to suggest that I should separate from Nigel, create a scandal, not see him for months and months, while I go off on a wild-goose chase after some anonymous individual who probably doesn't exist except in your overheated imagination? You're asking me to—"

"I'm asking you to do it for England." Sir John's voice was as flat as if he had merely asked her to go out and buy him a packet of pipe cleaners, and this gave an extraordinary conviction to the phrase. Damn him, thought Georgia, why does he make it so difficult for me to refuse? If he'd tried to cajole or bluff me into it, or said one more word about England my England, I'd have dealt with him easily enough. But he just sits there, looking like a worried but sensible small boy, and puts it out as a business proposition.

She turned impulsively towards Nigel. He was leaning against the mantelpiece; the smile he gave her was tender but absolutely noncommittal. She might have known that he would make no attempt to influence her, one way or the other. For a moment her heart rebelled against this: just for once couldn't he make a decision for her? No, it was not his way—or hers.

Sir John called her over to the window. One hand round her shoulders, he pointed up the street. It was the rush hour. A hundred yards away she could see the crowds hurrying home along the main thoroughfare. Typists, shop-assistants, business girls, tired yet moving with a gallant swing. She knew instinctively what Sir John wanted her to see there. His words only echoed what her own heart was telling her.

"Look at them," he said quietly. He might have been asking her to admire his roses. "They're not a bad lot, are they? Silly, vain, pert, ignorant, vulgar—some of them. But they've a grace of their own, haven't they? They've youth and independence and courage. They're England. And you know what the other side says— 'Woman is for the recreation of the warrior'—'Woman's place is in the kitchen'—all the rest of that neanderthal tommyrot. That's what would happen, though. No young man to meet her outside the cinema tonight. He's got a date with a sadist storm-trooper in a concentration camp. That'll spoil him for her." Sir John squeezed her shoulder, and his hand dropped to his side. "You can't let that happen," he said.

"But I can't stop it either," she cried incoherently. "It's not my line. You're asking too much. I—"

"Well, think it over. A day or two won't make much difference. Good-bye for the present." Sir John had taken up his shabby hat and his ash stick, and was gone before she had time to say a word. She hardly knew, now, what that word would have been. His homely, reassuring presence withdrawn, the whole business seemed infinitely more grotesque, yet somehow more inescapable too, like a madman's delusion.

"Nigel," she said, going swiftly across to her husband, holding him by the wrists, "what am I to do?"

"I should take it on. It wouldn't be for long. It's worth doing."

But even then Georgia could not quite make up her mind. "Why did you have to start all this, just when I was settling down to a nice comfortable old age?" she asked, allowing herself for once the luxury of being thoroughly unreasonable.

46

# 4. The Episode of the Amorous Cricketer

It was Georgia's habit, when she had to make an important decision, to go for a long walk. Though a highly civilized woman, perhaps because she was one, she believed that in the last resort decisions should be made — where women are concerned, at least — by instinct. Intelligence could and should provide the material, set out fairly the pros and the cons; but something deeper than intelligence must make the choice, ratify and execute the decision. Nigel was wont to say that this was a kind of moral cowardice — a specious excuse for letting the decision be taken out of one's hands. She partly admitted it, yet she had proved in experience that instinct on the whole knew what was best for her. Therefore she would walk and walk, till the warring arguments of her intelligence were too exhausted to squabble any longer, and when they had retired from the field the way would be made plain to her.

This morning, the day after Sir John Strangeways' visit, she put on an old tweed coat, went out hatless to the bus stop, took a bus to the Embankment, and walked eastward along Thames-side. A sea breeze gently fingered her dark hair. A tang of the sea rose up from the river. The river stretched away past mud flats and warehouses towards the sea, and beyond that lay many countries she knew and a few where she had never been. A few passers-by glanced curiously at the small, lithe figure, marching along with that solitary air as if she were alone in a desert and nothing in view but the horizon; they remembered, when she had passed them, that her face — for all its lack of conventional beauty — had been strangely arresting; the kind of eyes, the more imaginative might have remarked, which one would have expected to find gazing anonymous over a yashmak or far-sighted beneath an aviator's helmet.

The ebb-tide, piling up broken waves against the wind, seemed to be pulling at Georgia too, drawing her heart away to distant places as it always did. But the old fascination soon gave way to thoughts nearer home when she turned aside from the river and began threading her way through East End streets. Here, on all sides, were unforgivable poverty, indomitable vivacity. The green-skirted hills of Devon and these dingy, boisterous thoroughfares were each of them part of a country she loved — loved now with the heightened awareness both of a traveller who has seen many rival beauties and of one who, returning home, finds the beloved threatened by an insidious and mortal enemy.

This morning, superimposed upon the street scenes — the brightly-coloured coster barrows, the slatternly shops, the bustle and animation of the crowds, other images appeared, unnatural, shadowy intruders, as though the photograph of an ordinary room had been developed to reveal a ghost among the chairs and tables.

She seemed to feel silent, jack-booted watchers standing outside frightened houses, figures kneeling to scrub the pavements, children coldly excluded from their familiar playgrounds, the informer's whisper in the café, fear and suspicion like rheumatism fastening upon the easy intercourse of friends—all the vicious little tricks of modern tyranny.

But what can I do? Why must Uncle John pick on me for this kind of work? I should be an abject failure. And to separate from Nigel. "It wouldn't be for long." All very well to say that. Nigel doesn't understand, he still half-thinks I'm self-sufficient—"the Cat that Walked by Herself." So I was, till I met him. I shouldn't see the daffodils spring up in the orchard where I planted them last year. My good girl, there are more important things than daffodils. Yes, I know, but— And Uncle John is so devastatingly thorough. He'll arrange this separation, in every agonizing little detail, so thoroughly that it might just as well be the real thing. But you know, my lass, you're secretly itching to have a go at this English Banner or whoever they are, one more adventure, your last adventure, and then an honourable retirement. Adventure? Pooh! It'll probably be nothing more lurid than following seedy aliens in and out of Lyons' tea-shops, prattling away in expensive, boring drawing-rooms.

So it went on. Georgia walked faster, till she was too tired even for these futile thoughts. When she returned home at lunch-time, and received the telephone message from Alison Grove, she did not realize how soon the decision was indeed to be taken out of her hands. "Yes, darling, I'll come," she said. "Do we dress? And Nigel? Oh, just a hen-party. Very well."

Alison Grove was at once Georgia's friend and her despair. An exquisite little blonde figurine of a woman, who contrived to run a car, a service flat, and always to be perfectly turned out, no other visible means of subsistence than her salary as a society journalist, she lived a life which—for a woman of her many talents—seemed to Georgia quite incomprehensible. "But surely you don't really *enjoy* all these fatuous parties and receptions you go to?" Georgia would say. And Alison's turquoise-blue eyes would look more innocent than ever as she replied, "Well, you see, I'm an indoor girl, darling. And think of the pickings. I'm the Butterfly that Stamped." "Stamped on what?" "Oh, stamped on all the other butterflies, of course."

It was quite true. Alison was a consummately brilliant journalist who suited the *Daily Post* admirably, for that pushful young paper held its huge circulation by a process of alternately keeping its tongue in its cheek and sticking it out at all the celebrities of the day. Alison's gossip column, entitled "A Little Bird Whispers . . ." contained a masterly blend of snobbism and subdued derision. Society hostesses whose ears were sharp enough to catch this faint, derisive note had at first complained to Alison's editor, then attempted to exclude her. They very soon repented, finding that this gay little butterfly had the sharpest of stings. After her account of the coming-out ball of the Duchess of Speke's daughter —a ceremony from which the Duchess had given strictest orders that Alison should be excluded—society thought it best to accept Alison Grove on her own terms. For all that, Georgia still thought her friend was wasting her talents—an opinion she was to revise after the events of this evening.

At six o'clock Alison appeared, her coat opening on a superb white sheath of a gown that looked as if it had grown on her body like plumage.

"Oh, dear," sighed Georgia, "you always make me feel like something out of a rummage sale."

"An Eastern bazaar, more like," replied Alison, fingering the folds of Georgia's barbarically striped taffeta frock. "No, you win. You're Nature, I'm only Art. 'Nature I loved, and next to Nature, Art.' Come along, or we'll be late."

"Where are we going?" Georgia asked, when they were settled into Alison's little coupé and speeding westwards towards the by-pass.

"Well, it's a sort of country club. *Très snob. Très cad.* On the Thames. I think you'll find the atmosphere interesting. Oh, and let's have no polite feminine wrangling about who's to pay the bill. It's on the house. I'm writing them up, and they've darned well got to bring out their most expensive victuals in return."

"What a blood-sucker you are, darling!"

"I pay my way. So will you. 'At the smart Thameford County Club, fashion's latest haunt, I noticed Georgia Strangeways. The famous explorer was, of course, exotic in striped taffeta.' "

"If you hadn't spent a fortune on your wave, I'd ruffle your hair for you."

"A tomboy, as ever." Alison's laughter, tiny and delicate as her figure, tinkled like Japanese windglasses. "I didn't anyway. I paid Janice for my wave in kind—a lovely paragraph about her beauty shop. It's nice work if you can get it."

"You really ought to be exposed."

"Oh, well, we all have our little secrets, don't we?"

Little secrets! thought Georgia. If Alison knew what I had on my mind, it'd snap her in two—the fragile wee thing. Well, perhaps not so fragile. But it's odd to think of us playing about like this just now—butterflies

51

dancing over a volcano's crater. Tomorrow I suppose I must decide. Tonight we'll give ourselves up to such revelry as this ghastly club can provide. . . .

Revelry was not exactly the first word one would apply to the Thameford County Club, she decided when the car drew up to its imposing entrance half an hour later. The floodlights that bathed the Georgian façade in lustrous moonlight seemed less a glare of publicity than an act of homage to a national monument and its architect. Red-bricked, solid, yet of an exquisite purity and grace, the house slept in dignity, as though it had been called to its ancestors and found worthy.

"What a shame!" murmured Georgia, as they got out of the car.

"What's a shame?"

"To use this—this glorious shell for a lot of rich hoodlums in Bentleys."

"Sh! I have my living to make," Alison whispered. "Besides, you've not seen the inside yet. Who knows what a shell may hatch out?"

The door was opened by a powdered flunkey. It was perhaps at this point that Georgia felt the first qualm of uneasiness. Looking back on it, she thought it must have been the contrast between the spacious hall, the cool Regency decoration of white and green, the staircase that curved away up as gracefully as if it floated on air, and the wave of heat that came out at them. A damp, perfumed sort of heat, it was; they might have been walking into a conservatory.

The carpet gave like moss under their feet as they entered the lounge. Here, at small tables under a diffused glow of wall lighting, several people were drinking *apéritifs*. Lights and voices were alike discreet, as if subdued by the atmosphere of this beautifully proportioned room that breathed an older, more assured civilization.

"I shall begin to twitch all over soon," complained Georgia, sipping her sherry. "Steam-heating always gets on my nerves. Why should they make this place a cauldron? I—"

"Hush, my dear. A dark woman is coming into your life."

Georgia looked up. The door had opened and a woman entered—the proprietor of the club, Georgia suspected, though she inclined her head to the occupants of the room with a stateliness that suggested it was she, not they, who conferred a favour by being there. A rather overblown creature she was, but statuesque in her black lace gown. Georgia's attention was quickly diverted, however, by the man who followed her. He looked very old; he had the long, exhausted, parchment-skinned face of a Spanish grandee—the kind of face in which nothing seems alive but the eyes, which burn in an arrogant, heavy-lidded stare or film over suddenly like a saurian's. With a queer feeling of oppression, repulsion, she scarcely knew what, Georgia noticed that in this hothouse of a room he carried a plaid shawl over his shoulders.

Presently the strange procession came round to her own table. Georgia felt she ought to be bowing in a deep curtsy. She was aware of the old man's veiled eyes upon her. He might have been blind, and groping towards her by some sixth sense.

"I am very glad you could come, Miss Grove," the woman said. At once the spell was broken, for her voice—to Georgia's ear—had a synthetic quality, a note of falseness or vulgarity beneath its rich, drawling refinement. Alison, very much on her best behaviour now, introduced them.

"Madame Alvarez, our hostess. My friend, Mrs. Strangeways."

"Delighted to have you," murmured the woman. "Let me present my husband, Don Alvarez."

As though pulled forward on a string, the old man approached, took her hand, raised it to his lips. Georgia barely repressed a start of revulsion, for his hand was dry, brittle and cold as a lizard.

"You will find some quite interesting people here to-night, Miss Grove," the woman was saying. "Besides your own guest, of course." She inclined her head, and at once the old man's head bowed on his scrawny, tortoise neck with an equally grave inclination. "The Iberian ambassador is bringing a party. We expect Mr. Leeming—the banker, you know. And I believe Lady Mulcastle is coming. I hope you like our place, Mrs. Strangeways, what you have seen of it?"

"Oh, yes, indeed. It's quite charming." On an impulse, she added, "It's terribly hot, though, isn't it?"

Georgia's famous directness had shattered many façades in its time, but it made no impression on the two faces opposite her.

"My husband feels the cold so horribly. He's not used to our climate yet," the woman said. After a few minutes of stilted conversation, she moved away. The old man, who had not yet spoken a word, smiled suddenly at Georgia—a smile that gashed his face as though a parchment had been stretched too tight—and followed his wife.

"Mercy on us!" exclaimed Georgia when the pair were outside the room. "Who on earth is that preposterous old marionette?"

Alison giggled. "I told you you'd find the atmosphere interesting. He's the proprietor. Or should I say the husband of the proprietress? He lost his estates in Spain. That's the story, at any rate, and it's as good as any other. What do you think of the Madame?"

"Seville and Surbiton," replied Georgia tartly. "She looks rather discontented, doesn't she, in spite of the grand manner?"

"So'd you, if you were married to the oldest tortoise in the Zoo. However, we have our consolations. Perhaps Peter'll be here tonight."

"How you do jump about! Who's Peter?"

"Peter Braithwaite."

"Never heard of him."

Alison's turquoise eyes opened wide. "Oh, my dear! Do you never read the papers? Peter Braithwaite, England's mainstay in the coming struggle, the flashing young D'Artagnan of the tented field, the Mecca of schoolboy autograph-hunters, the—"

"Do shut up and tell me what you're talking about!"

"Peter Braithwaite. The cricketer. The English batsman."

"Oh, yes," said Georgia, feeling oddly deflated. Alison's talk had at first seemed to be leading in quite another direction—a quite impossible direction, she realized. "I do seem to have heard something about him. He's an amateur, I suppose."

"No. As a matter of fact he's a pro. But don't let that get you down. Peter is one of my leading sweetie-pies. You'll like him."

"A pro? What's he doing in this exclusive dump, then?"

"Oh, he's been taken up, you know," Alison replied vaguely.

Whether it was the effect of the steam-heating on her nerves or the result of her long walk this morning,

Georgia found herself in an abnormally receptive state. At dinner the food was excellent and the head waiter, informed no doubt of Alison's business here, flatteringly attentive. There was something about this club, though, that Georgia could not get the hang of. Its atmosphere was oppressive in more ways than one. Most of their fellow guests—it was difficult to apply any other word to the clientèle of the regal Madame Alvarez—were of the usual restless, pleasure-seeking crowds; but there were a few that Georgia could not place at all. The bald-headed man, for instance, sitting by himself at a corner table, whose eyes she caught every now and then fixed upon herself with an expression of strange vivacity and intelligence. Surely she had seen that face before somewhere? Among all these smooth, vacuous faces it stood out like flesh and blood in a gallery of waxworks. There were others, too: people whom she would not have expected to find in so exclusive a company. She was about to comment on this, when Alison nodded towards the door and said, "Here's Peter."

The popular cricketer was not exactly as Georgia had imagined him. He had a stocky figure, a broad, leonine face that looked boyish, full of vitality, not in the least spoilt. When, passing their table, he grinned at Alison, Georgia felt his charm like an electric shock; she felt it was there, a natural magnetism, not assumed for any one's benefit. Peter Braithwaite, too, though several hands were raised to greet him, went over and sat at a table by himself.

"Isn't he nice?" asked Alison.

"He's certainly alive, which is more than one can say for most of the— I say, who's that over there?" Georgia indicated the bald-headed man, who was now scribbling abstractedly on the back of his menu card. Alison did not know him. Presently she inquired of the head waiter.

"That is Professor Steele, madam. Professor Hargreaves Steele."

Goodness! thought Georgia. No wonder I seemed to recognize the face. It appears in the press often enough. Hargreaves Steele was one of the foremost scientists of the day, an expert on tropical diseases who had also written a number of popular text-books. Because of the publicity he received, the scientific fraternity inclined to look on him as a bit of a charlatan. His achievements in his own field, however, made this attitude difficult to sustain. Glancing again at the famous scientist, Georgia observed him placing the point of his menu card on a thumb-nail and spinning it round like a tee-to-tum, his mouth pursed in a grimace of impish absorption. Still with the same expression, he proceeded to perform a trick that involved a saucer, a tumbler of water, a sixpence and a bent match. He seemed entirely oblivious of any audience, and indeed no one but Georgia was taking the least interest in him. Which was a pity, Georgia said to herself, for his hands were the most dexterous she had ever seen.

Aware of the scientist's eyes upon her again, she looked away. Her gaze turned to Peter Braithwaite. It was quite a different kind of shock he gave her this time. At first she thought he must be drunk, but she realized he had not been here long enough for that. His mouth was hanging open a little, his hands gripped the sides of the table, his eyes were glazed in a look of—what could it be but the most besotted infatuation? Georgia felt a little sick at the dire change wrought in that merry, ingenuous face; sicker still when she perceived that it was Madame Alvarez at whom the cricketer was gazing with such flagrant self-betrayal.

The woman moved regally from table to table, inquiring if her guests had all to their satisfaction. Her husband was no longer in attendance. Georgia noticed sly glances among the other diners when Madame Alvarez approached the cricketer's table and he invited her to take the vacant seat. There was something about his imploring gaze and this overblown creature's half-coy, half-possessive response that turned the whole evening rotten for Georgia. She was a woman herself, though, and therefore she could not resist the feminine impulse to know what it was about Madame Alvarez that attracted the young man. She must have been twenty years older than he. Her beauty, like her voice and queenly air, was surely synthetic. Georgia could imagine her mask falling off under the stress of fear or anger, and revealing a character common as dirt. Those discontented lines, dragging down the corners of her mouth, explained her simply enough. But what explanation could there be for Peter Braithwaite? And Alison didn't usually make mistakes of judgment.

"This is a bit much, isn't it, darling?" she whispered to her friend. "I don't approve of baby-snatching."

Alison's eyes were wide and innocent. "Oh, *that*. I told you we had our consolations. Poor Peter, he does have a time."

"But what can he see in her?"

"Mystery. Mysterious womanhood. Or perhaps he's just being kind-hearted."

Alison's hand, though, was clenched very tight over her gold evening bag, Georgia noticed. There were some things, then, that even Alison did not take lightly. Well, if Peter Braithwaite could prefer that ageing, counterfeit creature to pretty Alison, he deserved whatever was coming to him.

She was relieved when Alison suggested that they should take their coffee in the lounge. It amused her, too, to see the stir made by her friend's presence there. Social climbers who had not achieved the rather dubious distinction of being mentioned in her column competed more or less openly for Alison's attention. Those who had been born at the top of the tree treated her with a guarded courtesy. Alison herself flitted like a butterfly from group to group, gossiping away in her inimitable manner, listening with the adorable tilt of the head which made men feel—poor, deluded things—what an intelligent, sympathetic woman she was. Not till they had started on a rubber of bridge did Georgia realize that her friend's gaiety was not tonight quite natural. For her, Alison was playing abominably badly, and after a couple of rubbers, excused herself from further play.

Georgia, too, decided she had had enough. She also wanted to make the acquaintance of Professor Steele, who seemed by far the most interesting person here. But the professor was to be found in none of the rooms downstairs. Georgia wandered off upstairs by herself, admiring the beautiful proportions of staircase and landing, the delicate moulding on the walls. She felt restless again. The nerve-tingling heat, the vaguely uneasy atmosphere of the whole place. Through a door on the landing she heard voices. Assuming it was another public room, she was about to enter when she realized that the voices were those of Madame Alvarez and Peter Braithwaite.

". . . No, you silly boy, I won't. You're much too young. Besides, you couldn't afford to lose the money."

"I might win. I know I'd win. I'm always lucky at games. And at love. Otherwise I'd not have found you, would I?"

59

"Darling Peter! But I won't let you. I—I daren't."

"Well, you might let me have a look. I've never seen roulette—"

"Sh! You're not even supposed to know—"

So that's it, thought Georgia disgustedly, moving away. That's what the place is for. A discreet, posh gambling den. I suppose that's where the professor has disappeared to.

Georgia felt a distinct sense of anti-climax. The climax of the evening, however, was yet to come. When, half an hour later, they were tucked into Alison's car and about to move off, Peter Braithwaite poked his head in at the driver's window.

"You forgot these," he said, handing Alison her gloves. Then, in a lower voice, "No luck yet."

Impulsively Georgia said, " 'No, you silly boy. You're much too young.' "

In the dim glow of the dashboard light, Peter Braithwaite's face showed surprise, but no trace of discomposure. His eyes twinkled at her. He threw up his chin and laughed merrily. "Good for you, Mrs. Strangeways. Well, you've had a look at the bowling, haven't you? Good-night."

"What an extraordinary young man!" said Georgia when they had moved away. "And what on earth did he mean by having 'a look at the bowling'?"

Alison did not answer at once. She drove half a mile on, then stopped the car and in a voice that Georgia hardly recognized, said:

"Peter's a brilliant actor. He needs to be, just now."

"I don't understand. You mean that he—he's not in love with that Alvarez creature?"

"He's certainly not."

"But—but why?"

60

Alison was silent for a while. At last, laying her hand on Georgia's, she said, "You had a talk with Sir John Strangeways yesterday evening . . . No, it's all right, don't get in a flap. You see, Peter and I are working for him. We were working for him tonight."

Georgia stared at her speechless for a moment, utterly dazed, unable to believe her ears. If she had drawn the favourite in the Irish Sweep—if Nigel had told her that he was a secret drug addict—if the Last Trump itself had sounded—she could not have been more dumbfounded than by this incredible revelation. Alison! The gay, fragile, exquisite Alison! And Peter Braithwaite, the Test cricketer! . . . At last she found her voice, and came out slap with a round and most unladylike oath.

"Well, I'm—! You dissembling little cat! Just a gorgeous humming-bird to look at but—"

"Now, I can't be both, really!" Alison's little glass-tinkle of a laugh rang out. "I told you there were advantages attached to the job of a society journalist. Pickings. Oh, yes, one picks up quite a lot. That's why Sir John picked on me for the work."

"Do stop this Shakespearean-clown patter. You mean, that club—"

"Yes. We suspected the place was being used as a cover by some of the people behind the E.B. movement. They're clever. Their shield has three layers, so to speak. On the outside, the place is all posh respectability. But they disseminate tactful rumours among the habitués that the place is used for roulette. It's all very vague, of course. The bona-fide visitors dare not broadcast the rumour, for fear of taking the rap for libel. If one of them wants a flutter, the Alvarezes tell him, with a fine show of righteous indignation, that he's come to the wrong shop. At the same time, it gives the actual conspirators an opportunity for meeting in secret—in an atmosphere of accredited secrecy. That's their tactic, you see: to use a comparatively venial illegality as a cover for downright treason. Smart lads. The roulette is just a sop to Cerberus. Peter's got the Madame as far as admitting that roulette is played there. Madame Alvarez is the weak link in their chain, and we're playing on it good and hard."

"But how do you know that it's not simply roulette?"

"Oh, they're playing for higher stakes all right. You'll have to take my word for it. We have no proof, though, yet."

Georgia was silent for a while, digesting all this. At last she asked point-blank, "Why did you take me there tonight?"

Once again Alison did not answer directly. Her fingers tightening round Georgia's wrist, she said, "Peter loathes that woman. Just to touch her makes him feel sick. But he's willing to go through with it. Right through with it, if necessary. You understand?"

"Yes, I see. I suppose this was Sir John's idea, the wily old serpent. Well, I think I'd have come into it anyway."

"Good girl." Alison started up the car, and they shot away toward London.

# 5. The Episode of the Two Dissemblers

When Georgia awoke the next morning it seemed that she must have dreamt the whole bizarre episode of Thameford County Club. The weeks that followed were like a dream, too, but the kind of dream in which only a faint, intermittent sense of unreality disturbs the apparently logical sequence of images. At such moments, disquieting though they were, she could feel little urgency about her position, little apprehension for the future. Even the parting from Nigel, painful as it had been, was far different from her expectations. Sir John had seen to that.

"You've got to do the thing thoroughly," he had said. "If they have the least suspicion that there's anything faked about it, you won't stand a chance of getting your foot inside their movement. What's more," he added with the brisk air of a seedsman's assistant advising an amateur gardener, "you'd make things exceedingly dangerous for both yourself and Nigel."

Planning the detail of their "separation" kept them

so busy that much of the sting was taken out of it. They worked out every move, every sordid business item, as though it were the real thing. At first the illusion of reality was so powerful that Georgia had to remind herself it was only make-believe. Soon, however, she surrendered to the illusion, for she realized that thus she would present a much more convincing front to the inquisitive.

"Good-bye, darling. Take care of yourself," Nigel said on their last morning together. They kissed passionately. She forced herself into a chair. There seemed no other way of resisting the temptation to stand by the window and watch the taxi taking him away. And that would never do; she must not allow even herself to suspect how bitterly this separation was hurting her; she had a part to play. Besides, one never knew that someone might not be watching.

From the cottage Nigel wrote appealing letters. Would she not change her mind, even now? Surely her decision to leave him was not irrevocable? Think how happy they had once been.

And she wrote back, no, it was over, their lives were too obviously incompatible. She had made a mistake in thinking she could settle down to the sort of domesticity he wanted. It had been all right for a while, but she was born restless, she wanted to go off on her travels again, she was determined to live her own life.

There were business letters too; about the cottage, the disposal of the furniture, the forwarding of her clothes and effects. He was to keep the cottage, she the London flat. Sometimes she felt wildly impatient at all this detail. It was like elaborately dressing a scene for a play that would never open. But she knew it was necessary. Their letters might, just conceivably, be intercepted. In any case, they kept all the letters they received, for the E.B.—as they had now come to think of it—would certainly make investigations before they let Georgia inside.

Then there were what Alison ghoulishly called "the official obituaries." Hints in the gossip columns, growing broader, becoming affirmations. Finally, an interview with one of the *Daily Post* feature-writers, to be reproduced next morning under the lurid headline, "Famous Woman Explorer Pans Domesticity."

After that—worst ordeal of all—the shock, sympathy, anger, curiosity, sly hints, well-meaning interference of Nigel's and her own acquaintances. "Your first appearance as a grass widow," Alison had remarked with some relish, "will be a tricky affair. What a pity you're so indecently fond of your late husband. You'll have to be coached."

And coached Georgia certainly was. During the fortnight that elapsed between Nigel's departure and the first hinting of their separation, Alison took her in hand. She would ring up and inquire innocently when Nigel was returning. She would take Georgia out to dinner or for an afternoon's shopping, and make off-hand, unexpected allusions to Nigel. Georgia soon learnt to answer these with a suitable blend of embarrassment and constraint. Knowing what terrible issues might hang on her being word-perfect, Georgia played up with the irritable concentration of an actress at a dress-rehearsal.

"Thoroughness and patience," Sir John Strangeways had said. "They're the things that really matter in our work." Well, they had been thorough enough. His own two visits to the flat a fortnight ago were to be explained, if any one should turn inquisitive about them, by the fact that, as Nigel's uncle and guardian, he had been trying to heal the rupture between them.

Everything seemed provided for. She was not to communicate with Sir John until she had obtained vital information, and then through a code which she had memorized. Her own instructions were simple enough: to make contact with the E.B. conspirators and find out the owner of the locket.

It *sounded* simple enough at the time. But, as week followed week and the date of the General Election drew nearer, Georgia's patience was severely tested. Nigel, the whitewashed cottage on the green hillside, the hedge she had never finished cutting, all were like memories out of some former life. They had receded to an immeasurable distance. Often, discouraged out of belief, she was tempted to throw up this wild-goose chase and return home. Discouraging the work certainly was. At first there had been a certain interest — excitement even — in picking up old threads, in the round of parties, concerts, social events which she attended, in playing the part of a woman who has regained her freedom. But the excitement soon turned sour on her tongue. Though she let fall hints of Fascist sympathies, expressed fears of what the next government would do, they all seemed to fall on deaf or indifferent ears, and nowhere did she come across a face that recalled the features of the woman in the locket.

At last, when she was almost driven to despair by this nightmare sensation of walking eternally down a dead end, things began to open up. Peter Braithwaite and Alison Grove arrived at the flat one evening early in April. There was no mistaking when Peter was in good spirits. His eyes snapped with an audacious gaiety, the infection of his vitality made you want to turn somersaults, to run out and push over a bus, to tell him your most intimate secrets. He sat wrong ways about on an upright chair, his arms crossed on its back, and announced:

"Alison and I think we've pottered about long enough. I'll be playing cricket soon, so it's time I got a move on. We're going to take the offensive, start bumping them a bit."

"Bumping who?" asked Georgia, rather mystified.

"Peter's mixing his metaphors," said Alison. "The point is, he's at last found out the room at the Thameford Club where these goings-on take place, and he believes some funny stuff is due next Thursday. We're going to gate-crash."

"We? But surely—"

"You've got to be there, Georgia," Peter said earnestly. "To take note of the assembled faces, don't you see? There may be some there that aren't frequenters of the club."

"But—it'll give me away completely. The E.B.'d not let me within a mile of them after that. Not that I've got any nearer myself so far. But still—"

"You'll be all right. Just listen to me. This is the way we're going to do it . . ."

That Thursday evening was not the first occasion when the habitués of the Thameford County Club had seen young Braithwaite a little the worse for drink. Moreover, they were people for the most part who could maintain their well-bred air of indifference against anything short of mass-murder in their midst. It was bad enough letting a professional cricketer into the place at all—of course, Braithwaite wasn't quite an ordinary pro—but he might at least behave himself when he came here. There would be a dreadful scandal, too, if Señor Alvarez realized what was happening between his wife and the young cricketer. Still, in the interests of decorum and their digestions, the habitués were willing to ignore a great deal.

Tonight, however, Peter Braithwaite tried them very hard. Madame Alvarez had not put in an appearance yet, it was true; it might be better if she did, for Braithwaite was becoming positively obstreperous, and no one in his party seemed able to control him.

The party consisted of Alison Grove, Georgia and her cousin, Rudolph Cavendish—an eminently respectable young Conservative M.P., whom Georgia, partly from policy and partly in sheer impishness, had invited to make a fourth. Rudolph had been glad enough at the opportunity to meet the celebrated cricketer, but now he was beginning to regret it. For the celebrated cricketer was leaning across the table, fixing him with a slightly unfocused eye, and remarking in resonant tones:

"Cavendish. You are Cavendish, aren't you? Yes, I thought so; I've a wonderful memory for faces. Well, Cavendish, I'm going to tell you something. 'S more about this club than meets the eye. Things go on which you'd scarcely believe. Oh, yes, they do. Don't dare to contradict me, Cavendish. The sticket here is wicky. Pardon. I should say, the wicket here is sticky. Distinctly sticky."

Rudolph glanced a little desperately at Georgia. "Why, that's news to me," he said.

"I dare say, Cavendish, if all were known, you'd find out a great number of things were news to you. Pray allow me to continue. I don't mind people having a little flutter—live and let live is what I say—but I resent, I bitterly resent this hole-and-corner business. If I want to gamble, my money's as good as any one else's—you agree?"

"Well, of course it is, old man."

"Don't interrupt, Cavendish. Now'z a well-known

fact that roulette is played in this establishment—"

"Pipe down, Peter. Pull yourself together," said Alison sharply.

"Aha, you're jealous." Peter wagged a finger at her. "My good friend, Madame Alvarez, charming woman, above approach—reproach, she told me so."

"Told you what?" asked Rudolph inadvisedly.

"Come, come, come, come, *come*, Cavendish. Get a grip on yourself. You may be an M.P.—I've only Georgia's word for it—but you're a rotten bad listener. She told me they played roulette here. Perhaps you're suggesting my good friend, Madame Alvarez, is a liar?"

"No. Well, no. But—"

"Exactly, Cavendish. You've hit the nail on the head. He may not be an oil-painting, but he has it up here all right." Peter tapped his forehead, beaming fulsomely upon the embarrassed Rudolph. "As you were about to say, why is any Tom, Dick or Harry allowed to play roulette here, and me not allowed? It's pure snobbery. Well, I'll show 'em. I don't want to play roulette especially, but I'll not stand for snobbery. I shall sacrifice myself," Peter concluded with some grandeur, "in the interests of the democracy of sport."

Peter had waited till most of the diners were at the coffee and brandy stage before commencing his performance. There was less come and go of waiters now, and Peter timed his most audible sallies for moments when none were within earshot. Georgia was apprehensive, though, lest he should overdo things and queer their pitch. He was far too good an actor to over-play the tipsy part; but Georgia recognized in him a latent recklessness which might lead him to over-play his hand in other ways. If she had been a cricket fan, she would have known that Peter Braithwaite's consummate skill as a batsman was slightly flawed by a tendency to "take a dip at it." The mercurial temperament which raised cricketing talent to the point of genius, also resulted in bad lapses. This apprehension of hers, together with a perfectly genuine embarrassment at the scene he was creating, gave her exactly the right air of fluster, humiliation and irritability when the moment came to make the next move.

"What's more," Peter said, "I'm going to do it now." He rose a little unsteadily to his feet. Rudolph Cavendish seized his coat and tried to pull him down to his seat, but Peter brushed his hand away.

"Leave me alone, or I'll knock you for six," he exclaimed dangerously. Everyone in the room was staring at them now.

Georgia made an apologetic gesture to the other two. "No. Leave him to me. I think I can manage him," she whispered, and taking Peter's arm, began to help him out of the room. "Come on," she said more loudly, "I'm going to see the fun too."

"Good lass."

Even when they were outside, in the deserted hall, Peter did not let up by a fraction. Leering at her with stupid cordiality, he said:

"Lot of pop-eyed stuffed-shirts in there. Don't like 'em. Just follow me now. I know the way."

They went upstairs. Peter tapped at a door that had "Manager" written on it. Madame Alvarez half-opened it and he thrust past her, Georgia hanging back on his arm.

"I'm terribly sorry," she said, with a flurried gesture. "I can't—Mr. Braithwaite's a bit above himself. Peter, do for heaven's sake come away and stop being a nuisance. I'm sure Madame Alvarez is busy."

"Never too busy to see *me*, are you, ducky?" Peter leant against the panelled wall, his hands behind his back, grinning amiably at Madame Alvarez. "I want to play roulette."

Fear flashed in the woman's eyes. One corner of her mouth dragged down, shaking. She rushed at Peter, tried to drag him away from the wall, shook him feverishly. Peter would not budge. She sat down at her desk, hiding her quivering hands beneath it. "No, Peter. Please. You mustn't."

"I want to play roulette. I want to play roulette. I want to play roulette."

"They're not playing tonight. Peter, darling, I implore you to go away. Mrs. Strangeways, can't you—"

Georgia had noticed the woman's hands searching under the desk. After more altercation, Peter said:

"If you've pressed that little button of yours, I'm going to press this little button."

He turned a knob, part of the moulding behind him, and pushed sideways. The panel slid aside. Only it was not a panel; it was a sliding door, six inches thick, sound-proof. Georgia was at his side, trying to drag him away. He pulled her through into the small anteroom that was revealed. Nothing there but furniture. He quietly opened a door on the far side.

Georgia was never sure what she had expected to see. A long table, perhaps, covered with papers, people sitting round, weapons even. There was a long table certainly, and people sitting round, but no papers. With a sick qualm of disappointment she saw that it was in fact nothing more nor less than a roulette table. The players' faces were turned in their direction, puzzled, indignant or startled, as they entered. Their silence was accentuated by the click of the ivory ball as it spun, slower and slower, round the revolving disk.

Not till the ball had come to rest did any one speak. Then, his head poking up like a tortoise's from the plaid shawl that covered his shoulders, Señor Alvarez said:

"What is the meaning of this intrusion?"

In that quavering, scratchy, yet somehow dominant voice—it was the first time Georgia had heard him speak—the theatrical little phrase carried a certain menace. It was as if a dead man uttered an invocation in a dead language. Peter, however, whom she had sensed going limp with disappointment at her side now rose to the top of his form. He shook a waggish finger at Señor Alvarez, and remarked to the company in general:

"Ah, naughty, naughty! An illicit gambling hell? T'ch, t'ch! Well, I'll promise not to tell the police, if you'll let me play."

"Throw this fellow out," said Alvarez to the croupier standing at his elbow. "Perhaps some of you gentlemen will assist."

"Here, I say," Peter exclaimed in an aggrieved voice. "What's the idea? I've as much right to play as any one else. I've got plenty of money. It's just damned snobbery, that's all. Isn't it, Georgia?" A look of bleary cunning came into his eye. "Of course, if you're going to turn nasty—well, the police might be interested."

"This is a private party. They are friends of mine. Now, sir, are you going, or must we expel you by force?"

Watching the heads of the roulette players turn, like spectators' at a tennis match, to and fro between Señor Alvarez and Peter Braithwaite, Georgia suddenly remembered something. She hoped her face gave away nothing of the revelation that had flared up behind it. To cover her excitement, she walked over to Señor Alvarez and said quietly:

"I very much regret this. Please forgive Mr. Braithwaite. He got a little drunk downstairs, I'm afraid. He's very young. I tried to restrain him, but he insisted on coming in here."

"Pray do not apologize, madam. It is I who should do so, for my seeming inhospitality. But you realize that my guests—" His old voice, slurring and rustling like silk, faded out into a courteous gesture.

"Come along, Peter," she said. "I'm sure Señor Alvarez will let you play some other night."

"I want to play tonight. With that lovely little ball. Whizz, whirr, clickety-click." Peter was thinking, she knew, that he must at all costs keep the foothold he had obtained here. He was thinking that he must watch them playing roulette, to make certain the game was not a blind. It was his last hope. How could she convey to him that there was no longer any need for it?

Señor Alvarez motioned away the croupier and the grey-moustached, military-looking gentleman who were now standing at Peter's elbow.

"One moment," he said. "Mr. Braithwaite, may I ask how you discovered our harmless little secret?"

"An open secret, old boy. Everyone knows roulette is played here."

"I do not make myself quite clear." Señor Alvarez' voice was still silkily courteous, but there was an undertone of harshness behind it, like the sound of a roughened finger rubbing against silk. "I must ask you how you found your way in here."

Georgia saw the trap instantly. It was only through Madame Alvarez that Peter could have learnt the secret of the sliding panel, but if he admitted this too readily the genuineness of his infatuation for the woman would at once become suspect. She dared not look at Peter. His intoxication was so convincing, it was impossible to feel that he had all his wits about him. She heard him, after a pause, say:

"Oh, dash it, I can't tell you that. I mean, it was just by accident. I happened to be fiddling with that panel the other day, and the jolly thing came away in me 'and."

Georgia's heart leapt with relief. Peter had taken the right line. There was exactly the right blend of hesitation, embarrassment and unconvincing candour in his voice.

"My wife didn't by any chance—"

"What the devil d'you mean, sir?" interrupted Peter, blustering. "I tell you, I found the knob by accident. I happened to be in her room out there one day, waiting for her to come in, and—are you suggesting I'm a liar?"

"Please, Mr. Braithwaite." Alvarez' hand sketched a deprecating gesture. The stretched, parchment face broke into a smile that Georgia found peculiarly chilling. "Believe me, we appreciate your—er—chivalry. It is, if I may say so, worthy of a better cause."

Peter's fists clenched. "I came here to play roulette, not to be insulted with oily compliments. Georgia, we'd better go."

"Oh, no, I insist on your staying. Perhaps you will take my invitation to play as an apology for any unintentional discourtesy of mine. I'm sure my guests will be charmed to—"

There was a general stir of assent. Preserving his air of slightly tipsy dignity, Peter allowed himself to be persuaded. Room was made for them both at the table. Georgia found herself sitting next to Professor

Hargreaves Steele. He, and the financier, Mr. Leeming, were the only two present whom she had seen at the club on her few previous visits. Georgia had more leisure to observe them now. The white-moustached man was introduced as General Ramson. There was a middle-aged man, with the melancholy features and heavily pouched eyes of the Russian nobility—Prince Orlov. There was a Herr Schwartz, pink and white of complexion, in a tight, high collar that might have grown into his fleshy neck. Beside the men, three ladies were playing. Two of them Georgia put down as "bazaar-openers," and left it at that for the time being. The third, a Miss Mayfield, was a younger, more striking woman. Her mop of flaxen hair and the complete absence of cosmetics on her face made her an incongruous figure in this company. A healthy, bouncing, keep-fit sort of girl, Georgia thought her—but the gambler's fever appeared in those forget-me-not blue eyes when the wheel began to spin again.

Indeed, as far as the evidence of her senses could go, Georgia was bound to admit that the whole company looked exactly like what they were pretending to be—rich, bored, more or less respectable people with a weakness for Dame Fortune. Their absorption in the game, their little stereotyped mannerisms in placing the chips or jotting down a calculation, the haggard tension that never quite broke through their polite poker-faces—all indicated the seasoned gambler. Georgia was discouraged by this, until she remembered that, if her instinct and Peter's information were correct, these people were indeed gamblers—and for higher stakes than they laid on the table tonight. Much more discouraging was the fact that among these nine faces there was not one which suggested the winsome, unforgettable features of

75

the woman in the locket. Well, why should there be? she asked herself despondently. If that locket did belong to one of the leaders of the conspiracy, he'd not be likely to put inside it the picture of any one who could be connected with him.

She found herself eyeing the jewelled watch on Miss Mayfield's wrist. Was there one of the E.B. disks hidden there too? The next moment a voice at her side was murmuring to her unbelievably:

"And what does John Strangeways think about all this?"

It was as startling as the sudden shrill of a telephone bell in a dark house in the small hours of the morning. Georgia perhaps was never again so near to giving herself away. It seemed minutes, though it was only a second, before she realized what Professor Steele had meant, and replied:

"I really don't know. Officially he'd disapprove, no doubt."

"I hope you're not a police spy in our midst," said the scientist, giving her one of his abrupt, playful smiles. Georgia smiled back.

"Oh, I won't tell on you. As a matter of fact, I shan't be seeing much of Sir John now."

"Are you really separated from your husband? It's not just a publicity stunt?" The professor's puckish grin made even this remark sound almost inoffensive, but Georgia replied in kind:

"I don't think Professor Hargreaves Steele is quite the right person to make charges of publicity-seeking."

"Madam, as one victim of the Press to another, I offer you my humblest apologies."

What an enigmatic creature he is, to be sure! she thought. Is he—could he possibly be one of Sir John's helpers too? Or was it just by accident that his questions came so near the mark?

Nothing else of moment happened that evening. Georgia took advantage of Peter's having had a short run of luck to persuade him out of further play. He left with her, giving an admirable imitation of a fundamentally decent young chap who has made a nuisance of himself, has sobered up, and is feeling a bit ashamed. He was very silent in the car, and when the three of them had got rid of Rudolph and were having a nightcap in Alison's flat, he said dismally:

"Well, there it is. Looks as if we'd been leading ourselves by the nose properly."

"Why so gloomy?" asked Alison.

"The boys were just playing roulette. A plumb wicket. To think I've gone through all that with the Madame for nothing. Do stop looking like a monkey that's found the king of fleas, Georgia."

"Not for nothing," said Georgia slowly. "Did you notice the way all their heads were turned to the door when we went in? It never occurred to me at first."

"Well, they'd been warned. The Madame rang that bell under her desk, which presumably meant that some rough fellows were going to burst in on their roulette."

"But don't you see? Several minutes elapsed between her ringing the bell and our entering. If it'd been a genuine roulette game, the only point in the bell would have been to warn them to conceal the evidence of the game. But they didn't conceal anything. They wanted us to believe they'd been rouletting all the time. But they made that mistake of looking up when we came in. Real gamblers, like they certainly are, would have been far too absorbed in the game to pay any attention to a door opening—the ball was still rolling, remember. Either the bell Madame Alvarez rang connects with the gambling-room, in which case, if the roulette was bona-fide, they should have concealed the evidence of it; or the bell does not connect with that room, in which case, if they were genuine roulette gamblers, they'd never have all looked up at our entrance. Therefore, which ever way you take it, the game was bogus."

Peter slapped his knee in an access of enthusiasm. "By Jove, you've got it!" he exclaimed, and took her hands, and danced her round the room.

# 6. The Episode of the Playful Scientist

The next day hung heavily on Georgia's hands. She was filled with a sense of anti-climax and doubt. Peter would be passing on to Sir John the information about those who had been present in the gambling-room last night. Their antecedents would be investigated, their movements watched perhaps. But surely the whole thing must be a mare's-nest? She perceived how flimsy were the arguments she had built upon that interrupted game of roulette. It was incredible to suppose that men like Mr. Leeming and Professor Steele, men of international reputation, should be involved in a melodramatic, hole-and-corner, entirely hypothetical conspiracy. Well, perhaps not hypothetical. Sir John was not given to alarmism. Peter and Alison must have had some evidence that the Thameford County Club was not exactly what it seemed, and her own instinct certainly told against Señor Alvarez. Alison, too, had informed them last night that Herr Schwartz was foreign correspondent of a Nazi newspaper, and it was well known that these Nazi journalists in England had more irons than one in the fire. Yet Georgia herself was no further advanced on her own mission. Indeed, if those respectable-seeming gamblers had been members of the E.B., it would be more difficult than ever for her to get a footing in the movement. It was difficult now to imagine that Peter's act could have hoodwinked them entirely.

Walking in Hyde Park, the mild April day blossoming all round her with tulips and tender, budding branches and the cries of children who somersaulted on railings or streaked erratically over the grass, Georgia felt the very despair of loneliness. Her knowledge seemed to cut her off from all this innocence and gaiety. She was like a prophet who sees doom imminent but is bound to silence, the weight of his knowledge suffocating his heart. Georgia's reverie was interrupted by a barking and gambolling at her heels — a Kerry Blue which had become fascinated by a stick she had absent-mindedly picked up from the grass and was dangling from her hand. She was about to throw the stick when the dog's owner, walking with a long, country stride, caught her up. It was Miss Mayfield — and looking very much more at home here, in her low-heeled shoes, tweed skirt and periwinkle-blue jersey, than she had looked at the Thameford Club.

"How clever of Gyp to find you," she said.

"Oh, were you looking for me?"

"No, not particularly. It's quite a coincidence, though, isn't it?" The girl blushed ingenuously, a little angry with herself, perhaps, for having nothing better than platitudes to offer a celebrity like Georgia Strangeways.

"You don't live in London, do you?" Georgia asked.

"How did you know? Well, I don't, as a matter of fact. Not much, I mean. My father has a place in

Berkshire. He's a trainer." She rushed it all out, not quite apologetically, not quite defiantly. Georgia said it must be fun—horses to ride, the downs wide open before you.

"Oh, it's all right, I suppose. I get bored, though. I'm sick of men who do nothing but chew straws. I suppose you're wondering what I was doing in that lousy joint last night?"

"Playing roulette, I imagine," said Georgia drily.

"It's all very well for you," Miss Mayfield exclaimed, pulling Georgia down on to a seat. "I mean, you can go exploring, you've done things, you're free as the air. You must understand what it is to crave for adventure —for any sort of excitement. And the world's such a drab, dreary place just now, isn't it?" She stretched her arms, looking in her ardour quite magnificent, a Nordic goddess. "I want to do things too. But Daddy—well, you know what fathers are like. He's a darling, but ghastly old-fashioned. He'd really like me to ride side-saddle, and sit at home in the evenings with a good book."

"He wouldn't approve of roulette, I take it."

"Oh, glory, no! He'd go up in smoke. That's really what I meant to—Look here, you're not going to tell any one about that, are you? If it got round to him, there'd be hell to pay."

"My dear, why should I tell any one? I was playing myself. It does seem to me, though," Georgia picked her words with delicately veiled contempt, "a pretty—well— decadent form of excitement. I should have thought you could do better than that. D'you play much?"

As she had hoped, her words stung. The girl tossed her flaxen hair in an abrupt, ungracious gesture. "It's excitement," she said sullenly.

"Excitement? With a lot of rich dagoes in that

hothouse? Watching a fatuous little ball twiddling round? Heaven help us!"

"Maybe there's more adventure in it than you think." The girl bit her lip and added quickly, "I mean, when you haven't much money, you get a real thrill out of winning—or losing. Anyway, they're not dagoes, not all of them."

Georgia raised her eyebrows, and the conversation lapsed for a while. Maybe there's more adventure in it than you think. Was Miss Mayfield being a thought too ingenuous? Or was she indeed the fanatic that she looked? Georgia could understand how the E.B. conspiracy would appeal to a girl like this. It would seem not so much a conspiracy as a crusade. Fanatics were necessary—and dangerous—to any revolutionary movement. Here might be another weak link.

Skillfully Georgia turned the conversation towards Nazi Germany, speaking with feigned admiration of the things she had seen there. She was rewarded by a gleam in the girl's eyes, a quickened breathing.

"Yes," she said, "it's wonderful. I've never been there, but I can imagine it all—the spirit of youth and confidence and hero-worship. Sometimes I wish we could have something like that in England—not Fascism, of course, but something adapted to our national character. Get rid of all these doddering old politicians and the greasy Jews and the agitators."

"I quite agree. We've given democracy a fair trial, and it's let us all down. It's a great ideal, I dare say, but in the modern world we have to be realists. Let the best people rule—even Plato said that—and the rest will be far happier for it in the long run."

Georgia had got so used to throwing out this kind

of bait in vain that it almost unbalanced her when Miss Mayfield took it.

"I say, you're not a member of the English Banner, are you?"

"English Banner? No. What's that?"

Miss Mayfield told her. She talked, of course, about the harmless organization which Sir John had already described to Georgia; talked with such naïve enthusiasm that Georgia found it difficult to believe she knew the sinister uses to which this organization was being put. However, when Miss Mayfield invited her to stay with them in Berkshire and attend a meeting of the Banner, Georgia readily accepted. There was more in this shy, abrupt, ardent girl than met the eye . . .

The conversation under the April trees faded from Georgia's mind next day, for events took a sudden, dramatic turn. While she was sitting at breakfast the telephone bell rang. It was Peter Braithwaite, asking her to come over to his lodgings at once. Georgia gulped down her coffee and took a taxi to St. John's Wood. Peter was waiting for her in the hall of the apartment house: his tanned, good-humoured face showed anxiety.

"Madame Alvarez has turned up. I'm in a proper jam," he whispered. "I've quietened her down a bit— she was almost hysterical; but I'm supposed to be at Lords, coaching some boys, at ten o'clock. Can you carry on for a bit? I couldn't get hold of Alison."

They went upstairs to Peter's rooms. He had certainly not exaggerated. The woman was in a state of collapse. Her regal bearing was gone. Without make-up, her face looked muddy-grey and sagging; she had the frowsiness of a woman who has been travelling all night in a crowded railway carriage. Her eyes were sunken and glittering in what seemed a fever of fear.

"I'm so sorry, Madame Alvarez. Are you feeling ill? Would you like us to get a doctor?"

"I'm not going back there," she muttered. "I'm not going back. Don't let them take me back."

"Why, of course not," said Georgia soothingly. "You're quite safe here."

"You don't know them," the dead, sleep-walking voice went on. "He locked me in my room yesterday. . . . I daren't go to sleep. I had to in the end . . . When I woke up I felt ill. I tied the sheets together and climbed out of the window. You don't understand . . . He frightens me."

The woman's head rolled from side to side and her eyes winced, as though the daylight hurt them. She was a pitiable sight, slumped in the chair like a broken-limbed doll; but pity was an emotion that Georgia could not squander now. She made Madame Alvarez finish the brandy which Peter had poured out. She knelt beside the woman, chafing her hands.

"Come now, my dear. Just tell us everything. We can't help you unless we know—"

"Rosa says her husband was very angry because she let us in to the roulette game." Peter glanced significantly at Georgia. "It wasn't her fault, of course. I've told her I'll go and explain to Señor Alvarez."

"I won't go back. I won't go back," the woman repeated dully. Georgia gripped her hands urgently. Something of Georgia's vitality communicated itself to Rosa Alvarez. She straightened her back with an effort, crying, "I mustn't stay here! He'll guess I've come here. Is that his car outside?"

"There's no car outside," said Georgia. "Take it easy, my dear. Your husband can't hurt you. Surely he'd never hurt you just because you were a little indiscreet over the roulette? Are you sure he's not jealous about — well, about you and Peter?"

"No. Not that. He always lets me go my own way. He's an old man."

"Well, it must be something else then." Georgia gazed fixedly into the woman's distraught eyes. It was as bad as the Inquisition, but it had to be done. "Wasn't it something more than the roulette? Something else that happens in that room? Wasn't it, dear? Why should he make such a fuss about a game?"

"Something else? I don't understand. . . . He told me no one must go into that room while they were playing. I told you not to, Peter. Why did you? I tried to stop Peter going in, didn't I?"

Madame Alvarez was shivering at intervals, like a fly-teased horse. Standing by the window, Peter had his hands clenched in his coat pockets. He knew Georgia must be ruthless, but he could not endure attending the operation as a spectator.

"I've got to be off now," he said. "Back at lunch. Georgia will look after you till then. You'll be all right, Rosa."

Georgia expected a scene, but the woman seemed sunk in apathy. With a gesture that Georgia was never to forget, Peter Braithwaite walked over to Madame Alvarez and tenderly kissed her forehead. A lover could not have done less. A Judas could not have done more. And Peter was neither, though he had to appear both.

After his departure, Georgia renewed her efforts to make Rosa Alvarez betray her associates. She used, with nervous shrinking and cruel tact, every feminine weapon of insinuation, sweet guile, sympathy, delicate bluff. At the end she had got no further. She was compelled to believe that Madame Alvarez knew nothing of what had really gone on behind the scene at the

Thameford County Club. Either that, or she was too ill or frightened to speak.

Georgia decided to launch a last attack. "Why did you say you were afraid to go to sleep?"

But, before Madame Alvarez could answer, there was a sound of altercation below, feet walking up the staircase. The landlady put her flustered head inside. "I'm sorry, m'm. I told them as Mr. Braithwaite was out." And she was pushed aside by two men who entered — Señor Alvarez, and the croupier of the roulette table, in chauffeur's uniform today.

Rosa Alvarez shrank back from them with a small, animal cry. The old man paid no attention to Georgia, but leaned solicitously over his wife, stroking her hair. She shut her eyes tight, as though the caress was a prelude to torture.

"My love, you gave me such a fright," he said in his old, paper-thin voice. "We didn't know where you'd gone. Luckily, I found Mr. Braithwaite's address in your book. Now you must come home and go to bed. You're not well. We'll send for the doctor."

Georgia had once seen a cat playing with a shrew-mouse. The mouse ran into an angle of the wall. The cat fetched it out with one flick of its paw. Again and again the mouse had run for refuge to the same spot, flattening itself into the angle of the wall, screeching like a slate-pencil, and again and again the cat had flicked it out. Madame Alvarez huddled back in her chair. It seemed as if she, too, was trying to make herself small, to sham dead. To her husband's patient entreaties she returned no sound — except, when he touched her, that jarring, desperate little cry. Georgia could stand it no longer.

"Just a minute, Señor Alvarez. Your wife came here in a hysterical condition, which I'm afraid your presence is exacerbating. She said she had been locked in her room all yesterday. She said you were very angry with her over that roulette business. I don't want to interfere, but she's evidently ill and I think we ought to get a doctor at once. If you leave her here, I assure you she'll be in good hands."

"I am sure of it, madam. But I could not think of putting you and Mr. Braithwaite to such trouble. If I may just have a word with you in private." The old man led her outside the door. His long, distinguished face broke into a melancholy smile. "You will understand, when I tell you that my wife suffers from recurrent delusions, a form of persecution-mania. Unfortunately—I shall never forgive myself for it—I did speak too severely to her about that little indiscretion, and it brought on one of her attacks. At such times she has to be—confined. And expert medical attention is needed. If it would set your mind at rest to accompany her home with us and speak to her doctor, pray do so. I realize how distressing this must be for you."

Georgia had had many difficult decisions to make in her life, but never a harder one than this. She distrusted Señor Alvarez' exquisite courtesy. Her instinct was to keep Rosa out of his hands. Yet, if she resisted him now, she would inevitably incur suspicion herself. On the one hand, a problematic danger to this woman (and she could not be sure that Señor Alvarez' explanation was not the true one). On the other hand, her own chances of getting at the heart of the conspiracy ruined. In an instant Georgia had weighed them up, and was saying:

"Why, of course, Señor Alvarez. She must go home with you. I'll come too, if I may. It's not a question of setting *my* mind to rest, but I think it might be a little comfort to her."

The drive back to Thameford was something she would have given much to be able to forget, even when she found out later that Rosa Alvarez was already beyond all help before she arrived at Peter's rooms that morning. She saw the woman, now comatose, to bed: had a word with Dr. Wilson, her medical attendant: returned to London and, from a public call-box, rang up Sir John Strangeways. Dr. Wilson's credentials would be investigated. Sir John's trusted men would keep an eye on the Thameford County Club, that was all she could do. . . .

A week or two afterwards, Peter Braithwaite came round to see her. He told her that Madame Alvarez was dead. "It's a dirty game, this," he said, walking restlessly about the room. "I don't like it. I was afraid they'd do it, but I couldn't raise a finger to help her."

"Do you mean they killed her? But surely—"

"Of course they did. Oh, Dr. Wilson gave a certificate all right, no doubt. They do things in style. No expense spared. He'll be one of them."

"What did she die of?"

"Some obscure disease. Alison inquired of the inconsolable widower. Poor Rosa—well, she did set my teeth on edge, but I'd like to lay my hands on that old fiend, Alvarez."

"But if it was a disease—surely you're not suggesting—?"

"Oh, it was all above board. Very neat. They even called in a specialist. They frighten me a bit at times, these chaps we're up against—the way they have everything at their finger-tips. No old-fashioned business of blunt instruments. Just a neat little dose of microbes."

"Peter, you're letting your imagination run away with you."

"No imagination about it. They're merely taking a leaf out of the Hooded-Men book. When the Cagoulard Conspiracy was exposed, the French police discovered a laboratory swarming with cultures of disease-bacteria. One of the Cagoulards confessed that these were prepared to be used against traitors within the movement. Laugh that off if you can. No wonder poor Rosa was afraid to go to sleep that night. She was afraid of having a shot of filthy microbes injected into her bloodstream. Her 'delusions of persecution' would explain away any charges she might make. I tell you, you've got to watch your step in the E.B."

Georgia reflected, well, if that is really true, Madame Alvarez must have been inside the movement after all. They'd surely not kill her just for having given away the secret of the roulette, and in that case they may suspect her of telling Peter or me something about the movement. It looks as if we should have to watch our step, too. As the weeks passed, however, Peter's suggestion seemed to her more and more fantastic. It was not till two months later, when Georgia had at last succeeded in finding her way into the councils of the E.B., that she realized how near the mark Peter had been. That scene, so innocent on the surface, so abominable beneath, bit itself deep into her memory.

A hot June evening. A dinner-party in Professor Hargreaves Steele's house at Hampstead. Their host's bald dome, whose tufts of a hair on either side gave him a faint resemblance to Mr. Pickwick, shone in the candlelight as he turned from one guest to another, now bubbling over with impish merriment like a Pooka, now dismissing some argument with incisive, almost contemptuous logic, now relapsing into a moment of abstraction when nothing of him seemed alive but his

restless, agile hands that performed little tricks of pres-
tidigitation while his mind withdrew into some abstruse
speculation of its own.

Georgia watched him, fascinated. In conversation, his
intellect so dominated the company that one could feel
it almost physically, as though it were one of those ir-
resistible elemental forces, so dear to the old writers of
ghost stories, which could smash their way through pad-
locked doors and shoulder strong men aside like wisps
of straw. Even his playfulness had something of the
lion's paw about it. Yet this weight of intellect was ac-
companied by no corresponding impression of character. There was no facet of character you could get a
grip on and say "this is the real man," only a series of
moods. Like an elemental, Professor Steele was somehow amorphous—he changed shape so fluently that you
could not pin him down to any one shape at all.

Each man's morality, thought Georgia, is a compromise between the strength of his character and the
strength of his environment. Where you have no character to fix the ratio, you get the genius and the lunatic,
to whom morality is meaningless. A genius is only a
specialized lunatic with special opportunities. For this
reason, Hargreaves Steele must be one of the most dangerous men in England: an elemental body that has immense momentum but no responsibility.

It amused Georgia to watch some of the women
lionizing the professor. He allowed them, metaphor-
ically, to stroke his mane, admire his teeth, even tease
him a little, but, if they got too venturesome, he would
knock them off their balance with one lazy, unerring
sweep of his paw. Later, no doubt, they would show
off the scars to their acquaintance. There were innumer-
able stories current of the scientist's scarifying retorts—

most of them told against themselves by the victims. One got a certain vicarious fame out of having been taken down a peg by Hargreaves Steele.

After dinner, he invited a few of them to inspect his laboratory. Here, among the tanks and the microscopes, he became a different person. Georgia understood why his colleagues sometimes referred to him as a "charlatan" or a "bit of a mountebank." He liked putting on a show. It was as though, entering the laboratory, he assumed the weird cloak of an ancient alchemist. His manner grew suddenly brusque, business-like, yet he manipulated his apparatus with a certain stylized flamboyance and an inward abstraction of eye that set his audience at a distance; they might have been watching him through the thick glass of one of his own tanks. The impression of a conjuror at work was increased by the scientist's assistant, a chubby, bristly moustached little man who in absolute silence set out the materials for each new demonstration, moving anonymously about the laboratory as if he were an automaton controlled by wireless from the professor's massive forehead.

One woman, a little bored with the performance, skittishly asked, "When are you going to show us where you keep all the wretched guinea-pigs you torture, Professor Steele?"

"Madam, in the eyes of science, you and the guinea-pig are equally suitable material for investigation. The difference is that you are more expensive to keep."

The woman, whose extravagant tastes had compelled her husband publicly to repudiate her debts, gave a brittle laugh. Professor Steele's mouth quirked in a complacent smile, like an amateur comedian whose gag has brought the house down. A few minutes later, when the professor was demonstrating an electric motor, one of the male guests asked, rather self-importantly:

"Why don't you use the Zinkessen model? I should have thought—"

"Because this one is better," replied the professor abstractedly, without even looking up.

When he had finished what Georgia called in her own mind his "set pieces," he unexpectedly took her by the arm and, ignoring the other guests who trailed round after them or moved back to the drawing-room, led her on a little tour of inspection.

"You've seen some of the effects on your travels, I dare say, Mrs. Strangeways. Come and have a closer look at the causes."

Pursing his mouth, he adjusted a powerful microscope. "That's *Cholera vibrios*. Active little chaps, aren't they? Take a peep."

Georgia saw what looked like a number of dark worms writhing and thrashing about, changing pattern like a demented wallpaper.

"Here are some tuberculosis bacilli. Rather dull. Most of us carry them . . . Bubonic bacillus . . . *Borfrelia berbera*—he's the parasite that causes African relapsing fever . . . Next, three different species of malarial parasite—*Plasmodium vivax, Plasmodium malarioe, Plasmodium falciparum* . . . Anthrax—ordinary-looking little beast, isn't he? . . . And here's the sleeping-sickness trypanosome . . . And if you come over to this microscope, I think we've got—yes, we have—the head of a tsetse fly, the one that transmits sleeping-sickness in Africa."

When he had finished, Georgia felt a little sick. "I suppose you're used to having all these filthy cultures about the place. I'd be getting up all hours of the night to see that none of them had escaped."

Professor Steele's eyes twinkled. "Twinkled" was perhaps an inadequate word for the scintillating, almost a little crazy look that came into them. He patted her shoulder.

"Don't you worry," he said. "I'll not let them out after you—not if you're a good girl."

The two other guests who still remained with them laughed merrily. Old Steele was in good form tonight. But Georgia's blood ran cold. She knew that the scientist's word had been a threat. She had seen too much of the horrors these vile, microscopic creatures caused, too much of the E.B. and Professor Steele, to be able to take the threat lightly. Rosa Alvarez perhaps, had been struck down from this bland, hygienic laboratory. She herself, a member of the movement now, had received her warning, delivered in innocent terms before two unconscious witnesses, like a bomb concealed in a Christmas cracker.

It was this scene, as much as anything else, that enabled her months later, when the leader of the conspiracy, the man whom the E.B. intended to make dictator, was in her power, to treat him with as little compunction as she would have treated one of Professor Steele's disease-carrying lice.

# 7. The Episode of the English Banner

That scene in Professor Steele's laboratory marked a new stage in Georgia's relations with the E.B., a stage which had opened during her first visit to Alice Mayfield's home towards the middle of May. Reviewing the whole affair a year later, she saw this visit in its true perspective. It reminded her of an occasion when, as a girl, she had been sailing on a friend's yacht to the Outer Hebrides. Barra, a sullen, black wedge, had risen over the horizon. The yacht had approached the island, nearer and nearer, till it seemed she must ram herself against those inhospitable cliffs: and then, almost in a moment, the opening of the sound appeared, at first as a narrow, angled rift in the cliffs, then a navigable channel, and they had slid through into the heart of the island, into Castle Bay where Kishmul's Castle, toy-like on its tiny rock, lay marooned in the farthest reach of the bay.

So it was with Georgia now. Driving hard at the outer walls of the conspiracy, until it seemed she must break herself vainly against them, she had found an opening with sudden, magical ease. . . .

On the way down to Berkshire that Friday afternoon, she summed up the information she had received from Alison and others about the Mayfield stables. George Mayfield, a cavalry officer and celebrated amateur rider in his day, now trained for Lord Chilton Canteloe. Chilton—"Chillie," as he was affectionately known by the millions who had profited either directly by his philanthropies or indirectly from the way his horses justified their backers' confidence—was a millionaire, still in his early middle age, but already something of a legend in the country, a figure as colourful in his way as the great Whig noblemen of the 18th century. Georgia, indeed, had suggested to her friend, half in fun, that he would be the ideal man for the E.B. to have chosen as dictator, but Alison had replied, "Oh, no. Don't go barking up that gum tree, my sweet. Chillie's all right. He's a grand chap. You wait till you meet him."

Georgia, however, was not to meet him on this visit. He was abroad, Alice Mayfield told her when she met her at the station. And a certain rapt, yet defensive look that came into the girl's eyes at the mention of his name suggested that here was another of Chilton Canteloe's easy conquests. Perhaps not so easy, thought Georgia. Alice is a proud prickly creature; she'd be a handful all right.

Five minutes' drive brought them to the Mayfield stables. The long, rambling red-brick house, the white picket-fences, the stables behind—all looked fresh as paint against the great ridge of downland already massed with shadows from the evening sun. The air was full of sound: the muffled stamp and clatter of horses, the clink of buckets, voices buzzing from yard and paddock, and above them a remote roaring as a flight of pursuit-planes — arrowed out like wild geese — passed overhead, homing towards their aerodrome beyond that shoulder of the downs. "We've got three aerodromes now, within a radius of twenty miles or so," Alice said. "Atterbourne, Hartgrove and Twybury."

"Don't the planes upset your horses?"

"Oh, they've got used to them."

"We've all got used to them, I suppose. Used to the idea of the air being the element of death."

"You're not a pacifist, are you?" Alice Mayfield asked sharply.

"Dear me, no. I dislike being killed without having a chance to hit back, though."

"I wanted to join the Civil Air Guard, but Daddy wouldn't let me. He thinks flying is not womanly."

"You should tell him to read Maeterlinck's *Life of the Bee*, then. Particularly the nuptial flight chapter."

"Daddy read a book? I should laugh. The book of form's the only one he ever opens."

"What's that, my dear?" said a voice behind them. "Hello, who've we got here?"

"Mrs. Strangeways. Let me introduce you. My father. Mrs. Strangeways is one of our guests for the week-end, Daddy, in case you've forgotten."

"Delighted," growled Mr. Mayfield vigorously pumping Georgia's arm up and down. "My little girl's talked a lot about you. Taken a fancy to you, yer know. I'm a bit deaf, so yer'll have to shout at me. Anno Domini, yer know. Why didn't yer bring yer husband?"

"Daddy! You know I told you —"

"She oughtn't to do it, at her age."

Georgia glanced rather wildly at Mr. Mayfield, but he was no longer talking about her. He was pointing with his stick at an old woman carrying two buckets of water along the lane. When she came abreast of them, he roared at her.

"Shouldn't do it, Mrs. Elder. Do yerself an injury. How's the rheumatism?"

"Middling, sir. I can't complain. 'Tis all this rainy weather we had in the winter."

"Get on with you! You're good for fifty years more. Wait till yer my age. It ain't the weather, it's Anno Domini, that's what it is. Feel it in me bones. The knacker's cart round the corner. Good day to you."

Georgia was attracted by this rumbustious old man, in his flat-topped hard hat, yellow waistcoat, slit-tailed check coat, and jodhpurs. He was a character. But it was easy to see, too, how Alice Mayfield's character had been distorted by him. The only daughter—she had four brothers, Georgia was to find—she had been alternately petted and harshly repressed by her father. He wished her to be a simulacrum of his dead wife, a "womanly woman," as Alice bitterly expressed it: while she, brought up in this masculine society, worshipping her brothers and at the same time envying them their freedom, could achieve neither the license of the tomboy nor the placidity of the feminine.

This impression was fixed firmly in Georgia's mind next morning. Waking early in the small, white-washed bedroom, she slipped on a wrap and went over to the window. In the almost level rays of sunlight, the downs to the west were picked out with such radiant clarity that it almost seemed as if every separate grass-blade stood visible. The hills surged up with a giant sweep on either hand, like Atlantic swells holding house, stables and village tiny and becalmed in their trough. Presently, over the brow of hill on Georgia's right, a horse and rider appeared. A chestnut horse, neck proudly arching as its rider held it on the summit in a statuary pose, the sunlight making a burning bush of the rider's flaxen mop of hair, a beacon on that solitary upland. Yet, for all the glory of the picture she made, there was a dejected droop about Alice Mayfield's shoulders, an air of one on the lookout for a relief that never comes. Motionless up there on the horse's back, gazing southward, she seemed to Georgia an image of "divine discontent."

There was a sentry in her pose, too. Georgia remembered the ghost of Yarnold Farm, and it struck her that here also was a strategic position: a house set in the middle between three R.A.F. aerodromes. A picture came unbidden into her mind. Flights of planes dipping and turning over the Houses of Parliament, while, within, an ultimatum was being delivered. Resign, or—

Irritably she dismissed it from her mind. That was the worst of fighting in the dark—you began to get fancies, to imagine enemies in every corner. The girl up above jerked at her rein: the horse shot forward, swiftly, smoothly, compactly as a torpedo; they were galloping along the ridge, galloping breakneck in a moment down the track towards the sleepy, dazzled village.

"Have you brought good news from Ghent to Aix?" Georgia called out of her bedroom window five minutes later. Alice Mayfield looked up at her, cheeks flushed, white teeth shining in a smile.

"I had a lovely ride. Did you see me up there?"

Yes, thought Georgia, she looks as innocent as the dawn. I must stop imagining things. Yet she was there in that hot room with Señor Alvarez and his associates: she couldn't have got there by accident.

The meeting that evening, when Georgia was initiated

into the English Banner, was no less innocent either, for all its oddity. Mr. Mayfield attended, though grumbling audibly beforehand about "all this tomfoolery of Alice's." Two of his sons, florid, well set up young men; one or two neighbouring farmers, a little overawed beneath their appearance of stolidity; a few "county" young things, larky and disrespectful; a parson; the head stable-boy, a gnarled, bow-legged, gum-chewing wisp of a man; Georgia's two fellow-guests—a landowner from another part of the district, and his wife; and a few R.A.F. officers, slick-haired, unobtrusive, talking their own language.

Proceedings opened with a ceremony, conducted by Alice's elder brother, Robert, who assumed for the occasion the robe and title of "Chief Banneret." The ceremony had that atmosphere of crankiness, make-believe and rather seedy mysticism which is apt to come over a religion or idea in its decadence. Georgia's chief feeling was one of embarrassed apprehension—the kind of apprehension one might feel at a séance lest the medium should misfire, or watching some pathetic old trouper in a travelling vaudeville trying to reproduce the talent of his palmy days. This part of the ceremony concluded with Georgia's induction.

"Do you believe in the principle of aristocracy, the rule and government of the Superior Person?" she was asked.

"Do you believe in the hereditary line of true aristocrats?"

"Do you believe in the privilege and responsibility of the Superior Caste?"

And so on.

Georgia contrived to keep a straight face, and was duly made a member of the English Banner. She was interested to note that she did not receive a disk such as Nigel had found in the locket; Sir John had evidently been right in saying that these disks were only current among the real conspirators. A sudden wave of homesickness came over her: she wanted to be able to tell Nigel all about this absurd ceremony, to hear his explosive laughter: nothing here seemed real at all.

After the ceremony was over, the Round Table took place. This high-flown title, Georgia discovered, meant nothing more than sitting round a table and airing grievances about the government, the servant-problem, the "crippling weight of taxation," the Socialist Party, the iniquity of hikers, speculative builders and tradesmen, the debasement of modern art, empty churches, football pools, chemical beer, birth-control, and other allied subjects. It was all very tedious and laughable, but at the same time one could see what admirably troubled waters the English Banner provided for the real conspirators to fish in.

Next morning, however, Alice Mayfield took her for a ride before breakfast, and it was high up on the downland, looking over the Sunday calm of fields and villages, that Georgia was at last admitted to the secret which had evaded her so long. They had reined in their horses to admire the view, and Alice suddenly asked her what she'd thought about the meeting of the English Banner.

"Do you want me to be polite or honest?" asked Georgia, seeing her opportunity.

"I hate people being polite."

"Very well, then. I thought it was a ridiculous piece of hocus-pocus. Not the idea itself—I wouldn't have joined if I'd thought that. But all the talk, talk, talk. So utterly peevish and feeble. Why don't they *do* something about it, instead of whining all the time? 'Aristocrats' whining over their silly little grievances. Haven't they any guts? Your brothers look as if they have, but they just jabbered away with the rest like a couple of Croatian café-conspirators. What a pitiful spectacle we were, complaining about the way democracy is ruining the Empire, telling each other how marvellous we are—born to rule, and the rest of it, and then just sitting back on our haunches! Heaven preserve me from that kind of self-righteous, do-nothing smugness."

Alice Mayfield was stung, as Georgia had intended, by the contemptuous reference to her brothers.

"We're not so futile as you think," she said indignantly. "Not all of us. Not Robert and Dennis. Or me. We're helping to get things done."

"Really? Writing letters to the *Times*, or what?"

Alice was white about the nostrils, but she controlled her voice. "What would you say if I told you that in less than a year's time, we'd have swept away the democrats in Britain and set up a real leader, a real leadership?"

"I'd say you were dreaming. A pleasant dream though."

"Would you come in? Our inner council believe you'd be invaluable."

"You bet I'd come in, if I thought you had any chance of success. I don't go on expeditions that are forlorn hopes, you know. Who is this leader, anyway?"

"I shouldn't be allowed to tell you, even if I knew. Only half a dozen people in the movement know his name."

"That's buying a pig in a poke, isn't it? How can you tell whether he's any good?"

"He's planned the whole thing—that's how we can

tell. The organization is simply amazing: only a great man could have done it."

Can this be true? Georgia asked herself. A movement with an anonymous genius behind it? Maybe Alice was stalling her off: it was not likely, after all, that a stranger would be entrusted with such vital information at the start. Yet she could have sworn the girl was telling the truth, or at least believed it to be true that the identity of the future dictator was only known to the leaders of the movement. And if this *was* true, it fitted in with everything Sir John had told her about the conspiracy. It minimized the greatest danger to which such conspiracies are open—the danger of the informer. Yet, in another way, it made it more vulnerable: for, if only one could find out who this arch-traitor was, one would kill with a single stone both the genius and the figurehead of the organization.

Georgia was careful to maintain her attitude of scepticism, but allowed herself to seem gradually more impressed by Alice Mayfield's enthusiasm. It soon became evident from her account that the movement was, as Sir John had suspected, divided into a multiplicity of watertight cells, so that a leakage would do the minimum of damage. Britain was divided up into six districts, each with its own organizer; each district, in turn, was composed of a large number of self-contained groups—the sub-districts, whose members for the most part had no knowledge of the membership or specific tasks of any other group. Alice Mayfield's job, Georgia imagined, was to keep contact between the Berkshire group and some of the "inner council" in London. It was for this purpose, no doubt, that she had been present in Señor Alvarez' club.

"You say the inner council think I could be some use.

Did they ask you to approach me, or was it your own idea? I should have thought they'd be rather suspicious of me — after all, I did marry into the police, so to speak."

"Good lord, I wouldn't have approached you unless I'd been told to. Our movement doesn't encourage its members to be indiscreet. You've been thoroughly investigated already."

It was not till the whole affair was over that Georgia learnt how thorough this investigation had been. And the cream of the joke was that it had been initiated by Sir John Strangeways himself. A month after her first visit to the Thameford County Club, he had taken aside one of his own men — a detective-inspector of the political branch whom he had good reason for believing a member of the secret organization himself, told him confidentially that some rather strange reports about Mrs. Nigel Strangeways had reached his ear lately, said she had refused to see him or explain herself, and asked the inspector to look into these rumours as tactfully as possible. The inspector, immediately reporting this to his local organizer of the E.B., was ordered to carry on with the investigation, just as Sir John had ordered, and convey any information he might obtain to the E.B. This achieved Sir John's object, which was to disassociate Georgia from himself, and at the same time got the E.B. interested in her. Her flat was searched. The letters from Nigel, proving that the break between them was final, were discovered. And, before long, the pro-Fascist tendencies she had so sedulously been showing came to the ears of the E.B. too.

Her first conversation with Alice Mayfield did the rest. Here was a celebrated, influential woman, evidently at a loose end, discontented with her present existence, disillusioned with the democratic régime: she was just the type that the E.B. could use. But the leaders of the movement, though they had all the confidence of men who are backed by unlimited money and allured by the prospect of almost unlimited power, did not take people on trust. They were very thorough, and this thoroughness was to bring Georgia to the very edge of disaster.

# 8. The Episode of the Proof-Copy

That summer brought a long heat-wave. On the fast wickets Peter Braithwaite flourished, runs flowing from his bat as inexhaustibly as the oil from the widow's cruse. At Ascot and Hurlingham, the balls and garden-parties and functions of the season, Alison Grove went gaily about her business. In thousands of offices, factories, slum-streets, the workers sweltered, looking forward to their brief August holiday. Behind and within all these normal scenes, like red and white corpuscles battling invisibly in the blood, the secret warfare between Sir John Strangeways' agents and the conspirators continued. It was a warfare without rules or mercy on either side. Even those who were engaged, apart from the general staffs, knew nothing of the battle but their own sector. In one sense, indeed, the battle had scarcely begun: at present there was only the manoeuvring for position, the skirmishing between outposts. Yet her isolation made Georgia feel like a combatant holding one yard of a line that stretched right across Britain, who had nothing but rumours to tell her how her comrades were faring.

Reading the papers, she gleaned vague hints of the E.B. offensive. An atmosphere of uneasiness was gradually, skillfully being created in the country. The Stock Exchange was restive, securities fluctuating for no apparent reason, like the disquieted air before a storm. Certain reactionary newspapers, without committing themselves too far, began adopting a new tone of scepticism about parliamentary government. Certain prominent men, in after-dinner speeches, in clubs, at school speech-days or the laying of foundation-stones, pleaded for closer collaboration with the totalitarian powers. The seeds of doubt and discord were being sown, like the tares in the parable, while England slept. There were other things, too — mysterious disappearances, unexplained suicides — the casualties of this subterranean warfare. Reading between the lines, Georgia could see the skill with which the E.B. were leading up to an atmosphere of crisis, were seeking to demolish little by little the Englishman's confidence in democratic institutions.

She herself, as a member of one of the London groups of the organization, was given the task of winning adherents to the movement from among her acquaintances — a task which exacted all her strength of mind, for it led in most cases to polite estrangement or positive hostility. But, knowing that the E.B. were testing her thus, she went through it unflinchingly. She had been told to give implicit obedience to any one who showed her an E.B. badge — a disk such as she had found in the locket; these were held only by the six district organizers, the inner council: but no one had yet done so, and she began to despair of penetrating further into the movement.

The necessity of wearing this detestable mask in public, the fearful strain of working for one side and at the same time appearing to work loyally for the other, began to tell on her nerves. She was glad therefore when she received an invitation to visit the Mayfields again—glad as an exhausted fighter might be when sent to a quieter part of the line. At least, one might have supposed it would be quieter. . . .

There was a new light in Alice Mayfield's eye, a suppressed excitement in her bearing, that were soon explained when she told Georgia that Lord Chilton Canteloe was to be one of the house-party. Georgia was excited, too. She was beginning to get ideas about this rich playboy and it would be interesting to verify them.

"Chillie," however, was not arriving till next day, and all thought of him was put out of Georgia's head by an incident that occurred as soon as they reached Mayfield's house. "Better come and pay your respects to Daddy," Alice said. "I wonder where he's got to?" They found him at last in his study, a room where he looked as little at home as would one of his own horses. His flat-topped hat lay on the desk beside him; there was a pencil in his hand, and he seemed so absorbed in a paper-covered book he was reading that he did not at first hear them come in.

"Hello, Daddy. I've—"

"What the devil? What d'yer mean by bursting in like— Oh, beg pardon, Mrs. Strangeways. Didn't see yer. How de do? Devilish hot today."

The old man had risen to his feet, slipping the book with remarkable dexterity under a sheaf of papers. It was while he pumped her hand vigorously up and down that Georgia remembered Alison saying, last time she had been here, "Daddy read a book? I should laugh. The

107

book of form's the only one he ever opens." And this book—the glimpse she'd had of it—didn't look in the least like that invaluable work of reference. It was surely an ordinary proof-copy? Which made it odder still. For if Mr. Mayfield never read a book, one might reasonably suppose it improbable that he had written one.

Georgia made no comment upon it at the moment; but later, when Alice was helping her to unpack, she remarked lightly:

"I didn't know your father was an author."

"An author? But of course he isn't! What makes you think—?"

"I thought he was going over a proof-copy just now."

There was a moment's pause before the girl replied, "Oh, that. No. Some publisher sent it to him. Asked him for his opinion of it. I suppose they want it for an advertisement. They send him books now and then like that—ones that are up his street, racing reminiscences and so on. He hardly ever looks at them, though, as far as I know. I suppose this one must have been written by a friend of his."

It sounded plausible enough on the surface. Georgia was well acquainted with some publishers' habit of sending out books to well-known people before publication, soliciting their opinion and angling thus for a little free publicity. They usually sent finished copies, not bound proofs, it was true; but not invariably. On the other hand, why should old Mr. Mayfield have whisked the book out of sight when they entered? He surely would not carry his robust contempt for literature to the point of such acute shame at being caught out in company with a book?

While she dressed for dinner, this curious little incident nagged at Georgia's mind. That she didn't tumble to its explanation sooner was due to her having never thought of George Mayfield in connection with the conspiracy. Alice and her brothers, yes. But their father, with his beloved horses, his quaint eccentricities, his one-track mind, seemed infinitely remote from the ambitions and subterfuges of the E.B. Yet it was odd about that proof-copy. It was not in character. And for anything out of character Georgia had an unerring eye. She was in the act of laying a trace of rouge along her cheekbones when it dawned upon her that here perhaps was the clue she had been seeking. What an admirable method of communication between the chief conspirators these proof-copies would be!

They might well expect their correspondence to be opened by John Strangeways' men. At least, it would be dangerous to send their most vital communications through the post, even in code: there was no code that could not be broken down nowadays. But who would think of intercepting a book, sent out by a reputable publisher with a request that the recipient should express his opinion on it? And, in a book of 100,000 words, there were enough combinations to baffle the most experienced cryptographer, even supposing the police tumbled to the trick. The publisher himself might well be above suspicion. It only needed a member of the E.B. in his office to get hold of a copy and send it out, indicating the vital words or letters in some prearranged manner.

Scarcely had the idea blazed up in Georgia's mind when reaction set in. What a fool I am! It's no good, she argued. However large and diverse a publisher's list, he would never at one given time have ready for publication enough books on different subjects to enable this method to be used. Besides, if I wasn't so jumpy that

I suspect everyone and everything, I'd surely admit that the leaders of the E.B. have no need yet for such elaborate tricks: there's nothing, after all, to stop them meeting each other.

No, the whole idea was fantastic. Yet Georgia was impelled by a desire to prove it so, as a child waking from nightmare is driven to investigate the wardrobe he has dreamed full of unspeakable things—just to make sure. She determined somehow or other to get a good look at Mr. Mayfield's proof-copy.

The next day, just before lunch-time, Lord Chilton Canteloe arrived. All that morning a restlessness, a sense of expectancy had hung over the house-party; Georgia felt its atmosphere both flat and keyed-up, like the electric air before a tropical hurricane: the guests moved about aimlessly, talked with spasmodic animation, then fell unaccountably silent, as though little wafted winds—precursors of a storm—were eddying through the house. Alice Mayfield was distrait, breaking off in the middle of a conversation to stare in front of her with unseeing eyes. Her father's voice could be heard outside as he cursed a stable-boy for some trivial misdemeanour. Lady Rissington, that famous beauty, whom Alison Grove had nicknamed "The Ever-Open Door," preened herself nervously at every available mirror. How absurd, thought Georgia, that one man should be able to create this extraordinary atmospheric disturbance, even though he is a millionaire and God's gift to yearning womankind.

And then, while they were all drinking cocktails in the L-shaped drawing-room whose windows looked on to the downs that folded their long shadows about them like wings and slept in the noonday sunshine, Chilton Canteloe appeared. He was in his middle forties, but looked younger than his age: he had the hyacinth-curling hair, the straight nose, the small, firm mouth of a Greek statue: his beauty of feature, Georgia had to admit, was superlative and of the kind that never seems to age: there was no trace of insolence or dissipation in the deep-set, audacious eyes that roved with interest among the company. "Hello, Chillie!" they all greeted him, and there was a stir and settling-down in the room as though some volcanic disturbance had taken place, cleared the air, altered every relationship there. Alice Mayfield was bringing him over to her. Georgia noticed with surprise and a vague sense of comfort that his gait lacked the incomparable grace of his head and shoulders: he walked a little clumsily, leaning forward, his arms swinging stiffly in front of him, rather like a bear; and this flaw in his physical perfection made him, paradoxically, more real for her, more homely and likable. There was something both shy and challenging in the look he gave her as they shook hands. "Well, what do *you* think about me?" it seemed to ask. She felt the full force of his personality directed for a moment upon her, isolating them from all the others in the room.

"This *is* nice," he said. "I've always wanted to meet you. I've heard so much about you."

There was not a hint of patronizing or of conventional falseness about it. His smile, boyish yet confident, created a kind of complicity between them, as though they were old friends meeting in a room full of strangers.

"Yes," said Georgia coolly, on an impulse, "we both like taking risks. We have that much in common, anyway."

She was aware of a small, stifled movement at her side. Alice Mayfield was not used to seeing her idol treated so familiarly. Or perhaps she felt a twinge of jealousy, perceiving in the words of those two the first flick and jar of rapiers, steel on steel, between two opponents who at the first touch recognize each other's quality.

"Taking risks?" said Chilton. "I thought you'd retired from active service. Are you planning another expedition?"

"Well, no. It's so exciting in England just now, isn't it? I feel we're on the edge of great events, somehow. The stay-at-homes will see the fun this time."

Gazing frankly into his face, she could find no trace of discomposure. Well, why should there be? There was no recognizable trace of the features of the woman in the locket, either. If she had hoped to force the issue, she had certainly failed.

Chilton laughed. "You sound as if you were going to start up a revolution or something. Yes, I think you'd make a good Joan of Arc."

"Well, if I do, you'll have to finance it. Voices aren't enough nowadays. But seriously, with all this international tension, something's bound to break before long, don't you think? What's the feeling in Germany now? I haven't been there for a couple of years."

"They're scared. Like us. Only they shout a good deal louder to hide it. But what do you mean by saying that the stay-at-homes would see the fun this time?"

Silently Georgia pointed through the window. A flight of bombers was crawling low across the sky.

"That's not my idea of fun," said Chilton Canteloe. But he said it perfunctorily; and Georgia, seeing the absorbed gleam in his eyes as they followed the bombers' course, felt an irrational conviction that he would indeed take a savage, childish delight in the blast, the mushroom smoke, the houses crumbling to rubble—the mere spectacle of destruction.

"I'd love it," Alice Mayfield said. "I know it sounds awful, but think of the sense of power, up there, fighting like gods in the air. I mean, bombing's pretty foul, but—"

"Alice is a blood-thirsty child," Chilton said. "A romantic with a taste for blood is a real terror. She ought to become a hospital nurse—that's the best cure."

Alice blushed, glanced angrily at Georgia as though she, not Chilton, had uttered those flippant, wounding words. Georgia was a little shocked at them too. Chilton, who evidently was a man of breeding and sensibility, could not have failed to realize how they would hurt the girl. That he could treat her with such teasing contempt argued some streak of cruelty, or at least of irresponsibility, in his nature. Well, he was a millionaire: men did not accumulate all that money without hurting a lot of people, one way or another.

"Weren't you a bit hard on her?" she said, when Alice had moved away.

Chilton eyed her curiously, almost as if deciding what reply would please her most. "I have to, sometimes. It'll be happier for her in the end if I've kept her—well—at arm's length. Don't you think so?"

"When a girl like that is in love, she'll thrive on rebuffs. She'll make herself believe that they show there's some response on your side. Indifference is the only thing for her."

"But supposing I'm not indifferent?"

Georgia shrugged her shoulders. "Then there's no more to be said."

Only afterwards did it strike her how odd this conversation was between two people who had never met each other before. If there was such a thing as love at first sight, perhaps there could be hate at first sight too, creating the same instant intimacy. Yet she had no reason to hate Chilton Canteloe: indeed, she found him charming and sympathetic. Now she had met him, she realized how admirably he qualified for the position of leader of the E.B. conspiracy. She had faced the naked light of his intelligence, his charm and force of character: she knew now at first hand what it was that dazzled his countrymen. But she had not the least reason for suspecting that he was associated with the conspirators. Her shock tactics during their first conversation had not gained one inch of ground. Moreover, she argued, if that proof-copy I caught old Mr. Mayfield reading is really one channel by which the leaders of the E.B. communicate with each other, Lord Canteloe must be considered out of it. If he wanted to send orders down here without attracting suspicion, he need only work out some code to be used in the correspondence he would quite naturally keep up with his trainer. It's fantastic to suppose that he would adopt this round-about proof-copy method.

There was no use milling around in her mind till she had seen the book, however. That night, when the guests were in bed and the house quiet, she crept out of her room. She found her way to Mr. Mayfield's study. She was prepared to spend some time looking for the hiding-place of the book, but it was there on the desk, under the papers where he had slipped it yesterday morning. Returning to her room, Georgia got into bed, flicked on her electric torch again, and began to study the proof-copy. *Fifty Years on the Turf.* One of the usual publisher's slips inside: "With the compliments of Eason, Swayne, Ltd. To be published on September 5."

Rapidly she turned over the pages. If Mr. Mayfield

was reckless enough to leave this book about on his desk, he might even have put a mark on the relevant page. No luck there. Nor did there seem to be anything phoney about the text. An hour passed, and Georgia began to despair. Somehow or other, the person who had sent the book to Mr. Mayfield must have conveyed some code with it. Yet, if the object was to avoid suspicion, in case of the parcel's falling into the wrong hands, he would not have dared to put in an enclosure with it. Enclosure? Oh hell! Georgia muttered: the usual covering letter that publishers send out with their complimentary copies. Why didn't I think of that? Such a letter often has a reference number, and by this means Mr. Mayfield could safely leave the book about: it was as harmless to him now as a bomb with the detonator removed. Georgia was getting out of bed, to restore the book to Mr. Mayfield's study, when the publisher's slip dropped out of its pages. She bent down, and suddenly the slip seemed to stand out unnaturally large before her eyes. September 5. Publishers rarely had proofs ready so long before the date of publication. Could this be the clue she was searching for?

She turned to page five, read it word by word, examined it carefully, held it up against the light of the torch. No, there was nothing there. Try September. The ninth month of the year. She turned to page nine, page ninety, page ninety-nine, but in vain. She had a feeling, though, that she must be growing warm. Multiply the number of the month by the date. Five nines make forty-five. And on page forty-five, sure enough, she found it. Beneath certain letters there were faint indentations, made perhaps by pressing a blunted point of metal on the paper: they were invisible to the eye, but her sensitive finger-tips could feel them. She spelt out the letters, and it was as if the atrocious crime they spelt was taking shape in her own head.

"Wildiedangerousarrangeaccidenturgent."

It was enough. Georgia crept out again, replaced the proof-copy where she had found it, and returned silently to her bedroom. Lucky that it was she who had tumbled to this. No one else might have been able to interpret it. "Wildie" was the nickname of one of the R.A.F. officers who had been present at the English Banner's meeting during her first visit here. Wildman: a square-faced, blue-eyed lad—a bit of a James Cagney to look at. Evidently he had become dangerous to the E.B. conspirators in some way: perhaps, like the unfortunate Rosa Alvarez, he had merely been indiscreet: or perhaps he was another of Sir John Strangeways' agents who had found his way into the movement and had been discovered. At any rate, the E.B. centre had told the Mayfields to arrange an accident. They had contacts in the aerodrome, no doubt. A mechanic in their pay. It was damnably easy. "Arrange accident urgent." Nothing had happened yet. Alice Mayfield had mentioned Wildie's name last night. She had said—oh, God!—she had said that Wildie was giving a display of aerobatics at Hartgrove Aerodrome tomorrow afternoon. There was to be a big air-pageant there, and the whole house-party would be driving over to watch it.

For hours, till the sky paled with dawn and the first impassioned chorus of birds began, Georgia sat propped up in bed, thinking, planning against time. Once again she had become arbiter of life and death. It should be comparatively easy to warn young Wildman of what was coming to him: but, if she did and the "accident" were averted, suspicion would at once fall upon her. She had showed curiosity about the proof-copy from the start. The E.B. would deduce that she had read it and warned Wildman. Her own life, from that moment, wouldn't be worth a farthing. She did not mind this so much: what worried her to desperation was that her last chance of reaching the central secret of the E.B., to which she was now so close, would be irretrievably lost. It was a young airman's life against the lives of millions—the life of England. If only Nigel were here, or Sir John, to advise her! She felt the responsibility pressing upon her with the suffocating weight of a nightmare.

At last, when the faint gleam of dawn shone on the window-panes, she began to see light. She knew what she must do. The whole affair, in a sudden gleam of enlightenment, took on a changed complexion. A risk would have to be taken. If she failed, if her calculations went wrong, she would be a murderess. So be it.

With the fatalism and aplomb of the seasoned campaigner, who has made a decision and knows it irrevocable, Georgia Strangeways turned over in bed and went to sleep.

# 9. The Episode of the Nebuchadnezzar

Hartgrove Aerodrome lies on a plateau of the downs, extending over many acres of turf which has been laid and levelled so that from a distance it resembles the fairway of a golf course. The landing-speed of the pursuit planes stationed at Hartgrove is so great that they need a smooth run to ensure safety. This Sunday afternoon, clouds bowled across overhead, trundling their great shadows along the expanse of the downs, while in their intervals the sun shone down on the brick-red hangars, the neat houses where officers and men lived, the roadway bordering the flying field, now lined with cars whose enamel and chromium flashed back the sunlight. On the field's southern edge the spectators were arrayed, their talk mingling with the humming engines of a flight of silver planes that stood in the centre of the field, airscrews flickering, ready to go up for formation-flying. Mechanics and officers strolled about, in blue uniforms or white overalls, giving the whole scene a gala air. No one but herself, thought, Georgia, seemed to pay attention to the motor-ambulance and fire-engine which faced them on the far side of the aerodrome, small as toys.

She must give no sign of what she knew. She must concentrate all her forces on playing the part of a woman who has come to see an air display, who is used to danger, who is not expecting death. For they were watching her: she was certain of it. It had been proved this morning. She would not, in any case, have dared to telephone from the house to the aerodrome: that was too risky. But, when she had gone out after breakfast, Robert Mayfield had fallen into step beside her, offered to post the letter she carried in her hand and save her the trouble of walking into the village. "Oh, no thanks," she said, "I'd like a little walk." Robert stared down at her, his expression both puzzled and obstinate. "Well, we'll both go." He was going to be present if she should telephone from the post-office. And that, she thought now, might mean one of two things. And, if it didn't mean what she thought it did, she was about to kill an innocent man.

A loud speaker boomed hollowly across the ground. There was a crescendo of engines. The silver flight leapt forward, raced over the sward, launched imperceptibly into the air, and made a great climbing sweep like pigeons released. Attaining height, they frolicked about in the sky, moving all together as if some bird-like instinct directed each dip and turn and dive. Georgia watched them, fascinated, her fears forgotten for a moment. Then she felt a hand on her elbow. Alice Mayfield was saying, "You met Wildie last time, didn't you?" — and she was looking into the sparky blue eyes of the young officer. They talked idly for a few minutes. She noticed the slender strength of his wrists, imagined them tugging vainly at some jammed control while his plane went spinning about his ears like a catherine-wheel. She had only to say the word now. The others, Chilton, the Mayfields, Lady Rissington were grouped at a little distance, almost—she thought—as if by common consent they wished to offer Wildman this last chance. She saw Chilton giving her a curious, measured scrutiny. With an effort that seemed to drain all the blood out of her body, she kept the conventional expression on her face, maintained the slight, conventional talk. She knew she could stand very little more of this. Then, at the very moment when her hands were going out of their own accord in an imploring gesture to Wildman, a great, rising whine came down at them out of the sky.

The silver flight, still locked together in formation, had gone into a power-dive. They dropped shrieking from the high clouds, down and down, faster than falling, as if some god—angry at their presumptuous sporting in heaven's face—had seized them up in his fist and flung them down at the earth like a handful of shining pebbles. They came at the field like meteors. And then, at the moment when the eye already saw them plunged deep into the earth's heart, they swerved up and away in a roaring curve.

"That was wonderful," Georgia exclaimed. But young Wildman had left her side: she could see him strolling across to a solitary, yellow plane that stood on the concrete outside one of the hangars.

"What a nice young chap he is," she said to Alice. The girl's eyes swerved away from hers. "Oh, yes. Yes, he is." Chilton Canteloe was watching them both, Georgia noticed, with the guarded, whimsical, slightly superior air of a man watching two women who may any moment break into a furious quarrel. It flashed over her mind that Chillie was not, in any case, absolved from suspicion because of the proof-copy. Alice told her once that only the six district organizers of the E.B. knew the identity of its leader. It might be true. There was a certain bravado about Chillie, a boyish delight in the theatrical, which might lead him on to consorting incognito—like the young king in the romances—with his own followers. It would tickle him, she imagined, to send out orders that Wildman be killed, and then come down to watch the reactions of the executioners.

"Well, there he goes," Chilton said to her. "Good luck to him."

The yellow plane floated away off the ground.

"I hope nothing happens to him," said Georgia, looking up seriously into Chilton's face.

"Why should anything happen to him?"

"Well, stunting puts a terrific strain on the machine, doesn't it?"

"Oh, well, they go over every inch of it beforehand, you know."

The crowd gasped. You could hear the sigh above the drum of the engine. Wildman was taking his plane along, a few feet above the ground, one wing depressed, like a broken-winged bird trying to scuttle away from the guns. Presently he straightened, rose up almost on his tail and gained height. It was as if the plane were romping and tumbling with some invisible playmate up there. Skidding, sidling, wobbling, somersaulting—the most amazing exhibiting of crazy flying Georgia had ever seen. If something was going to happen, it must happen soon. The terrible stresses to which Wildman's airy clowning subjected his machine would find out any weakened spot: she could feel those stresses within her own body, tearing her apart centrifugally.

121

"God!" someone exclaimed. "He can make that kite talk."

Lady Rissington, that languorous, bored beauty, gave a little cry. Young Wildman went into a spin. Georgia glanced up to Chilton Canteloe. He was gazing fixedly, not at the plane, but at herself. She did not bother to decipher his expression: she knew now for certain what it meant. Controlling her voice with a last effort, putting the faintest note of apprehension into its casual tone, she remarked:

"Surely he's cutting it a bit fine, isn't he?"

Young Wildman was certainly cutting it fine. His plane was still spinning down, helpless and silent as a dead, yellow leaf, to the very furthest margin of safety. But Georgia's heart was singing. Her ordeal was over. Wildman was safe: he had never been in danger, except from his own audacity. She had called the E.B.'s bluff, staked that brilliant airman's life on its being a bluff, and won the show-down. She hardly heard the roars of applause as he cut in his engine and pulled the plane out of her spin.

Driving back in Chilton's car after the display was over, she remembered most the tension on the faces of Robert and Alice Mayfield before Wildman had gone up, and the way Chilton had been looking at her when every other eye on the field was hypnotized by the weaving plane. Last night she had come to the conclusion that the whole business of the proof-copy must mean a stratagem directed, not against Wildman, but against herself. Her attention had been called to it a little too blatantly at the start. Had it been a genuine message from the E.B., Mr. Mayfield would never have left it lying so ingenuously on his desk. Nor would the clues to such a diabolic plan have been so simple, or the plan

122

itself so nakedly set out. The E.B. had still been suspicious of her. The Mayfields had arranged that, if she were indeed a spy, she should be made inquisitive about the proof-copy, and discover its secret. They had watched her like lynxes then, to see if she passed on a warning to Wildman: Wildman might even be in the know himself. Well, she had survived the ordeal, had given no sign that she had read the message in the proof-copy, or that—if she had read it—she wished to obstruct their plans. They could doubt her allegiance no longer. But it was neither this, nor her relief at not having sent a man to his death, which made Georgia so vivacious at dinner that evening. She felt a wild, half-incredulous excitement, as a hunter might who has come upon the spoor of some legendary animal . . .

When the week-end party broke up, Georgia returned to London and sought out Alison Grove. She recounted in detail the events that had taken place at the Mayfields.

"Things don't seem to have been too cosy for you," said Alison. "Well, I'll pass it on to Sir John. Poor dear, he's still very worried, and I don't see this is going to help him much."

"You don't? The heat must have curdled your brains, darling."

"Schoolgirl abuse! Why *are* you so cock-a-hoop?"

"Chillie's asked me to stay at his place next month."

"You don't let the grass grow beneath your feet, do you? But what about it?"

"Just this. I think Chillie's our man."

Alison's blue eyes opened wide. "Oh, no! Now that's too much! You can't make me believe—why, he's got everything already. He's got money, power, immense popularity. A man like that would never risk it all for—"

"When that young chap Wildman was doing his

stunts, Chillie had eyes only for your humble servant," said Georgia stubbornly.

"He's probably fallen for you."

"Oh, dear no! Chillie's more fallen for than falling, and you know it. He was watching me to see how I'd take it. I'm never mistaken about a thing like that. Which means that he knew about the proof-copy and the plan to make me give myself away. Which means that he's in the E.B. movement himself. But Chillie wouldn't play second fiddle in any show, and he has all the qualifications Sir John and Nigel proposed for the leader of the movement."

"You're dreaming. He's just a playboy at heart."

"Yes. And that's why he's so successful and so dangerous," said Georgia very seriously. "Life's just a game to him, maybe, but he likes making the rules himself, and he has the money to make them, too. Now listen. You can help me here. I want to put over a little test. It won't absolutely prove anything, whether it comes off or fails, but it may give me another bit of probability. This is what you've got to do . . ."

Mrs. Ryle's parties were famous. She had been one of the "Bright Young Things" of the twenties, and fifteen years of happy marriage to John Ryle, now a Cabinet Minister, had not taken the edge off her larkiness. There was nothing she liked better than to invite a number of maliciously ill-assorted guests, play them off against each other and watch the repercussions. She was also fond of putting the most self-important people through the hoop: indeed she had a way with her that made them almost enjoy the circus themselves.

This evening, after dinner was over, she announced in her most robust tones, "We're going to play Nebuchadnezzar. John, you pick one side, and I'll choose the other."

An elderly gentleman, permanent head of a Civil Service department, stirred uneasily. "Nebuchadnezzar? What is that, Mrs. Ryle? I hope you're not expecting me to eat grass?"

"I'm sure the hay diet would be very good for you, my dear. But we'll let you off this time. Nebuchadnezzar is a kind of charade. We all played it like mad when I was a foolish young girl."

"A charade? Oh, but really, Mrs. Ryle—"

"Now, don't start making a thing about it," she said firmly. "Nobody could reach your position in Whitehall without being a born actor. Besides, you'll be all right, you don't have to *say* anything. It's a dumb charade. Just the thing for the Silent Service."

Quelled by this flow of rather sinister compliments, Sir Thomas Park allowed himself to be led out with the rest of Mrs. Ryle's team.

"Now then," she said remorselessly when they were outside. "The word will be Abel. We'll finish with a Cain and Abel scene. What about A? Agag? Artemis? Absalom? All a bit threadbare."

"St. Athanasius," suggested Chilton Canteloe.

"My dear man, what do you know about St. Athanasius?"

"Nothing. But I can easily imagine it. Park could appear as Athanasius, dictating his creed, while three of us—"

"No. I don't think that would be at all historical. Besides, the bishop might object."

"Alcibiades, then. A scene from his private life. That would knock them."

"It sounds rather risqué to me. Platonic love is one thing, and Socratic love another. Still, art should have

125

no frontiers. We'll settle on that. Abel. B. What about the B?"

"Browning," piped up Sir Thomas unexpectedly. "A rattling good play that was. What the devil was it called? 'The Brownings of Wimpole Street,' that's it."

"Barretts, dear, Barretts. Yes, that'll do. I," Mrs. Ryle added masterfully, "will play the part of Mr. Barrett."

After the usual flippant wrangling, the rest of the word was disposed of. The first scene having been played out with considerable *réclame*, Mrs. Ryle's side retired to make ready for the second. Their leader threw open the cupboard of theatrical properties. "Elizabeth Barrett must have some sort of wig," she said. "This'll do, perhaps." She took out a heavy, ringleted affair and tried it on Sir Thomas Park. "No, my dear. Nothing could make you look like an invalid poetess." She tried it on two of the women: then on Chilton Canteloe. "Ah, that's better. You're Elizabeth B. Now go and swathe yourself up in this lace. Run along. And don't forget to put some powder on. The canary of Wimpole Street was not suntanned. Sir Thomas, you will sustain the rôle of Robert Browning: you must be suave, but passionate: success is your middle name, remember."

"I always think Browning was a bit of a bounder," replied Sir Thomas.

"I'll leave you to bring out the nuances of the character. Now for the rest of you . . ."

The Barrett-Browning scene was always remembered, by those who had been present, as Mrs. Ryle's greatest triumph. Ably seconded by a corpse-pale but winsome Elizabeth, and Sir Thomas' wonderfully caddish Browning, she gave Mr. Barrett full value. She sneered, rampaged, snubbed, exuded the very essence of patriarchal tyranny. Even a maid, who had peeped in at the drawing-room door with a message for her mistress, was held spellbound and evidently so affected by the scene that she entirely forgot to deliver the message.

Not merely forgot the message, but after watching for a few moments through the slightly-opened door, slipped away, took off cap and apron, and emerged from the house as Georgia Strangeways. Much as she admired Mrs. Ryle's rendering, it was not Mrs. Ryle she had come to look at. She had come to look at Chilton Canteloe, wearing a wig of black hair parted in the middle, with ringlets falling to the shoulders. And she had seen his face amazingly transformed thus into the face of the woman whose picture was in the locket claimed by Major Keston. There could be no mistaking it. The link was made at last. It was just conceivable that some unknown X might be the real owner of the locket, might have picked up that daguerreotype by chance and used it to conceal the E.B. disk: but, in view of what Georgia knew about Chilton, this must be considered too much of a coincidence.

In the taxi, Georgia was exultant, yet a little worried. The question was—had Pamela Ryle and Thomas Park carried it off without raising Chilton's suspicion? Had there been any difficulty in getting him to wear that wig? Alison would tell her tomorrow. It was Alison who had suggested to her friend Mrs. Ryle the plan by which Chilton and the locket should be connected. Pamela Ryle was staunch as oak, Alison knew, beneath her old whims and escapades, and she had been willing to fall in with Alison's suggestion without inquiring too deeply into the reasons for it. Sir Thomas Park was the repository for so many secrets that he could be trusted not to give away even the most apparently insignificant. Mrs. Ryle had asked him privately to suggest Elizabeth

Barrett as one of the scenes for the Nebuchadnezzar, for Alison thought the whole thing would thus appear more spontaneous and be less likely to put Chilton Canteloe on his guard.

Indeed, but for the ill-timed enthusiasm of Lady Rissington, who was also at the Ryles' party, everything would have gone off without a hitch. Pamela Ryle had seen to it that the men of her side changed their clothes in her husband's study, where there were no mirrors. There was nothing here to show Chilton his resemblance to his grandmother—the woman in the locket. He was entirely absorbed in his rôle as Elizabeth Barrett, till, when the scene had ended, Lady Rissington rushed up to him out of the audience, took his arm, screaming, "Oh, Chillie, you look positively divine! Do come and look at yourself. It's a knock-out," and led him up to a mirror on the wall.

Chilton Canteloe regarded for a moment the tilted, coquettish head with its drooping ringlets, the face that gazed at him out of the mirror, so strange yet so familiar. "Yes, the effect is rather stunning, isn't it?" He turned away, smiling speculatively over Lady Rissington's head at the guests sitting there. He walked out of the room with that lumbering, bear-like gait of his, and found Mrs. Ryle.

"Do you mind if I use your telephone?" he asked. "There's something I forgot to tell my secretary before I came out."

"Of course. You know where it is. You're not on in the next scene, are you?"

Still in wig and Victorian lace, the millionaire went out into the hall. He dialed a number. He spoke quietly:

"Is that you, David? . . . Canteloe speaking. Will you find out where Mrs. Nigel Strangeways was between nine-fifteen and nine-thirty tonight. Also her husband . . . Yes, I know that. Please don't interrupt. Put B20 and B23 onto it. Yes, I want them to start at once. Good-bye."

Chilton returned to the study, took off the wig, stared at it for a few seconds; then, with an expression which few people had ever seen on his face, he twined his fingers almost lovingly in the silky, black hair and, breath hissing through his distended nostrils, began to pull. He did not jerk out the handful of hair. He pulled at it steadily, as if he wished to prolong the torture of some woman whose dark head he was holding down. He went on, steadily pulling, till at last that lock of hair was dragged up by its roots. Then his mouth straightened again, and he took a comb, and began carefully combing the hair over the little bald patch he had made on the wig.

"Those two were the only ones who saw it," he muttered, "unless Keston was lying. Foolish of me . . . still, one can't be too careful. Damn all this caution! It makes me sick. Not for much longer, though."

He went into the next room, smiling with gay, confident charm at Mrs. Ryle and the rest of her side, who were just returning from the third scene of the charade.

# 10. The Episode of the Most Popular Man

Up till now, Georgia had not been able to grasp the full implications of the E.B. There had been moments—the affair of Rosa Alvarez, the sinister episode in Professor Hargreaves Steele's laboratory—when she had felt its breath chill on her neck. Yet even these, by their sheer melodrama, put an aura of unreality around the whole business; while the amateurishness, the cheapjack reactionary sentiments, the pathetically idealistic or merely disgruntled attitude of the E.B. rank-and-file with whom she herself had been working, prevented her from taking the situation with consistent seriousness. Like many highly intelligent people, Georgia was inclined to under-estimate the enormous potential strength of stupidity. Like herself, millions of men and women in England, though the last ten years had given them so many object lessons in the way a few really determined, unscrupulous men can exploit this stupidity and apathy, were still saying "That sort of thing cannot happen here." Even Georgia, who was seeing it begin to happen, could not quite believe her eyes—so difficult was it for English people of her class to shake from their eyes the scales which long security had grown there. "One has heard of engineers being hoist by their own petards," she said to Nigel when the whole affair was over: "I'd never realized how a nation might be betrayed by the sheer perfection of its defence-mechanisms."

Georgia, however, was brought wide awake at last by two events that occurred shortly after Pamela Ryle's party. The first of these was so trivial that she herself hardly noticed its significance at the time. The second made perhaps the biggest journalistic sensation since the Great War.

The night of the Ryles' party, Georgia got out of her taxi a few hundred yards from her flat, slipped quietly in and went to bed. She had sent her maid out for the evening. She had not been in bed half an hour before there was a ring at the outer door. Slipping on her dressing-gown, she went to answer it. A policeman stood outside, a large, fresh-faced, polite young man, his helmet tucked under his arm.

"Sorry to disturb you, ma'am," he said. "Saw a chap hurrying down the street just now—he seemed to have come out of this block, so I thought I'd better make sure he hadn't been breaking in anywhere. You heard anything suspicious?"

Minor public school and Hendon Police College stuck out all over the young man's bearing. Georgia screwed up her eyes against the light, passed the back of her hand over her forehead.

"No. I've heard nothing. I've been in bed—a headache, but I'd have heard him if he was in any of the rooms, I think."

The policeman inquired politely whether she had been at home all the evening.

"Yes," she said. "But why should you think this chap was a criminal? And can't you arrest people for loitering with intent?"

"He wasn't loitering, ma'am. Far from it. Came haring past me like a streak. I thought I recognized him, though. And, if he's the chap I believe he is, we can pick him up any time. One of our regulars." The policeman grinned at her. "Suppose your maid didn't hear anything?"

"She's out for the evening."

"Don't mind if I have a look around, do you? Just to make sure."

He went solemnly round the flat, even poking a nose into her bedroom. Finally he took himself off, saying how fearfully sorry he was to have been a nuisance and expressing the hope that her headache would soon be gone. Georgia wrote down the number she had noticed on his uniform. No doubt it was just a coincidence that somebody should be inquiring about her movements on this very evening when it was essential that the E.B. should not know she had been out of the house at all. But, if the young policeman and the suspicious character were fakes, she'd be able to find it out very quickly.

Next morning, when Doris brought in her tea, the girl was evidently excited—and faintly disappointed not to have found her mistress murdered in her bed. The copper had been round to every flat in the building last night, to see if anything was stolen. Loudly Doris lamented that she always missed the fun.

"And was anything stolen?"

"Well, not as you might say stolen. But he nearly caught the burglars, a couple of them, running away. Must have surprised them before they'd got to work properly."

Just another scare, thought Georgia. If my polite young copper had really been an E.B. agent in disguise, he'd never have bothered to go into all the other flats: too dangerous for him, besides: somebody might have recognized he wasn't the regular policeman on this beat, and started talking. Wait a minute, though. Wouldn't he have taken the risk? In order to find out if any of the other occupants of the flats had seen me go out or come in last night? He'd not be apt to take my own word for it that I had not gone out.

"Do you know this policeman, Doris?"

"Oh, yes m'm. A nice boy, he is. Real superior, too. That Millie, in Number Two—fancies herself, she does, it'd make you laugh—when he went in there last night she tried to get a date out of him—been trying for months now, the artful cat—but nothing doing with our Mr. Robert."

So Millie could vouch for the young policeman. That was that. An over-zealous officer he might be, but not a bogus one. Georgia dismissed him from her mind.

It might never have recurred to her, had not Mrs. Tinsley, the occupant of Number One flat, whom she met by chance in the hall later that morning, begun talking about last night's visitation. The constable, it seemed, had been remarkably pertinacious in his inquiries. Had Mrs. Tinsley heard any movements in the flat above? (The flat above hers was Georgia's.) Had she seen or heard any one going in or out since nine o'clock?

"Of course, I hadn't," said Mrs. Tinsley with some heat. "I kept on telling him nobody could have been up in your place—except yourself: you'd come to borrow some aspirin off me and then gone to bed. These young policemen are becoming a menace. They'll do anything for promotion."

Thank heaven our flats don't boast a night-porter, and I made my exits and entrances as quietly as I did, thought Georgia.

At six o'clock that evening Georgia rang up Sir John Strangeways from a friend's house. She was still a little impatient of the precautions that had to be taken in communicating with him, but she followed his instructions meticulously. When they had spoken the code-sentences by which they recognized each other, she said:

"The experiment was successful."

"Good. Well done. You must stick to him now—a lot will depend on you. Find out what his arrangements are. You know."

"I wish you'd keep your policemen out of my hair." Georgia gave him a brief account of the visit yesterday night, and told him the constable's number.

"I'll have inquiries made. Don't trust any one you're not sure of. Well, good luck."

That was all. But it was more than enough. Though Georgia had lived often enough in lawless places, she found it difficult to adapt her mind to the idea that here, in England, a blue uniform might cover an enemy. The servant, Millie, had recognized the policeman as the regular one on the beat: yet there seemed little doubt now that he had invented the story of the man running away in order to find out whether Georgia had left the house that evening. It was quick work on the part of the E.B. What unnerved Georgia, though, was that it had been done with the full panoply of the law. She had a vision of the E.B. stretching out its tentacles into all the places she used to believe most secure. Sir John had warned her at the start that the movement had a certain foothold in the police, the army, the Civil Service; but it had needed that polite young constable to bring it right home to her. From now on, she would not know who was friend, who was enemy.

Well, she had her job. She must stick to Chilton and "find out what his arrangements are." In Sir John's crisp, business-like tones, it had sounded like nothing more important than the plans, say, for a summer cruise. Yet on those plans history was now balanced. And what chance had she, supposing her alibi of yesterday night did not convince the E.B.? About as much chance as a bug under a steam-hammer. Only Georgia's remarkable buoyancy of temperament, the self-confidence that had carried her through so many difficult places, prevented her falling into despair during the next few days.

It was on the Saturday morning that the great news-story broke, overwhelming her own worries and activities as a beaver-dam might be overwhelmed by the tidal wave of an earthquake. The trap she had set to catch Chilton Canteloe, to identify him with the woman in the locket, seemed a niggling, irrelevant thing in the face of this enormous counter-stroke—no stronger than the wisps of flax that Samson burst with one heave of his muscles. Georgia opened her papers that morning, and their headlines smacked her across the eyes. The press had certainly let itself go.

"MILLIONAIRE PLANS MILLENNIUM," one paper shrieked.

"CANTELOE'S CURE," howled another antiphonally.

"CHILTON'S CHALLENGE," chimed a third.

Pouring herself another cup of coffee, Georgia lit a cigarette and read quickly through the various stories. They boiled down to this. Last night the millionaire had given a dinner to a number of prominent industrialists, bankers and scientists. The speech he made had evidently been issued to the press beforehand, for the papers carried it verbatim. It put forward a plan for the abolition of unemployment in Great Britain.

In brief, a network of co-operative enterprises was to be set up all over Britain, among which the unemployed were to be distributed. Each man should follow the trade to which he had been accustomed, while those who had not yet learnt a trade would for the present provide the unskilled labour. As far as possible, each co-operative should be self-sufficient: but the necessary goods which any one of them could not manufacture would be exchanged by a system of barter with commodities produced by some other co-operative. The scheme was on a heroic scale. Whole communities might be transplanted to places where they could work under the best conditions. On the other hand, it did not necessarily involve a depopulation of the derelict areas. "The desert," Chilton had quoted in his moving peroration, "shall blossom like a rose." There was coal and iron in the earth, there were fish in the sea. It was pernicious nonsense, Chilton declared, to say that the unemployed did not want work. All that you needed was a scheme by which the fish might get to the miners, the coal to the fishermen.

This co-operative scheme would not injure the normal trade of the country, he pointed out, for by it the unemployed would be transformed into one vast, self-contained unit, living by the exchange of its own commodities until such time as world economic conditions allowed them to be reabsorbed into the normal productive life of Great Britain. The scheme would apply not only to manual labour, but to unemployed architects, engineers, doctors, teachers, clerks — all of whom could find a place in the co-operative communities.

136

Chilton Canteloe emphasized that, by this means, all the derelict agricultural land could be brought into cultivation again, thus helping to diminish the danger of starvation in the event of war. Moreover, each co-operative would have its own deep-shelter against air-raids, and could send out "Defence Workers" to construct such shelters in the big towns. These two points, the latter especially, were given great prominence in the press accounts, for they concerned matters over which the public had been growing more and more restive during recent years.

Until the scheme was properly on its feet, it would be subsidized by a loan, in which Lord Canteloe was prepared to sink £1,000,000 himself. The interest would accrue from a certain percentage of the co-operative commodities which would be set aside and launched upon the home or foreign markets. As to this loan—and now Georgia began to see light—it should be a government loan: but, if the government was unwilling to adopt the scheme, Chilton offered to run it himself. He already had the support of a number of influential persons who were present there tonight. This was no Utopian plan, he concluded, no lunatic philanthropy, but a scheme which had been worked out by experts and approved by hard-headed business men. Great ills demanded heroic remedies. No man's personal interests or prejudices should be allowed to outweigh the terrible fact that two million of our countrymen were being condemned to a living death.

Georgia turned to the leading articles. They were for the most part cautious and noncommittal. A scheme backed by such weight of authority could not be dismissed with a little editorial persiflage. At the same time, it was evident that Chilton's speech had not been given to the papers in time for their experts to make a thorough examination before the paper went to press. His scheme, therefore, had a day's start to impress public opinion: it was a jump ahead of any expert criticism: and a day's start, Georgia knew, will work wonders. The timing of Chilton's stroke roused her to unwilling admiration. Political genius is often a matter of perfect timing, and she realized, as never before, what Sir John and herself and all the rest of them were up against. Her musings were interrupted by the arrival of Alison Grove, looking like a butterfly dishevelled by an unseasonable gale.

"Well, the lid's off now, my dear," she said. "I don't believe even John Strangeways knew this was going to break."

"Do you think Chilton is at all sincere over it? It can't just be a gigantic piece of spoof. His backers—"

"The people backing the scheme are mainly high-ups in the E.B., you can bet your pants on it, my girl. This scheme only need be coherent enough to hold water for a few weeks, while it's making its impact on public opinion. The man in the street doesn't give two damns for expert verdicts. Suppose the present government refuses to consider the scheme, shows up all its weak points: the man in the street won't bother about that, he'll say to himself, 'Here at last is someone making constructive proposals on the three subjects that've been most on my mind—the unemployed, food in war-time, real security from air-raids. And, as usual, the government turns it down. To hell with governments! Why can't we have Chillie running the country?'"

"Yes, that's true. He's certainly got wonderful tactical skill. Reading his speech, I found a sort of disillusionment and discontent with parliamentary government

138

even creeping over myself. It's very skillful, the way he injects a note of scepticism, a good-humoured but weary contempt for the muddle parliament has made of everything."

"Believe me, if there was any doubt before, there's none now. He's the most popular man in Britain today. You can't imagine the sensation this has made in Fleet Street. And all the way along here I kept being bumped into by people with their eyes glued to their newspapers. If ever the E.B. are allowed to make their coup, there's not going to be much difficulty in putting over their dictator now."

"Yes. He'll have the better part of the two million unemployed at his back, for one thing. And there's nothing Nazi-ish about it to arouse their suspicions, either. No talk of labour camps and so on."

"That's his genius. The leopard that changed his spots. It doesn't look like Fascism: it doesn't sound like Fascism: it doesn't smell like Fascism. But—" Alison shrugged her shoulders.

"It's odd, his coming out into the open like this so soon after I began to get proof that he's the man behind the E.B."

"Don't flatter yourself, my dear. Spoof or no spoof, his scheme has taken longer to work out than that. You're just a nice little woman to him. Or perhaps a nasty little nuisance. Depends how much he's found out. Blast Lady Rissington and her mirror!"

"It makes me feel like Mickey Mouse trying to ride a whale."

"Even a whale's got its weak spot. It's your job now to find it."

Alison crossed her pretty legs, and went on, "Yes, Chillie's got the politicians in a cleft stick. The present government daren't ignore his scheme since he's threatened to run it himself if they do, and that puts them in a false position. The Opposition can't use it as a stick to beat the government with, because — although there's a certain flavour of Socialism about it — it's been put forward by a group of capitalists. He's taken the wind out of everyone's sails."

Georgia walked over to the window, stared out unseeing at the opposite houses, the trees in the square now limp and dusty after the summer months. It was a familiar scene, but today the ordinariness of it did not comfort her. She thought of Nigel, who had gone to live with a friend at Oxford: they had lived here together and had been happy, but now she felt like an exile for whom the unreality of the present clouds even the past happiness. Shaken by a spasm of intolerable longing, she turned away. On with the motley, she thought: on with the make-believe. It can't last for ever. Either they'll find me out, and Hargreaves Steele's filthy bacilli will do the rest; or else we'll beat them, and I can become an ordinary person again. Oh, Nigel, if only we could have been doing this *together*!

# 11. The Episode of the Clock-Golf Course

Georgia's first sight of Chilton Ashwell was on an August evening. She had travelled up to the Midlands by train. At the main-line station she was met by a chauffeur, who tucked her solicitously into the Rolls-Royce and drove fast through the mining district from which a part of Lord Canteloe's wealth was derived. They were model villages, having sprung up out of a new coal-field during the last twenty years, the groups of red-brick houses arranged in crescents, their gardens blazing with flowers. There was nothing here to remind one of all that lay beneath, except the black-faced miners, tin-helmeted, their cans slung over their shoulders, bicycling home from the day shift, and the pervasive, indescribable tang which burning slag-heaps left in the air.

After a drive of eight miles, the car turned off through the park gates and whirred up an avenue of beeches that rose, smooth and metallic like organ pipes, into the evening sky. An occasional pheasant, alarmed by their approach, rocketed screeching away. Rabbits lolloped leisurely across the drive in front of them. Then the drive curved, the screen of trees and bracken fell away a little, and Georgia saw the west front of Chilton Ashwell, all its windows glowing like opals in the late sun. The grey, Palladian façade looked infinitely peaceful: its elegance had an ethereal quality, as though this house still lay in the dreaming mind of its creator, and might vanish into thin air at a touch. On the lake swans sailed with their dreamlike motion, arched their necks superbly. The stone-balustraded terrace, the formal gardens had the swept air of a place from which men have long since departed, where only history remains. You could not imagine this house in any other setting, or that green park-land opening to reveal any other house.

Yes, thought Georgia, Chilton Ashwell is everything he claimed for it. But I must not let myself be lulled into oblivion by all this. He shan't try his stately-homes-of-England stuff on me. Walking up the broad, shallow steps, already half under the spell of this house, she forced herself to remember that here, in the heart of England, England's ruin was being planned.

She was shown into a high-ceilinged, homely room, where a number of the party were congregated. Chilton Canteloe's face lighted up when she appeared. In flannels, his hair rumpled, he looked more boyish than ever: he strode across the room with his stooping, bear-like gait, and took both her hands for a moment.

"How nice to see you. And you got here quite safely? Do you want some tea?"

"No, thanks. I've had it. I do think your house is perfect." Georgia glanced round, a little bemused by all these conflicting sensations. Most of the men, she noticed, were in flannels. "Have you all been morris-dancing?"

Chilton threw back his head, and roared with laughter. "Morris-dancing! What a tortuous mind you have! Never content with the obvious. We've been playing cricket."

"It's all one to Georgia," said a familiar voice. "She doesn't know the difference."

"Peter! I never knew you'd be here. Have they thrown you out of your county side?"

"We've no fixture today. So Lord Canteloe asked me to play for his team against one of the local pits. Eh, they're terrors, your miners. Ah've been boomped all over," said Peter Braithwaite, throwing a Nottingham twang into his voice.

"We don't dope our wicket here," said Chilton grinning. "Shows you up properly, Peter, my lad, when you've got to play on a piece of honest turf."

The friendly banter was so English, Georgia thought bitterly: like the whole atmosphere of Chilton Ashwell which, in spite of its owner's millions, achieved that paradoxical English blend of the idyllic and the cosy. At dinner, too, when they were talking about Chilton's plan for the unemployed, and Georgia—acting her part —remarked that perhaps his recent travels in Germany and Italy had helped him to formulate it, Chilton replied passionately that he hoped we should never model ourselves on continental methods, the English spirit was a thing apart and must always create its own forms.

Studying his magnetic, brown, gold-flecked eyes, which could turn so easily from playfulness to an almost tigerish fury of concentration, Georgia was inclined to think he really meant it. His belief in himself was so implicit that he could never doubt, at the moment, the truth of his own words. He was a self-deceiver on the heroic scale, and of that stuff dictators are made. If a man is only vulnerable at the point where his self-confidence leaves off, Georgia asked herself, where is Chilton's weak spot?

Tonight more than ever she realized how invulnerable he was. Among the guests there were two women at least whose beauty was worth a king's ransom—the dazzling, blonde, patrician-featured Lady Rissington, and Mrs. Mainwaring with her loveliness that glowed in the candle-lit room like a ruby or a smouldering coal. It was plain that he had only to lift a finger and they would follow him anywhere. Yet his manner towards them was affectionate, teasing, whimsical, without either the puritan's stiff reserve or the libertine's aggressiveness; they might have been his kid sisters just out of the schoolroom: and, oh my, don't they know it, Georgia thought with secret amusement, watching their subtle or undisguised efforts to capture his attention.

She was the more surprised when after dinner they began dancing to the radio gramophone and Chilton sought her out first, leaving the two professional charms to bite their thumbs together. He danced perfectly, absorbed in the steps, the usual clumsiness of his gait altogether gone. I am now not merely in the lion's den, but in his very jaws, Georgia said to herself: it gave her a feeling of temerity and faint astonishment. Well, he's only a man, after all. He feels like a man, his fingers are warm on my back, so snap out of it, my girl.

When their dance was over, he took her out onto the terrace. The park was stretched before them, its smooth contours seeming to stir in the universal rhythm of sleep. Below, the lake glimmered, and riding swans were like drowned ghosts of moonlight. The music throbbed out again behind them.

"Why are you looking at me like that?" asked Georgia, turning to meet his eyes.

"How am I looking at you?"

"As if I was a new kind of equation your teacher had chalked up on the blackboard."

"Perhaps you are, Georgia. I can't quite place you."

"Do you always have to place people?"

"When they might be dangerous to me—yes."

Georgia's voice was cool, interested, not in the least betraying how his words had shaken her. "How could I be dangerous to you?"

"If you don't know that, nobody does."

A silence fell, broken by the flurried squawk of a moorhen among the reeds below. There was something formidable about Chilton's silence, his refusal to press her at all. She felt his enigmatic power circled about her, mingling with the spell of house and moonlit park.

"This is a very odd conversation, considering we've only met once before," she said at last.

"We're neither of us ordinary people," he replied indifferently. "Do you suppose we should talk about the weather?"

"It's a safe subject, especially when you're with a *dangerous* person." She underlined the word. Two could play at the game of cryptic remarks.

"I don't play for safety. Nor do you, judging by accounts."

"There's not much risk for a traveller today. Only dirt and fatigue. I never minded them much."

"Travelling. Oh, yes," said Chilton politely. He linked his hands behind his neck. "But were we talking about travel?"

Georgia made no reply. Her silence stood up to him like an ice barrier. His voice deepened. "I believe you've

145

no idea what an electrifying creature you are. You make the Mainwarings and Rissingtons of this world look like dumb celluloid close-ups. A woman like you could—"

He broke off, put his hand under her elbow and took her back into the house. No, thought Georgia, it's absurd. Fantastically absurd. Yet perhaps this is the way to do it—the only way I could do it. It must be the resistance in me that attracts him: he's so used to women crumpling up at his feet: he senses this resistance; but how far does he suspect its real cause? Did he mean I was dangerous to the man, or to the future dictator?

She had no opportunity that night for talking to Peter Braithwaite alone. Next morning, though, when Chilton was in conference with his secretary and his agent, Peter asked her to have a round of clock-golf with him.

"I can't play clock-golf," she said.

"That's all right. I play it like a master. You'd be surprised."

The lawn lay between waist-high hedges of beech. At the far end stood a miniature marble temple, built by some 18th century Canteloe who liked to admire his panorama from a classical vantage-point, abandoned now to spiders and golf-clubs.

"A good place to talk," said Peter cheerfully. "You can see any one approaching, quite a long way off. And one can always hide behind that marble oddment if they start shooting."

"Are you expecting to get shot? I thought you'd come here to play cricket!"

"Oh, I'm doing a bit of that on the side. Alison told me you'd begun to play the big fish."

"Were you surprised?"

"After the things I've come across these last months,

146

I'd not have been surprised to hear that Canteloe was the Grand Lama of Tibet in disguise," said Peter, hitting his ball negligently over the hillocky turf to the lip of the hole. Georgia followed suit, with pronounced ill-success.

"I wish there weren't all these horrid little bumps in the grass," she complained. "It's not fair."

"As a matter of fact, clock-golf is usually played on a level surface, not a sort of championship golf green like this. I suppose Canteloe wanted to make it more difficult. He fancies himself as a games-player. A gardener told me that his Lordship laid this out himself not long ago. Beats me how he gets time for all this, what with planning for the unemployed, organizing a revolution and being groomed for Britain's dictator."

"Don't stop playing, Peter, and be careful what you say. There's someone watching us out of a window in the east wing, with field-glasses."

"Field-glasses? What does he think we are? A couple of long-tailed tits?"

"There's such a thing as lip-reading, Peter. Keep your back to the house if you're going to throw off any more slander about our host."

They played the remaining holes. The young cricketer was quite accustomed to being watched by people with field-glasses: he kept running his ball up to the pin, his slender wrists moving neatly, lazily.

"It's a very lopsided sort of clock, isn't it?" said Georgia. The little numbered disks from which they played did not, as usual in this game, form a circle, but were dotted irregularly about the lawn.

"Canteloe is a very lopsided sort of man," Peter replied.

After they had finished the game and Georgia had

declined another, they went to sit in the marble summer-house. Two caryatids, blank-eyed, supported the door. You could see Chilton Ashwell and its rolling parkland all laid out below, scorching now in the summer heat. A herd of deer, motionless and painted as wooden toys, was congregated among the shadowing oaks away to their left.

"Canteloe seems to have taken a fancy to you," said Peter at last.

"I can't quite make out whether he's a bit suspicious of me, or whether it's—well, natural interest. The latter, let's hope. It might come in very useful."

"Don't, Georgia," the cricketer exclaimed with unusual intensity. "You mustn't let it come to that. It didn't matter so much with me. I'm just a chap who can hit a cricket-ball hard. But you're different. You're really worth something."

"My dear Peter, what are you—"

"I can't get Rosa Alvarez out of my head." He shivered in the dry, lizard-like chill of the summerhouse. "It was bad enough leading her up the garden path. Well, she asked for it, I suppose. She was a stupid, greedy, frightened woman, if you like, and I was the young hero in a Secret Service play, risking worse than death for his country's sake. All right. Let it go. But I killed that woman. I'm responsible for whatever filthy thing it was that Alvarez and the E.B. did to her. Yes, I know, all in a good cause. But a good cause doesn't make a dirty trick clean. Sounds silly, but I feel as if I'll have to expiate Rosa's death somehow."

"I do understand, Peter," said Georgia gently. "But you can't keep the rules when you're fighting anything as big and unscrupulous as the E.B. You've got to set your teeth and plunge into the muck."

"I reckon there are limits. I wouldn't like to see you laying for Canteloe—well, in that way. It'd save a lot of trouble if I shot him straight off." He chuckled grimly, half aware of his own naîveté. Georgia had forgotten how dizzily his temperament could swing him from hilarity into the deepest gloom. That was the damnable thing about this business—you lost track of your friends, you got calloused and insensitive to everything but the enemy's movements, like fighters in a guerilla war.

"We'll have to get hold of his plans before we shoot Canteloe," she said.

"Well, here he is, coming along with that cod-faced secretary of his. You'd better ask him for them."

They giggled at each other, keyed up to action again, back in a brittle, polished world of make-believe that shuddered like thin ice under their feet.

"Very well, David, you'll see to that, then?" said Canteloe. The secretary turned back to the house, his black morning-suit and bald, bland head looking absurdly incongruous amid these sylvan surroundings.

"And what are you two conspiring about?"

"Peter's just given me a frightful licking. He's a master at clock-golf. I'd back him against Henry Cotton."

A faint shadow of petulance appeared on Chilton Canteloe's face. He gazed speculatively at Peter for a moment, then challenged him to a game. Perched on the window-sill of the marble summerhouse, Georgia watched them. They both played with almost uncanny skill: but, whereas Peter struck the ball nonchalantly and did not seem to mind whether he won or lost, Chilton was all rigid, furious concentration. The little white balls ran, dipped, curled over the undulating turf: after the first time round, the opponents were all square: they decided to play another twelve holes. Georgia found herself desperately willing Peter to win. It was as if great issues hung on the result. Chilton obtained a lead of two holes; but Peter, pulling out a flash of extraordinary brilliance, holed out in one twice running and pegged him back: then he started to go ahead.

Chilton cracked. He couldn't do anything right: his ball shot far past the mark or only crawled half-way towards it. In a moment, Georgia realized he wasn't trying—or rather, that he was deliberately playing badly so that victory would leave a nasty taste in his opponent's mouth. It was incredible. This man, who already controlled so many lives and might in a few months' time be controlling the destinies of an empire, was sulking like a peevish schoolboy over a footling little game. He couldn't bear to be beaten at anything. His morale would crack up under pressure. It seemed of immense significance to Georgia: never again would she think of Chilton Canteloe and the E.B. as invulnerable, invincible: she would no longer be fighting a power huge and resistless as Fate—only a man who lost his temper at clock-golf.

It did not occur to her at the time that her presence exacerbated Chilton's defeat. She was thinking, rather, how great his egotism must be to permit him thus to sulk in public. A less self-confident man would have made some attempt to conceal his pique.

When the game was over, Chilton gave her a wry, ugly smile, and without a word went abruptly off into the summerhouse.

"He doesn't like losing, does he?" whispered Peter. "Sh!"

Chilton Canteloe, having put his putter away, emerged again between the two caryatids. For a moment his Grecian face seemed inhuman as theirs. He surveyed the putting-green that lay mapped out beneath the summerhouse.

Lips curved in a remote smile, nostrils distended, legs planted apart, he looked in that instant, thought Georgia, like a general surveying a battlefield. Then his expression relaxed, he chatted to them good-humouredly for a few moments, and set off towards the house.

"Girlie's recovered her poise," said Peter, nodding at Chilton's retreating back. "Hey, Georgia, are you going off into a trance?"

Georgia was standing between the two caryatids, gazing over the clock-golf course as Chilton had done. What had brought that imperious, secret expression into Chilton's face? She stared at the green, and gradually its contours shaped themselves into something familiar.

"Peter, come up here," she called softly. He stood on the top step of the miniature temple beside her.

"When is a clock not a clock?" she asked.

"All right. You tell me."

"When it's a map. A nice, bumpy contour map. Peter, you're going to play some more golf. You need practice. Go round the course, playing two balls. Start at Number One mark, hit the balls up to the hole, then stroll after them. Only put one foot in front of the other, so I get the distances measured out in feet. If any one's watching from the house, they'll think you're just pottering about: your feet will be screened by those beech-hedges. Walk back from the pin to the first tee, then measure out the distance between that and Number Two mark—knocking the balls along in front of you. I'll do the counting: you concentrate on walking naturally. I want the number of feet between each successive tee, and between each tee and the pin. Take some cross measurements, too. That'll help, as I shall only be able to calculate the angles roughly."

"O.K. But what *is* all this about?"

"It may be a boss shot. But I have an idea that this green represents a map of England. The bumps and ridges—well, look, can't you see a suggestion of the Pennine Chain over there, and the Cotswolds, and the Chilterns? And, if I'm right, maybe the position of the hole and the twelve starting-marks will tell us something."

"Good Lord! But, look here, do you seriously suggest that Chilton would lay out a plan of the doings right beneath everyone's noses?"

"It sounds crazy. But he *is* a touch crazy. He's the kind that gets a kick out of tempting providence, reckless, a bit of an exhibitionist, too. We know that he laid out this green personally. Just now he surveyed it—well, like looking down on all the kingdoms of the world. He snapped out of his sulks right away. He was seeing things in perspective again. Can't you imagine him coming up here, brooding over it like a Napoleon, drawing inspiration from it—the map of England, and he's the man who's going to change it? And at the same time getting a sort of schoolboyish fun out of the idea that his plan, which the Secret Service is bursting itself to get a sniff of, is staring up out of this green with oh such an innocent expression on its face? Do get on with it," Georgia added irritably: "It's probably just another hunch of mine gone wrong, but get on with it!"

Watching him through the summerhouse window, she sketched out on paper a rough plan of the green and filled in the measurements as Peter paced them out. The insect-drone of a lawn-mower came over from the cricket-ground where this afternoon Peter would be facing the local talent. There were faint, spasmodic cries from the tennis-courts, and once or twice a peacock gave its outraged scream. The sounds wove themselves into a background for the tap of Peter's club, the stir of her own pencil on the paper. . . .

An hour later Georgia was sitting behind a locked door in her bedroom. The map of England lay open before her. First she must establish what spot on the map corresponded with the hole which lay in the centre of the putting-green. Why not Chilton Ashwell itself? She made some rough calculations, scaling her own plan till it fitted the map. A stab of misgiving struck her. Unless Chilton had planned out his green accurately to scale, she would get no further. Well, the E.B. paid great attention to detail, so perhaps their leaders had done likewise. The question was—what did the numbered disks on the green represent? There were twelve of them. Wait a minute, the E.B. had divided up the country into six districts, with an organizer over each. Supposing the odd or the even six disks indicated district centres? She suspected that the Mayfield stables in Berkshire was such a one: and she knew there was an arms-dump beneath Major Keston's house in Devonshire. Breathing hard, Georgia calculated distance, plotted positions. She had three given points—Chilton Ashwell, Yarnold Farm, the Mayfields. Yes, the points on her plan which corresponded roughly to the two latter places were both even numbers. But they corresponded too roughly, that was the trouble. Number Six fell between twenty and thirty miles north of Yarnold Farm, for instance: the Mayfield point was too far north, also. It looked as if the whole thing would be a wash-out. Her plan must be far more accurate than this if it was to be of any use to Sir John.

Her first point of reference might be wrong, though.

She was only assuming that the centre of the green indicated Chilton Ashwell. If her other two reference points were given their approximately correct position on the map, the central point would fall farther south, between twenty and thirty miles south—would fall, she muttered excitedly, as near as nothing slap on Nottingham. Nottingham, the centre of England! Yes, why not? Nothing could be more symbolic, or more likely. There was a huge armaments factory near Nottingham, for one thing.

Now she had these three points firmly fixed, it was possible to plot the others with fair hope of accuracy—Northumberland, Norfolk, Berkshire, Devonshire, Carmarthen, Cheshire. She had half expected the odd numbers to coincide with the great cities of England, but they fell at random and she was inclined to discount them. Thinking it over, she began to change her opinion that the even numbers denoted the bases of the six district organizations: some of these, at least, would surely be in big towns. Major Keston's house certainly was an arms dump. Why should not the other five be the same?—great reservoirs of arms which had gradually been filling during the last two years, dotted widely over the country in strategic positions, from which—when the time came—arms could be distributed to the centres of the rising.

Georgia locked her plan away, and sat back with a sigh. Half her work was now surely done. Even though her calculations could not indicate accurately the positions of the E.B. arms reservoir, they were near enough to enable Sir John to draw a cordon round these districts at the first sign of trouble. Unless the arms had already been distributed from them, the rising was as good as crippled.

# 12. The Episode of the Nottingham Earthquake

Though Chilton pressed her to stay longer, and Peter hoped she would come over with some of the other guests to see him playing at Trent Bridge on the Wednesday, Georgia returned to London on Tuesday. She wanted to make sure that her plan would be conveyed safely to Sir John Strangeways. She believed, too, that her early departure would heighten Chilton's interest in her, for he was a man little accustomed to having his pressing invitations so firmly declined.

By leaving when she did, Georgia missed an incident that—in more ways than one—shook Nottingham. She was not there at Trent Bridge when the bails fell off the wickets though no ball had been bowled and no wind was blowing. If she had stayed, she might not have lost a friend, but equally she might well have lost all chance of penetrating deeper into the warped and complex mind of Chilton Canteloe.

On Tuesday morning after Georgia had gone, Peter

155

Braithwaite was sitting rather disconsolately on the terrace. He felt out of place here, and a little bored. He tried to fix his mind on tomorrow's match. Trent Bridge was not one of his lucky grounds. He must not start cutting those fast out-swingers of Joe Marston's this time till he'd got properly set—Joe knew his little weakness a sight too well. Cricket. There'd be no more cricket if the E.B. succeeded; they'll all be too busy forming fours and yapping "Heil, Canteloe" at each other. Well, give him his due, Chilton probably wouldn't stop the cricket. But to be fooling about with bat and ball when this hellish infernal machine was ticking away in England's heart—that got you down.

Rosa Alvarez got you down too. When Georgia was about, it didn't seem so bad: she put life into you, made you feel right on top of your game, made you feel the game was worth a candle. Playing up to Rosa had seemed a good game too, at the time. But now you could only remember that flushed, silly, terrified face—the way you'd handed her back to the executioners without a murmur, half glad to be shut of her, kidding yourself that you'd just done your duty and England Expects and all that ballyhoo. Well, get on with it, then: do something to justify your place in the team: why not have a snoop round in Chilton's study, for a start? Jerusalem! What a hope!

For all that, Peter got to his feet and moved silently along the terrace to where the French windows of the study opened out on the summer day. Though he had worked long enough for Sir John, off and on, he could never quite rid himself of the feeling that he was in the middle of one of those spy dramas he had acted in several times himself, where red lights flash over doors and hands appear out of panelling and papers marked "Secret" in red ink are strewn about in full view of the audience.

As he approached the study windows, a telephone bell rang inside. He stood still, gazing out across the park, listening hard. He was supposed to be playing tennis with the other guests, so Chilton would not expect any one to be here. Presently he heard the voice of David Renton, Canteloe's secretary, saying:

"From Mr. Blackham. He's sending Goltz up, sir. He'll be passing through at 4:15. Do you wish to speak to Mr. Blackham?"

"No. Just leave the address for Goltz. He knows where to find it, presumably?"

"Quite."

There was the slight ting of a receiver laid down on its rest. Canteloe began dictating a business letter to his secretary. Peter found it all very above-board and boring. He'd have to find his way into the study some other time: those two were evidently in for a long session.

He walked down to the tennis-court, and stood watching the players. For such an indolent-looking houri, that Mainwaring girl wields a ferocious racket, he thought. Seeking to retrieve a hard shot down the side line, Mrs. Mainwaring slashed under the ball and hit it out of the court into a shrubbery. Peter hurried to retrieve it.

"Oh, thanks, Mr. Braithwaite," she said, giving him a lustrous glance. "You know where to find it? In that laurel bush, I think."

Peter tossed the ball over into the court. There was something peeping out at the back of his mind. "You know where to find it." When had somebody said that before? Of course. Chilton. Leave the address for Goltz.

He knows where to find it, presumably? Well now, that was surely a little peculiar. If this Mr. Goltz was "passing at 4:15"—passing through what? the village? in a car? by train?—why couldn't someone simply tell him the address? "Knows where to find it" almost suggested that the address was hidden in some way. A curious method of doing business.

The young cricketer's mood of depression cleared up like an April sky, replaced by that tingling in the veins, that sense of buoyancy and clear-headedness which for him always precluded a big innings. He decided to keep a watchful eye on David Renton. If there was anything shady about Goltz, he would not be coming to the house, for it was part of Chilton's policy never to give E.B. agents any reason for identifying him with the movement. The secretary would have to "leave the address for Goltz" further afield.

Peter must allow the secretary to lead him to Goltz, then he must follow Goltz. He packed his bag, put it in his two-seater, and at lunch announced that he would be leaving Chilton Ashwell in the afternoon; he had to join up with his team at Nottingham, in readiness for tomorrow's match.

"Can I give you a lift into the village?" he asked David Renton, who had said that he would be going in to fetch a parcel from Ashwell station.

"No thanks. I haven't time to walk back, so I'd better take one of our own cars."

Shortly after 3 p.m. the secretary went off. Peter got into his own car and followed at a respectable distance for the three miles into the village. When they reached the first houses of Ashwell, he closed up a bit. Lucky this *is* the road to Nottingham, he thought: it's my lucky day. His quarry did not, as he had half expected, stop at the post-office, but went straight through the long village street and, just short of the railway bridge that spanned the road, turned sharp right, making up the station approach.

Peter's mind worked in a flash. He had planned to see where David Renton stopped, let him depart again, then inquire himself whether there was a message for Mr. Goltz. His natural modesty had blinded him to the fact that Peter Braithwaite would be recognized anywhere in this cricket-loving county and could never pass himself off as Goltz. He realized it now, however; in the hundred yards that separated him from Renton's car, he altered his plans. Sweeping past the end of the station approach, he went under the bridge and turned right, up towards the goods yard. He could see a string of empty coal-trucks in the siding, they would screen his car from Renton's eyes. He drove up quietly, got out, stood under the lee of a coal-truck to light a cigarette.

The little branch-line station, its name picked out in stones amid a pattern of bright flowers—the stationmaster's pride—dozed under the afternoon sunlight. There was a smell of creosote from the sleepers. A voice from the opposite platform carried lazily through the air.

"That's raight, Mr. Renton. I put it here, ready for you. Joost saign this invoice. Can y' manage?"

Renton and a porter went together into the waiting-room.

"I heard you've 'ad yoong Braithwaite up at Chilton Ashwell. A nice bat, he is. I fancy Joe Marston'll have him tomorrow, though. He never could play Joe. They're a bit soft, these Soothern chaps."

Still talking, the porter emerged from the waiting-room. He was followed in a minute by David Renton, who carried his parcel under an immaculate, black-sleeved arm. Next moment, Peter heard the engine of Renton's car start up and saw it move decorously down the decline into the village. He leapt into his own, and followed Renton again. The secretary did not stop anywhere in Ashwell, so Peter could reasonably assume that the message must have been left at the station.

Mr. Goltz was not due till 4:15. That gave Peter rather less than half-an-hour's grace. He drove his car into a garage, took out his bag, and walked up to the station. As far as he could tell, Renton had stopped nowhere except for that minute he had been alone in the waiting-room. But how the blazes did you leave an address in a waiting-room? Peter discovered soon enough the answer to that. The cricket-enthusiast porter had retired to some sanctum of his own, and Peter had a clear run in to the stuffy, white-washed room whence Renton had taken his parcel.

It was undeniably, almost aggressively, empty. There was nothing but dust on the long table and the benches: in the fireplace there was nothing but cigarette-ends and orange-peel. Perhaps Renton had given the porter the address, to be passed on to this Goltz. No, the very essence of all the E.B. tactics was that nothing should be done which might give any one—even their own agents—a line on Chilton Canteloe. Discouraged, Peter moved over to the far wall of the waiting-room. "Well, I'll be—!" he exclaimed.

That white-washed wall was the answer. The address was written there in pencil. It was one of the two or three dozen names and addresses scrawled up there, together with inscriptions of a less reputable nature, by the summer tourists who alighted at this station for a day's outing among the bracken and swarming flies of

Sherwood Forest. Peter could not help laughing at his own discomfiture. He might as well be looking for one particular lump of coal in Newcastle. No doubt Goltz had been told exactly where to find his address on the wall. Well, he would certainly have to wait for Goltz now.

He filled in the time by disguising his appearance a bit, for he did not want to be recognized here by the porter or any chance traveller. Peter always carried a few theatrical properties in his bag: when rain washed out play, he would amuse the teams with his deft little character-sketches. He gave himself pince-nez, a drooping, wispy moustache, and brushed his hair out to fall lankly over his right temple. He looked like a professor of chemistry in a provincial university, or a melancholy but quite prosperous grocer. Thus disguised, he bought a first-class ticket to Nottingham and returned to the waiting-room.

A long mineral train clanked past on the up line, the trucks jolting and clashing as the train gathered speed down the bank. Then there was no sound but the clucking of the station-master's hens from across the line. At last the wires under the platform's edge whirred, and a distant rumble followed. The 4:15 was due. Peter stood up, opened his bag, and dropped one or two articles on to the floor.

When the man in the green pork-pie hat entered the waiting-room, he saw a fussy, disconsolate figure stuffing a pair of pyjamas into a bag. The man hesitated a moment. He had not expected to find any one here. He looked around quickly, walked over to the communicating door of the ladies' waiting-room, glanced at something written on the wall level with its handle.

"This is the gentleman's?" he asked the other traveller, a faint guttural note in his voice.

"The gentleman's? Oh, I see. Oh, no. That's along the platform."

The man hurried out. Peter straightened, studied the place on the wall where Goltz's eyes had rested. Yes, a name and address. "Sam Silver, 420 Easthwaite Street, Nottingham."

Peter went on to the platform, peered short-sightedly up and down. The porter was fetching a crate out of the goods van at the top of the train. The man in the pork-pie hat marched back along the platform.

"Pardon," said Peter timidly. "This *is* the Nottingham train?"

The man nodded brusquely, got back into his first-class carriage. Peter followed him in, tripping awkwardly over his bag.

"Very inconvenient, these local trains," said Peter. "No—er, I mean, no conveniences."

The man stared at him with undisguised contempt. "The English trains! Ach!" Then he pointedly settled down behind his newspaper. He was a thick-set man, about Peter's own height, with a clipped, stubbly moustache which did not mitigate the hairless impression that is given by a Prussian head. Peter, glancing at him, altered his plans. He had only intended to follow Goltz, then communicate the Nottingham address to Sir John. But why shouldn't he become Goltz, just for today? There was time to play Goltz today and beat the Notts men tomorrow. Here at last might be the opening he was looking for.

He began a flow of dreary small-talk, which Goltz after a while could no more ignore than a man can ignore the dripping of water on his forehead. Peter studied his tones of voice, the abrupt, hacking gestures he made with his hands. Whoever was expecting Goltz at the other end might conceivably have met him before; though the watertight-compartment organization of the E.B. made this improbable.

Fortunately, Peter had travelled on this line before. He remembered that, after Bulthorpe station, the train climbed a steep incline with a wild heath at the foot of its embankment. Five minutes before they reached Bulthorpe, he got up to look at the map on Goltz's side of the compartment. Turning to sit down, he tripped over the man's feet.

"Oh, I say, I'm awfully sorry," he said, leaning apologetically towards Goltz. The next instant he had let fly a blow which caught the man on the point and knocked him cold. Peter tied Goltz's feet and hands with the straps from the man's own suitcase: he whipped out some adhesive plaster and strapped it over his mouth: he emptied Goltz's pockets. Then, as the train slowed down into Bulthorpe, he pushed the senseless body under the seat.

Let's hope nobody tries to get in here, he thought. Pretty safe. First-class compartments are not much in demand on this line. He stood in the window, scowling, prepared to repel boarders, but there were no passengers on the platform. The train started off again, clattered round a curve, approached the stiff incline of Bulthorpe bank. Peter dragged out Goltz's body, now beginning to twitch and stir a little. He wedged open the door, and tipped the body out: its fall should be concealed by the steep wall of the embankment down which it was rolling. Well, that takes care of him for a bit, he'll roll down into the heath and stay there till we send someone to pick him up.

Peter stood by the mirror, clipping his moustache till it resembled Goltz's. With Goltz's pork-pie hat, that would serve for the present. He began to examine the articles he had taken from the man's pockets. Not much information could be gleaned from them, but, such as it was, it was invaluable. Inside his watch an E.B. disk was pasted. His diary had an entry for tomorrow, "Nottingham, 8:30." So Goltz was not due at Sam Silver's till tomorrow morning. Well, that would give Peter more time; unfortunately, it would also leave more time for the real Goltz to be discovered.

Alighting at Nottingham, he went into the hair-dresser's at the station hotel, and had his hair clipped short. Then he sought out a smaller hotel, registered there as H. Goltz, and settled down to examine Goltz's suitcase in the privacy of his bedroom. It contained, among other things, some overalls, a suit of dark-grey worsted, and some blue-prints which, not being an engineer, he could make head nor tail of. He remembered his car, left at the garage in Ashwell. When Goltz returned to the fold, he would have no possible reason to connect the droopy-moustached individual, who had attacked him in the train, with Peter Braithwaite, the cricketer. But it would be as well to leave no loose ends lying about. Peter went along to the hotel where his own team were staying, and sent up a message to Frank Haskings, the wicket-keeper, a close friend of his. He had removed his moustache in a public lavatory on the way, but he came in for some chaffing at Frank's hands about the convict cut of his hair.

"Frank, I had to leave my car in Ashwell. Will you borrow one and drive me over to fetch it? And please keep all this to yourself. I'm—well, for one thing I shan't be sleeping here tonight."

164

"Oh, a dame? Well, that's your business. Did she tell you to get your hair cut, too?"

Frank's entirely gratuitous inference gave him another idea. When they reached the Ashwell garage, he took its proprietor aside and fiddled suggestively with a one-pound note.

"Look here, if any one comes snooping round, you might forget the fact that my car was left in here this afternoon. Fact is—well, there's a lady in the case, and I don't want—"

"That's all right, Mr. Braithwaite. You drove in this afternoon for a minor repair, and you was off again in ten minutes' time. How'll that do? Hope you gets a century tomorrow. I'm an old Middlesex supporter myself, see?"

That's that end stopped, thought Peter, driving his car back to Nottingham. The garage is at the extreme end of the village, and it's fifty to one nobody could have noticed me putting the car in or taking it out.

He garaged at Nottingham, resumed his disguise, and returned to his hotel. There, he wrote a brief report of to-day's events which would go to Sir John Strangeways through the usual channels. He also wrote a note to Frank Haskings, telling him to put the police on to Sam Silver, of 420 Easthwaite Street, urgently. He would hand this note to the hall-porter when he went out tomorrow morning, asking him to have it delivered at Trent Bridge ground if he himself had not returned by eleven o'clock.

That was all he could do by way of precautions. The rest must be left to luck and his own recource. He was taking a grave risk, he knew. But he was tired of playing for keeps with the E.B. The same blend of audacity and impatience that, on the cricket field, compelled him sometimes to take a dip at a bowler who was pegging him down, in the hope of knocking him off his length, possessed him now. They might get his wicket. Well, let them. It was better than pottering about. . . .

Easthwaite Street, a long, squalid thoroughfare, lay under the shadow of Nottingham Castle and its towering rock. Just before eight-thirty next morning Peter was standing outside Number 420. "*S. Silver, Furniture Dealer*" was the legend over the shop-front. Peter marched in, with the jerky, military stride of Mr. Goltz. A small man wearing a baize apron and a gap-toothed smile appeared from behind a clutter of furniture like a rabbit out of a burrow. I hope to God there are no passwords or anything, prayed Peter. He clicked his heels and said:

"Mr. Silver?"

"That's me. What can I do for you, sir? Looking for a nice bedroom suite perhaps?"

"My name's Goltz. You are expecting me," Peter rapped out. The silence that followed took him by the throat like a fog. The little man was staring at him dubiously, scratching the thinning hair on top of his skull. Was that crack about the bedroom suite a password? Did he have to reply, "No, I want a couple of mahogany sideboards," for instance? Staring back at the man with all the Prussian insolence he could assume, Peter took out Goltz's watch.

"It is eight-thirty," he said. "We must get to business." He allowed the watch-cover to flip open, exposing the E.B. disk on its back. That brought Sam Silver into camp all right. Bidding Peter follow him, he retired towards the back of the shop, led the way down a ladder into a basement stacked with second-hand furniture, opened the door of a large wardrobe that stood against the wall, and stepped inside it. It was done so quickly that Peter had scarcely time to savour the oddity of the proceedings. Does the local E.B. hold its meetings inside a wardrobe? he asked himself, feeling all the bewildered interest of Alice in her Wonderland.

This wardrobe was a unique one: it had no back. Or, rather, its back was a door in the wall — a door that led into a dark, low passage, along which Peter now followed the beam of Mr. Silver's torch. He remembered that the ground beneath Nottingham was honeycombed with these passages, burrowed out of the sandstone by prehistoric hands. He remembered, too, the use to which the Cagoulards had meant to put the underground warrens of Paris. It would be wise now to turn back. He could easily get away now, and he had learnt the secret of the furniture shop. But that strange mixture of happy-go-lucky daring and deep fatalism, which made up Peter Braithwaite's character, led him on. Another hundred yards, crouching along the low-roofed passage, moving always perceptibly downhill, and they arrived in an immense chamber brilliantly lit with electricity which must be generated on the spot. Two men were working at a metal lathe. A third, at the far end of the chamber — Peter did not need any scientific knowledge to be sure of it — was filling bombs. The underground room was both a munitions factory and an arsenal.

"Here's Mr. Goltz, boys," said Sam Silver, and ducked back again, more rabbit-like than ever, into the warren.

The men looked up from their work. The place grew instantly silent. Peter could hear nothing but the faint hum of a dynamo from beyond the opening at the other end of the room. One of the men, a big, greasy-faced fellow with a nervous tic that kept fluttering beneath his left eye, came up to Peter and put out his hand.

"Pleased to meet you, Mr. Goltz. My name's Tooley. We've been at sixes and sevens here since Mr. Haines went sick. Now we can get going again."

Peter felt a stab of apprehension. Goltz had been sent to supervise the munitions-making. How much longer could he sustain the part of Goltz now? He clicked his heels, ignored Tooley's hand, barked out harshly,

"So. Goot. Above here is what?"

"You needn't worry. We're too far down for any danger of interference." The man jerked his thumb at the roof. "Up above's a piece of waste land, and a derelict factory. Now, if you'll step this way, sir. This cutter — Harry's spoilt two jobs on it already. Seems it's got out of alignment."

Peter bent studiously over the machine. It might have been the Koran for all he knew about it. Well, nothing like taking the offensive.

"So," he said. "This machine has been mishandled. I must return to my hotel and fetch some tools."

"Mr. Haines's kit is here, sir. You were to use them."

Tooley led him over to a bench littered with drawings, scribbled formulae, and instruments. Peter glanced at them in dismay. He must get out. At any moment his ignorance would be betrayed. He made a hacking gesture with his hand, exclaimed gutturally:

"Ach, these are no goot! We need a — how do you say it? — verbinderungschaft?" And let's hope none of them know any more German than I do, he thought, for I don't know a word of it. He stalked angrily away, feeling three pairs of eyes boring like cold steel into his back. He was five feet away from the opening of the passage when Sam Silver appeared again. Something in his rabbity face told Peter that all was up with him. He made a dash for the passage, hurling the little man aside. But it was too late. The passage was blocked—blocked by the stocky body of the real Mr. Goltz.

It was a good fight while it lasted, but five to one is too great odds, even against a man who knows that defeat means death. They knelt on him, kneeing him into the floor. Breathing hard, Mr. Goltz bent down and brutally tore off Peter's moustache. The jerk of pain sickened him.

"You see, gentlemen?" said Goltz.

"By God! A bloody spy!"

Then they had him tied up, spreadeagled on one of the work-benches. The faces round him gave no hope. It was their lives or his. The close-set eyes showed all the viciousness of frightened men who can revenge their own fear on another's body.

"Who are you? Who sent you here? If you tell us everything, we shall make things a little easier for you," said Goltz.

"Oh, take a jump at yourself."

"So." It was like an echo of his own voice. Yes, thought Peter, with a flicker of pride even in this extremity, I got his intonation just right.

Tooley said, "Put the bleeder's fingers in that vice. He'll talk."

Pain ground into him, furrowing his flesh like grapnels. After a while he fainted. They waited till he came round, and then started again. He lost all track of time. There was nothing in the world left for him but this agony, and his determination not to speak. He knew that the pain must win in the end. Later—hours or minutes later—there was a lull. Words were running blindly in Peter's head, running, flickering to and fro behind a mist. He strove to capture them, they would help him to resist a little longer, painfully he pieced the lines together out of his shattered consciousness—

> . . . *For the field is full of shades as I near the shadowy coast,*
> *And a ghostly batsman plays to the bowling of a ghost,*
> *And I look through my tears on a soundless-clapping host*
>   *As the run-stealers flicker to and fro,*
>     *to and fro,*
> *O my Hornby and my Barlow long ago!*

"Will you talk now, damn you?"

*As the run-stealers flicker to and fro.*

A great flash of pain burned across his whole body, and everything went dark again.

The M.C.C. flag, drooping above the clock-tower. The tiered, white seats all round. The wide glass windows over the Members' Balcony. The news-reel cameras on their tower. A cluster of figures watching from a factory roof. This was Lord's Cricket Ground. He recognized it. The Australians, in their bunchy, long-peaked caps, small, bronzed men, all on their toes, fighters to the last ditch. He patted the crease. He looked up at the scoreboard. His score was ninety-eight. The bowler was running up—that loping indefatigable stride. The ball was pitching a little short, well to the off. He flashed his bat at it in a sweet, controlled square cut. Backward point, cover point left standing. The rattle of the ball against the stand merged into the louder roaring of the crowd. The roaring came nearer. It was in his own ears.

Water splashed over Peter Braithwaite's head. The real voices began again.

In spite of everything, a miraculous sense of strength welled up in him. His head was suddenly clear, but he knew this clarity would not last long. He had had his vision, now he must obey its prompting.

"All right, I'll talk. I can't stand any more of this. For God's sake give me a drink and let me stand up," he said, surprised by the weakness of his own voice. They had to guide the water to his mouth. He stood up, staggered, clutched at the work-bench for support. He was all in, they knew. They'd made a sorry mess of him. Half in horror at their own handiwork, half with a kind of respect, the men made way for him as he swayed and staggered over the floor.

That was their mistake. Before they realized what he was after, before any one could lay a hand on him, Peter's feet had carried him in a drunken, faltering rush across to the bench where, on first entering, he had noticed the man filling bombs. With his right hand—his left was horribly crushed—he took up a bomb. The charging figures stopped dead a few feet away from him, as if they had been checked by an invisible ray. They began to back, showing their teeth, surly or whimpering. Instinctively they pressed themselves close against the wall, leaving Peter's way clear to the far entrance of the underground passage.

But he could not make it. He knew that. They would not dare to attack him for fear of detonating the bomb, but he had not enough strength to carry him through the passage. Already he felt the mists swirling back. Tooley had said they were deep down here. Peter hoped

171

he was right. He didn't want to kill innocent people.

He tossed the bomb meditatively up and down in his hand. So, on the cricket-field, he would juggle with the ball at the end of an over before throwing it to the new bowler. The action was quite unconscious. Peter was only deciding where he could best throw the bomb in order to make sure that the whole dump would go up; but it made the five men wince and shut tight their eyes.

"Here, look here, mate," one of them quavered. "Call it quits. We'll let you go. Straight, we will."

Gritting his teeth, Peter Braithwaite came away from the support of the bench. He'd take it standing up, not like those quitters grovelling against the wall over there. His last words were characteristic, and not unworthy of his life and death.

"Well, I always did like fireworks," he said, and with the unerring, side-arm flick which had surprised many confident run-stealers before now, he jerked the bomb bails-high at a heap of cases in the far corner of the arsenal. . . .

A policeman, passing along the road that bordered the waste land, felt the earth shake beneath his feet. A great, thudding, suffocated cough and rumble seemed to come up from the earth. The policeman had been brought up in a mining village; he had heard that kind of noise before, and knew what it meant. But there were no pit-galleries under here. The derelict factory caught his eye. It was tottering, collapsing, falling in upon itself and sliding down to the ground like shale. "Here, what's all this?" said the policeman from force of habit. He blew his whistle and started running out onto the waste ground. . . .

At Trent Bridge the second over was just beginning. Joe Marston ran up to bowl; but before he reached the crease the green turf quivered and the bails fell off the wickets at both ends. Joe Marston stopped dead. "Eh, lad, it's an earthquake," he said to the umpire. A wag in the crowd yelled out:

"Hey, Joe, you're putting on weight!"

The crowd roared. It was as good a valediction as any for Peter Braithwaite.

# 13. The Episode of the Unforced Landing

Thus, in dark passages, innocent villages, street corners, shady little shops, and no less behind the plate glass of great offices or the elegant façades of country mansions, was waged the undeclared war between Sir John Strangeways' men and the E.B. As the year turned towards autumn, Chilton Canteloe's campaign for his unemployment plan alternated with European crisis and rumour of crisis to keep Britain's nerves on the stretch. Like the first symptoms of a plague, ugly incidents began to break out sporadically over the country; a riot here, an attempted assassination or unexplained piece of sabotage there, sudden panics on the Stock Exchange, hints and rumours flawing the calm surface of English life. Public opinion was bewildered and growing resentful. The European dictators continued on their triumphal path. Our own government, thought the man in the street, seemed to have lost its nerve entirely; it made concession after concession abroad, while at home it was dilly-dallying over the Chilton plan that had so

174

kindled public enthusiasm. This inarticulate resentment was cleverly exploited by the E.B., whose policy was, by constantly embarrassing the present government, to discredit the principle of parliamentary government altogether.

The events of the autumn soon put out of people's minds that nine-day wonder of August, when the headlines had flared with "Disappearance of Test Cricketer." This sensation relegated to a quarter-column of an unimportant page the seismic disturbance which had been felt throughout Trent Bridge ground and its immediate environs. Several newspaper humorists had made cracks about the relative news-value of earthquakes and English cricketers, but no closer connection was made between the two events as far as the public was concerned. Frank Haskings, who had received Peter's note and directed the police to 420 Easthwaite Street, was sworn to secrecy. The police had found Sam Silver's basement with its furniture curiously deranged by the blast of the explosion. Digging through the blocked passage, they discovered enough to tell them what had been going on in the underground chamber. Sir John Strangeways got it announced that a secret arms-dump of the I.R.A. had accidentally blown up; in private, thrusting out of his mind the merry face of Peter Braithwaite and the familiar figure he would never again see at Lords, he set to work on the plan he had received from Georgia.

Georgia herself, though Sir John sent no word, had put two and two together. So when, a week after her departure from Chilton Ashwell, Chilton rang up and invited her to lunch at the Berkeley, she knew that she would now be facing her most difficult ordeal. Chilton might well suspect that her relation with Peter

Braithwaite had been more than a personal friendship, though of this he could surely have no proof. At the same time, she must act the part of a woman who was a member of the E.B. and thus could make a pretty accurate guess as to what had really lain behind the "Nottingham earthquake" and Peter's disappearance. It was going to be a ticklish business.

Many heads turned in the Berkeley dining-room when Georgia and Chilton entered. Indeed, she felt her own head in danger of being turned by the obsequious array of waiters clustering round their table, the gorgeous sheaf of dark-red roses that Chilton had ordered for her, the solicitous way he arranged for her comfort. She felt like a favourite aunt taken out to lunch by a charming schoolboy nephew. His pleasure in her company seemed almost *naïf*, as if playing the host was a new and entrancing game for him.

She could not help being flattered, too, by the way he deferred to her opinion. He had considerable holdings in China, and asked her about the Chinese "backdoor," the road recently constructed by Chiang Kai-shek to the Burmese frontier. Having travelled in this country, though not since the road was built, she could give him a fair idea of the conditions and the potentialities for transport which the new road opened up. Absorbed in this subject, she was taken unawares when Chilton said:

"And, talking of travel, where's Peter Braithwaite pushed off to?"

"Peter? I only wish I knew. I simply can't understand it."

"You don't think he'd got into any trouble, or had a brainstorm or something, and decided to go off on a trip?"

176

"Oh, no, that's impossible. He seemed perfectly himself last week-end, and he'd never go off and leave his team in the lurch like that, unless he'd gone crazy. Besides, with all the rumpus the papers have been making about it, he'd have been found by now."

"Well, then, what was it? Suicide? He never seemed that type to me. Murder? Kidnapping? That's an idea! Kidnap Peter Braithwaite and sting the M.C.C. for a whacking ransom. They'll need him in Australia."

Chilton realized at once that his flippancy had struck a jarring note for her. "I'm sorry, my dear," he went on, "he was so full of life and humour, it's difficult to think anything serious could have happened to him. I was forgetting what a great friend of yours he is."

You smooth, handsome devil, you weren't forgetting anything, Georgia thought. You like operating on people's feelings without anaesthetics.

"Yes," she said slowly. "I don't feel I really knew—know him well, though. I got the impression that there's more to him than the cricket-field idol. I wonder—"

"Yes?"

"This I.R.A. dump that blew up at Nottingham. You don't suppose Peter was mixed up in that somehow?"

She contemplated Chilton from under her long lashes. His gold-flecked eyes expressed nothing but surprise and incredulity.

"Why, however—?"

"Well, he might have been working for the police. After all, he *was* seen last in Nottingham. The police said the bodies were unrecognizable, but it may just have suited their book not to admit that Peter—"

"Oh, come now, Georgia, that's fantastic. You'll be saying next that it wasn't an I.R.A. dump at all, but a German plot or something." He gave her one of his

177

most engaging smiles. "Now, if any one gives me the impression of living a double life of that kind, it's you."

Georgia glanced back at him candidly, her brown eyes twinkling. "And why do you pick on me, sir, for these dreadful insinuations?"

"You're a woman in love with adventure. Everyone knows that. And you have the ability, the means to gratify it. Instead of which we find you trotting round dull house-parties and lunching with me at the Berkeley. It's very suspicious. There must be something behind it."

"Perhaps lunching with you at the Berkeley is an adventure?"

"I wish I could believe you meant that," he said in a different voice, gazing deep into her eyes.

"For a middle-aged, provincial woman? Of course it is."

"Don't belittle yourself, my dear. It's not in character."

They were like two deadly enemies, groping for each other in a pitch-dark room, thought Georgia. There was a certain wariness about Chilton, even when his words, his tone of voice, made love to her. Even had she been willing, she believed that to yield to him would not solve her problem; beneath his attentions, his lively interest, lay the profound indifference of the egoist. She could only hold him by keeping him at arm's length.

Georgia decided that the moment had come for an attacking move. Attack was the best defence, and it was vitally necessary to dispel his suspicion that she might be working against him. Burying her face in the sheaf of roses he had given her, she said:

"I wish I knew how far I could trust you."

"Trust me? You sound very much *en grand serieux*, my dear."

"Have you ever heard of the E.B.?" she asked, not looking up.

His fingers twiddled the stem of his wineglass. "The E.B.? It sounds very mysterious. What is it?"

She could tell by his voice that he had been disconcerted. She went on to describe the harmless mysticism of the English Banner, very much as Alice Mayfield had described it to her months ago. And Chilton made much the same comment as she herself had made to Alice.

"My dear! Playing at mediaevalism? Surely *you're* not taken up with that kind of nostalgic nonsense?"

Well, well, she thought with secret amusement; to think that I should be trying to convert the leader of the E.B. to his own movement. She said:

"Put like that, it is nonsense. And the English Banner is a bit absurd and cranky. But don't you think the principle behind it is sound? The principle that some men are born to rule the rest? I used to be all for democracy, but recent history doesn't show it up in a very favourable light. Look at the mess England has been making of things lately."

"Have you gone fascist?"

"You can't frighten me with words. I don't like their methods, but they get things done. We don't want that kind of fascism over here. We might create a new brand of aristocracy, though, a home-made product. I'd have thought you would approve. That speech of yours, when you first launched the Chilton Plan—you sounded impatient enough with parliamentary government. And there's yourself." For the first time she looked straight at him, her eyes glowing. "You have all the qualities of a great ruler—"

"Now, my dear. You flatter me."

"—Except ambition, should I say? Except the nerve for responsibility."

"I'm responsible for quite a lot already."

"Oh, I don't mean your high finance, your unemployment plans, your philanthropy and your racehorses. Can't you think bigger than that? You'd be—" She broke off sharply, as though afraid she would betray too much.

"And what is all this leading up to, little Georgia?"

His glance was quizzical. He was evidently enjoying the joke, and she believed he had no idea now that she shared it. But there was a suppressed excitement in his face too, a thinly-disguised leaping of pride.

"Leading up to?" she replied cautiously. "That's really for you to say. Leading up to a leader—a man who could be a great leader. If he had the right organization behind him."

"But, supposing there was such an organization, wouldn't it have chos—wouldn't it choose its own leader?"

"I don't know anything about that. All I know is that the best man should, and would, get to the top."

Chilton laughed pleasantly. "Well, good luck to him. I'm too lazy. I can't keep up with you and your voices, Madam Joan of Arc Strangeways. You won't make me a Dauphin of your storm . . . Unless—"

"Unless?"

He leant forward over the table, picked up one of the roses, and touched her thin brown hand with it. "If you loved me, I might do great things. Yes, I might surprise myself."

"No, Chilton. Please . . . Not yet."

There was a short silence. Then he said, "So you're Dedicated to the Cause, are you?" He had recovered his gay, bantering manner. For the rest of the lunch he teased her and flirted with her gently. Georgia felt convinced that the load of suspicion had been taken off his mind. The position between them, though, seemed to have developed into a stalemate, and such it remained for the next three months. They went about together a great deal, few days passing when Georgia did not receive from him a present of flowers, an invitation to dinner, theatre or concert. She for her part kept up towards him an attitude of cool, elusive affection; at intervals she hinted at the existence of the E.B., but Chilton—as elusive here as herself—refused either to promise his support or admit any complicity. It was a war of attrition between them, whose incidents gave her a deeper understanding of his complex character but brought her no nearer to the E.B.'s secret—the plans for the rising which, she was convinced, must be in Chilton's possession.

Time was growing short. Georgia was burdened by the knowledge of how much depended upon her. Sir John Strangeways could only take direct action against Chilton as a last resort. The millionaire's influence in the country was so great that, if Sir John took the offensive—intercepted Chilton's correspondence, for instance, or sent agents to ransack secretly his town and country houses—and they were discovered, his own position as head of C. Department would be in the gravest jeopardy. Besides, he did not want to explode the mine prematurely. "Give them rope and they'll hang themselves" was the motto of his department. But, Georgia feared, Chilton was a person who made other, less desirable uses of the rope you allowed him. . . .

It was not till the last week of November that the break came. Chilton had invited her to another house-party, and was flying her down to Chilton Ashwell in his private plane. He was in terrific good spirits that afternoon, like a schoolboy who has received an unexpected half-holiday. He piloted the plane himself. Now and then, out of sheer exuberance, he gambolled with it in the air, then turned towards her his flushed face and sparkling eyes as if to make sure that she too was enjoying the fun. The green checker-board of the country streamed and tilted beneath them. Chilton pointed down, put his lips to the speaking-tube.

"All the kingdoms of the earth, Georgia. Don't you feel tempted? Or would you rather have the sun and the sky? Look, I'll lay them at your feet."

He turned the machine over and they were flying upside down, the illimitable sky beneath their feet. Georgia could not help being charmed, exhilarated by her enemy's love-making. He carried it off so much in the grand manner. Not long afterwards they flew over a sprawling, industrial city. Chilton came down low, so that she saw the honeycomb of streets and houses enlarged. Towards the town's outskirts there lay an open patch of green, with small figures scurrying over it.

"Oh, look, they're playing football," she said. "I haven't seen a football match for ages."

"Well, you shall see one now. We'll go and watch."

At first Georgia assumed that he intended to fly to and fro over the playing-fields; but he cut out his engine and began to circle down, and she realized with a pang of horror that he intended to land down there amongst all those tiny midgets whose faces were already beginning to turn up to them like white flowers opening in the sun.

"No, Chilton, you mustn't," she exclaimed. "I didn't mean—it's too dangerous. You'll get into fearful trouble."

" 'She lived in storm and strife.' Another adventure for you, my dear. Besides, the engine's cut out. I expect the petrol-feed is choked. Better to land here than on one of those roofs."

He grinned mischievously at her. So that's how he proposes to get away with it. Pretend it was a forced landing. He must be mad. Of course he's mad.

"Stop showing off, Chilton," she cried. "It's contemptible."

But he paid not the least attention. Showmanship on this scale left you gasping. You might as well have accused the Great Ziegfeld of showing off. They were very low now. The playing-fields and those small figures, some breaking wildly to either side, a few seemingly paralyzed in the airplane's path, rushed towards them with horribly-increasing momentum. A larger figure dashed out and pulled two of the smaller ones aside. Georgia realized that they were children who had been playing here, who at any moment might be cut down in swathes by the hurtling machine.

When they had come to a standstill and Chilton opened the plane door, he was confronted by an angry group of men and women. They looked ripe for lynching him. Furious with him as Georgia was, she could not help admiring the blend of effrontery and authority with which he carried it off. Stooping in the narrow door, he yet contrived to dominate that cluster of people. He jumped down, shook hands with the man who had dragged the two children away from the plane's path, apologized for his forced landing, reassured himself that no one had been hurt, explained why he had been forced to come down here, invited the two children into the plane, kissed them and helped them up—all in a few moments. Then he set to work to repair the imaginary defect in his engine. By the time the inevitable policeman appeared, Chilton had finished his "repair." "My name's Canteloe—Lord Chilton Canteloe," he told the policeman, and after that the affair became a mere formality. What's in a name? thought Georgia disgustedly. If he'd killed half a dozen of those children, he could still have brought himself out of it.

"Now you're not really angry with me, are you?" he said, taking her arm. "I told you nothing would happen."

And Georgia, who dared not alienate him too far, let him lead her on to the touchline, where they watched some of the bigger boys playing football for a while.

"You know, you might have killed some of them," was all she said.

"Well, I didn't. Don't fuss, my dear, it's not like you," he replied indifferently.

At that moment Georgia perceived the whole depth and implication of his irresponsibility. He was infinitely more dangerous than a man who has a positive lust for killing and destruction. Such a man sooner or later is betrayed or driven mad by his own lust. But Chilton simply did not care much, one way or the other. Without venom or compunction he would brush aside people who blocked his way, just as he had so nearly swept away those children standing in the path of the plane. He had, abnormally developed, the egoist's profound indifference to all human life but his own. He had the splinter of ice in his heart.

But how well it was concealed! Who would have guessed that these children meant no more to him than buzzing flies, when he and Georgia walked back to the plane once more. The children came running from all over the field. Chilton waved gaily to them, smacked

184

their bottoms, had them in a minute cleared away from the course so that he could get a good run up into the wind. They were all hero-worshippers from the word go. Chilton, opening his pocket-book, called out to them:

"I'll fly back over the field and throw these two ten-bob notes out of the plane. Whoever touches one first, keeps it. No grabbing, you young ruffians. And don't spend it all on drink."

They were off, to a shrill, ragged volley of cheering. Chilton circled and flew back, throwing out the notes downwind. Georgia could see them fluttering away, and the crowd of children swaying backwards and forwards below, like flowers, their white faces upturned.

# 14. The Episode of
# the Terrestrial Globe

Looking back later upon the events of that desperate year, Georgia was to reflect how tiny had been the straws that had shown her which way the wind was blowing. An uncut hedge was her introduction to the E.B. conspiracy; a half-open door finally revealed to her the truth, and ushered her into the most tense and dangerous week of her whole life. During this week the whole force of the E.B. was mustered against her. She was a fugitive who carried next her heart, as a refugee might carry her firstborn through a country where every man's hand seemed hostile, the safety of a civilization. Though she always denied it, Sir John was probably right when he said afterwards that no other living woman could have won against such odds.

It was late afternoon, and the mist was beginning to settle down over the oaks and rusty bracken of Chilton Ashwell, when they touched down on the landing-field. The leaden, midland mist gave the house a lack-lustre appearance and tarnished the waters of the lake. But

Chilton's good spirits, that air of suppressed excitement he had manifested all day, seemed quite unabated. Later, as the other guests arrived, Georgia realized its cause. It was a gathering of the clans. Mr. Leeming, the banker, with his wizened face and inevitable tube of digestion tablets; Hargreaves Steele, the puckish mouth and fanatic eyes; the great armaments-manufacturer, Almayne Kennedy, who looked like a sideman in a fashionable church—and maybe was: they were all here.

"You must treat them nicely, Georgia. They're the chief backers of the Chilton Plan. So mind your step, and keep a watch on that witty, outspoken tongue of yours," said Chilton. "You'll be playing hostess for me, remember."

The Chilton Plan, she thought. What an excellent cover for them. And I'm to be hostess to the leaders of the E.B.—the tragic irony is laying itself on thick, I must say. It looks as if things were going to start moving soon.

The Friday evening passed off without any incident, except that Chilton and Georgia won a considerable sum of money off Mr. Leeming and Lady Almayne Kennedy at bridge. They seemed almost instinctively to understand each other's play. The long duel of wits had created this sympathy between them, so that they could lead each other on with audacious bids that kept their opponents guessing all the time.

Next morning Chilton went into conference with his associates. Georgia would have liked to listen at the door; but, in broad daylight, with servants passing up and down the corridor, the risk was too great. It was purely by accident that, just after the conference had broken up, she happened to be passing the study door when Chilton's secretary came out, and before he closed it behind him she noticed Chilton standing by his desk, in profile to her, his hands stretched out over the big globe that rested on a corner of the desk. His mouth was graven in that dreamy, conqueror's smile which she had seen on his face three months ago when he stood in the doorway of the marble summerhouse and gazed down on the clock-golf course.

Georgia did not pause for a moment outside the door, but Chilton's gesture and expression bit deep into her mind. At odd moments during the day it recurred to her. There was something symbolic about the way he had been standing there, alone in the room, with the terrestrial globe beneath his hands. But was there not something more—or less—than symbolism in it too? By an association of ideas Georgia began to link the globe with the clock-golf course. The latter had contained a secret; might not the globe also hold some clue, the whole secret of Chilton's ambitions? After all, she mused, the plans must be hidden somewhere here. They were not things one would keep in a safe, because the safes of men like Chilton Canteloe are obvious targets for burglars, which would mean either exposure or blackmail. And why else should the mere touch of his fingers on the globe bring that rare, enigmatic, omnipotent sort of expression to Chilton's face?

Her job was to get hold of those plans. Well, she must start somewhere, and she must certainly start soon. She decided to try the globe on Monday night, when most of the guests would have departed and there would be less danger of interference.

Georgia's long experience as a traveller had impressed on her the importance of detail, of being prepared for any contingency, and at the same time had taught her not to worry about the unknown factor that might crop up at any moment to upset all calculations. The unknown factor now was the globe itself. She might be unable to open it; or her hunch that it contained the plans might very well be wrong. So much had to be accepted. Assuming I do get possession of the plans, she asked herself, what next? First, I must as far as possible memorize them, in case the E.B. succeed in getting them back again. Second, I must discover the best method of conveying them to Uncle John. To memorize them, I shall probably need four or five hours at least, which means I should not leave here till the next morning. In any case it would be difficult to get away at night with all the cars locked up in the garage and the chauffeurs sleeping above.

I must leave, then, all open and above board, on Tuesday morning. But suppose Chilton finds the plans are missing? I'd never reach London alive. Well, my girl, the answer to that is for you to take Chilton with you— ask him to fly you back in his plane. Ask nicely, and he'll do anything for the little woman. And it will ensure you getting at least to the London airport in safety.

The daring of the plan brought a sparkle into her pensive eyes. She went off straight away, and asked Chilton if he was returning to London on Tuesday and could take her with him. Yes, he was, and he would. He'd fly her to the Isles of the Hesperides, if she only said the word. So far, so good. But these were only the bold outlines of a plan; filling in the detail, working out alternatives in the event of something going wrong, took up all the time she had off from being sociable with her fellow-guests and eluding Chilton's ardour. Those two days he turned all the batteries of his charm upon her, as though in an unconscious knowledge that zero-hour was fast approaching. There were moments when he almost convinced her that this was the reality and all her suspicions of him only a plausible but incoherent nightmare.

At last Monday night came. Half-past twelve chimed from the clock downstairs. Georgia got out of bed, dressed in black coat and skirt, crept from her room on to the landing, down the broad sweep of the stairs. Chilton had gone to bed earlier than usual, to get a good sleep before their early start next day. Now she was in the great hall. The eyes of all those painted Canteloes on the walls—she could imagine them following her in the dark with their insolent curiosity. She shut the study door on them. Stay outside and mind your own business, my popeyed friends. The study curtains were drawn close. Good. Georgia put her small torch back in her pocket, and switched on the shaded light over Chilton's desk. Now for the globe.

There it stood, bland, shiny, uncommunicative, telling her little she did not know about the countries mapped on its surface, and nothing about the business on hand. Topical yet absurdly irrelevant phrases floated across her mind as she fiddled with the globe, trying to find a secret hinge, a spring, a way to open up the obstinate brute. Showing the world to the world. This dark terrestrial ball. Globe-trotter all at sea with a globe. The cubic area of a sphere is . . .

No, it was no good. The damned thing was all one piece. Or its hemispheres as firmly welded as creation itself. She had drawn the wrong number. Yet the picture of Chilton standing here on Saturday morning, his fingers carressing the globe, refused to budge from her mind. She strove to recall exactly the position of his hands as she had seen them then. It seemed a forlorn hope, for the globe might well have been turned round since. But she persevered, gently pressing the smooth surface, over and over again, shifting her fingers slightly each time, till at last there came a faint, reluctant click from somewhere in the globe's big belly. At the same instant, a section of it was depressed by the pressure of her right hand, and she found she could slide it inwards, exposing a gap ten inches square. Trembling a little with excitement, she put her hand into the hole, felt a mechanism of rods and springs, then, deeper down, papers. Sheaves of paper. Eureka! She began cautiously to pull them out from the globe.

"She put in her thumb and she pulled out a plum and said what a bad girl am I." The familiar voice froze her dead. "Wouldn't you like a bit more light on the scene, Georgia? It'll try your beautiful eyes, reading all that stuff."

Chilton Canteloe switched on the central lights. The revolver in his hand was pointed at her stomach. He said quickly:

"And don't yell for help, because if you do this gun'll go off and I shall have to explain that I thought it was a burglar and shot you by mistake, Georgia darling, you twister, you little bitch."

Georgia recovered her self-control in a moment. she had not come entirely unprepared for this. She flipped over a few pages of the document she had taken from the globe, then looked up at him, her eyes shining.

"So it *is* you, Chilton," she said enthusiastically. "I *knew* it. I was sure you must be our leader, but I had to prove it to myself. Why ever didn't you tell me? You could have trusted me. I was sick of all this mystery-making. A good many of us are, for that matter."

Chilton stared at her with sleepy interest. His tousled hair, the slim body in the dark-blue silk dressing-gown, made him look twenty. He said:

"It's a good performance, but it's wasted on me."

Georgia's eyes opened wide. Her voice quavered pathetically. "Chilton, don't. You—you don't think I'm—?"

"I know you're a spy. We suspected it at the start. Then you lulled our suspicions for a while, I admit. But not altogether. That's why I kept you near me. I wanted to have my eye on you."

She knew he was lying. He was not the man to confess, even now when she was in his power, that she had taken him in so thoroughly. She wanted time to think, to plan the next move.

"You're making a terrible mistake. I've been heart and soul in the E.B. from the beginning. It's lost me most of my friends. But—don't you see?—I had to make certain that the right person was at the head of it. I tried to make you tell me, but you wouldn't. Then, the other morning, I saw you with this globe in your hands, and I had an intuition—"

"Intuition! Georgia, you're losing your form, you're getting rattled." He smiled at her pleasantly, almost regretfully. After his first outburst, he had controlled himself to this gentle, teasing manner that frightened her far more than any threats.

"There's a little gadget in that globe," he went on, "which rings a buzzer in my bedroom when it's opened. I'm not so simple as you thought, my dear. I'm sorry a burglar-alarm should have come between us, though. I was growing quite fond of you."

"Well, what are you going to do about it? Hand me over to the police?"

" 'The warm water of your mawkish police'?" Chilton quoted. "Oh, no. I'm afraid you've got yourself into hotter water than that. You'll have to be—disposed of."

"I see. And what good will that do you?"

He shrugged. "Isn't that obvious?"

Georgia knew she must change her tactics; there was no use telling him the tale any longer.

"It's not obvious at all," she said, the deadly quietness of her voice matching his own. "John Strangeways knows all about you. I recognized you at the Nebuchadnezzar party—the woman in the locket. And we know the position of your six armament dumps, too. The clock-golf course was a mistake. You should try and conquer your habit of showing off."

Chilton crossed his knees, transferred the revolver to his left hand, lit a cigarette with the right.

"That's better," he said. "Now we know where we stand, we can be more cosy. What a nuisance women are! That means I shall have to shift my dumps before we get going. Well, these things can always be managed."

"Yes, I know, money talks. There's just one thing you egoists lousy with money forget. And that is, the country's full of decent people who don't take bribes and look upon your values as utterly contemptible."

"There are quite enough who *do* take bribes, my dear. Besides, there are more ways of bribing a man than with money. You can offer power, excitement, revenge, or a dream of better things. My dream is selling very well just now."

"Your dream! It's a dirty delirium, that's all. It hasn't even a hope of coming true now. Our people have got you taped. Even suppose you start your rising at all—a few innocents will be killed, and a few enthusiasts. Then you'll collapse. Chilton Canteloe will get away, no doubt, like other scared, shady financiers before him. I can imagine you, rotting away somewhere in South America, the would-be dictator, growing fat, dirt under his fingernails, beginning to stink—a pathetic figure you'll cut, for any one who has pity to waste. . . . Why are you clutching that revolver so tight? Look, your knuckles have gone white."

"I should very much like to take you into the cellars and beat you to a pulp. Perhaps I shall, but—"

"Listen to the Nazi-imitator! Can't you be more original? You're just a spoilt, vicious child, eaten up with vanity. A Prince Charming who's begun to grow old and threadbare. A contortionist going stiff in the joints."

It was not so much her words as the lashing contempt of her voice that stung Chilton Canteloe. For months he had been exercising all his charm upon her, taking her final response for granted. The contemptuous indifference she now showed hit him in his sole unguarded spot. He stared at her uncomprehendingly, his lip pouting like a sulky boy's. She thought for a moment that he was going to cry. Then he controlled himself and said:

"Yes, you're quite clever. But not clever enough. You think the E.B. rising is going to fail. You're quite right. *I intend it to fail.* You see," he added naïvely, "there's a world of difference between cleverness and genius. Cleverness adapts itself to fate, genius adapts fate to itself. The great man has the courage of his own immorality—he stands above morality."

"I seem to have heard all this before."

"That plan you're hugging to your bosom—you may read it before you die, if you like, it's quite immaterial—we'll call it Plan A. But there's also a Plan B, which you and the rest of the second-rate snoopers know nothing of. It's much simpler. I could write it on a sheet of notepaper, but I prefer to keep it in my head. Have you ever wondered why the rank-and-file of the E.B. have not been told the name of their leader? Perhaps not. You lack subtlety. You've got a niggling, second-rate mind, like that hired keyhole-watcher, your husband."

"It's wonderful how unimpressive you are in the rôle of Genius Through the Ages," she chuckled.

Chilton sprang up and smacked her across the mouth. "As I was saying, there's this Plan B. I should like you to realize what you've been up against. It should comfort your last hour to know that you could never really have been expected to succeed."

At first Georgia thought he was bluffing; then that he was off his head with megalomania. As he talked, however, revealing Plan B and the depth of his own infamy, she realized he was neither a bluffer nor a lunatic. She perceived, too, the real secret of the clock-golf course. It was a symbol not so much of the E.B. organization as of his own intention to betray it. He had not anticipated that any one would read the secret of that green turf, yet it was a revelation—an unconscious one, perhaps—of his double treachery.

For Plan B, as he had said, was simple enough. Chilton intended the rising to take place in the way mapped out by Plan A. Arms would have been distributed from the secret dumps to the revolutionaries a week or two beforehand, while his agents were creating a panic on the Stock Exchange and disseminating rumours that the new Popular Government was on the point of involving us in a war with the Axis Powers, taking away the small man's savings, socializing industry. Then, when the country had been keyed up to the right pitch of bewilderment, indecision, hysteria, the rising would break out. Leading Cabinet Ministers would be kidnapped or assassinated, Broadcasting House and the B.B.C. stations in the provinces would be occupied, the Civil

Service thrown into confusion, the daily papers compelled to close down or print under E.B. orders; and finally, when the nerve centres of government were paralysed, an ultimatum would be delivered to Parliament backed up by flights of bombers over Westminster. Parliament must hand over to the E.B. council, or they and half London would be destroyed.

"At this point," said Chilton, with that infectious smile which Georgia now loathed like the plague, "at this point, when the E.B. await the setting-up of their dictator, I shall intervene. I shall call a conference of the E.B. leaders, put it to them that they must not be led by their initial successes into thinking that the whole country is theirs, and suggest a compromise. My key men on the E.B. Inner Council are, of course, aware of this manoeuvre and have a majority vote. They will vote me into the position of Guardian of Public Safety. A good idea, 'First Guardian,' don't you think? The English like the idea of being looked after, without having to admit any filial piety. You see the point of all this? I shall be announced to Britain, first as a mediator, then as First Guardian of the Committee of Public Safety. The politicians have utterly failed to control the situation; the country is in a state of anarchy; the public confusion and my own personal popularity will do the rest. The man in the street will have no idea, certainly no proof, that I was behind the original rising. The E.B. rank-and-file may think what they like—they'll have no proof either—that's why I have been so careful not to let the identity of their leader be revealed to them. Most of them will accept me, either as their real leader or as the best compromise. A few may kick; they'll be dealt with. I should add that my partners—my future partners in the Axis—are awaiting events with great interest.

Should we have more difficulty than I expect in over-coming opposition at the outset, they have promised to lend me a hand."

"I see," said Georgia disgustedly. "All you and your precious E.B. amount to is a sort of Fifth Column, first to give your jack-booted friends an opportunity for at-tacking England, and then to stab us in the back while we're being attacked. You're even more contemptible than I imagined."

Chilton Canteloe rose to his feet, the silk dressing-gown rustling, the revolver steady in his hand. He went on as if she had not spoken.

"Another advantage of my position will be that I can get rid in a perfectly legal manner of any of my associ-ates whom I distrust. Our countrymen dislike purges; but, in a state of emergency, they're willing to bury their heads in the sand and let someone else do the dirty work for them—provided it's done with all the legal parapher-nalia, a chaplain in attendance, and officials to sign the document in triplicate. Yes, if any one cuts up rough, I can dispose of him in the most correct manner. Far more correctly, I'm afraid, than I shall dispose of you, Georgia." Chilton had quite recovered his good humour. "Oh, dear, what a pity I have to kill you. I feel you would have inspired me to even greater heights."

"When you've finished talking, you might get on with it. Or haven't you the nerve? I suppose even your dirty work must be done by proxy."

"What a heroine! Game to the last! You ought to be in a book. I've not had time to arrange the details of your demise. And I'm sure you want to read Plan A. We'll say half an hour, shall we? It'll give me time to consult Hargreaves Steele. Lucky he stayed over tonight. I don't know whether he's got any of his maggots with him. If not, I'm sure a fertile brain like his will be able to think up something. In the meanwhile—"

He motioned with his revolver. Georgia was almost tempted to fling herself at him. A bullet would be better than Professor Steele's iniquities. But she restrained herself. She had half an hour, and she knew Chilton's secret now—knew him for a double traitor, a traitor both to his country and to the E.B. movement itself. She must give her knowledge a last chance of survival. She picked up her bag and the papers, and walked in front of him out of the room.

The revolver close behind her, she was forced to walk into the east wing of Chilton Ashwell. The wing was temporarily closed; she knew that if she called for help it would not be heard. They reached the top floor, and he pushed her into a small bedroom.

"The light's in working order, I see. You'll be able to read," he said. "I'm afraid there are no sheets on the bed; but perhaps that's just as well—a dangerous girl like you might tear them up for a rope and let herself out of the window like heroines do in books when there's a fire. Well, so long. You've had your adventure, haven't you? Oh, but one minute, though."

With a sense of revulsion that stiffened her body to stone, she felt his hand ruffling through her hair. He gave it a little tweak, just enough to hurt her.

"No, I thought you didn't use hairpins. But I had to make sure. You're such a resourceful girl, aren't you? And they say locks can be opened with hairpins. Now just let me look at that bag of yours."

Not taking his eyes off hers or deflecting the muzzle of the revolver, he ran his hand through her bag, laid out its contents on the mantelpiece. Then he glanced at them.

"No skeleton keys. No tablet of cyanide," he said, crowing over her a little. He was not a graceful winner. "No, Georgia, you disappoint me. You're not such an efficient spy as I should have thought. In half an hour's time, then."

# 15. The Episode of the Foggy Morning

Locked in the stuffy little bedroom, Georgia's first instinct was to get some air. Opening the window, she looked out. It was a dark, foggy night. The wall went sheer down; there was no parapet, no drainpipe or moulding to offer a slight hope of escape that way. She bit her lip thoughtfully. If the worst came to the worst, she could throw herself out of the window; better this than being left to Hargreaves Steele's devices. Perhaps that was what Chilton wanted her to do. She imagined him waiting for the fall, taking off her clothes, dressing her body in her nightgown. He could say she had been sleep-walking, it would save him a lot of trouble.

With an effort she wrenched her mind away from these useless speculations. She looked at her wrist-watch. It was nearly quarter to three. How time flies. At ten past three. . . . Forget it, you still have time. She examined the lock of the door. It was a stout, old-fashioned one. Chilton Ashwell was built to last. And there was nothing in the room with which the lock could be forced. There was nothing in the room but an empty washstand, a small arm-chair, a cupboard, and the bed with a pile of blankets on one end.

The foggy night air blowing in made her shiver. She did not like to shut the window; with it open, she felt not quite so hopelessly the prisoner. She lay down on the bed and pulled the blankets over her. She tried to think of Nigel, the Devonshire cottage, the lovely landscape now drawn out in the clean lines of winter. But Chilton Canteloe's smiling, merciless face came between her and the comforting vision. His words wove backwards and forwards in her head, like an argument one has thought of too late. "A heroine," he had called her mockingly. "You've had your adventure." "Like heroines do in books when there's a fire."

A fire! Georgia's heart leapt up. He had all unwittingly offered her a hope of release. By heaven, he should have his blasted fire! She couldn't force the lock, but she might burn down the whole door. Her hand went to her mouth, swollen where Chilton had hit her. Fire was the one thing she had always, from a child, been terrified of. Well, there was always the open window if she failed.

But how could she start a fire? You can't just set a match to a door. On the mantelpiece were laid out the contents of her bag, amongst them a nail-file and a petrol-lighter. Thank goodness she had filled it this morning. She stabbed the file into the mattress on which she had been lying, ripped it along, pulled out the flock in handfuls and piled it against the door. She opened the cupboard doors. The shelves were lined with paper. She crumpled paper under the flock, unscrewed her lighter and poured the petrol over the heap. Then she put a match to it.

In the draught from the window a flame blazed up. Carefully she nursed its precarious life, adding paper, then a drawer from the washstand, then, as the fire began to draw more steadily, piling the rest of the mattress on it. Would Chilton and Steele hear the crackling, wherever they were? Skirmishing flames began to venture farther afield, licking along the wooden panelling on either side of the door. Fog and smoke stung Georgia's eyes, rasped her throat. The crescent of fire was advancing towards her in stealthy little rushes. It was coming too fast. No, it was dawdling, Chilton would be back before . . .

Hurriedly Georgia stuffed the papers inside her dress, stowed in her pocket the money that lay on the mantelpiece; she could not be encumbered with a bag now. The door was a sheet of flame now, and in a few minutes the whole room would be a furnace. It was either the door or the window for her. She wrapped the blankets close about her head and body, and threw herself against the blazing door. The panels gave, but the lock still held firm. Sobbing with the agony of flame and smoke, Georgia recoiled, reeled back to the window, gulped the harsh, foggy air. Then she picked up the armchair and ran at the door again, ramming it with the chair. This time, in a shower of sparks and a great swirl of smoke, the door fell outwards.

Georgia flung down the blankets and sped along the landing, down the narrow stairs. At the bottom was a green baize-covered door which shut off this part of the house. Georgia felt for the handle, turned it. Chilton had locked the door from the outside. She was still in a trap and soon all the landing overhead would be ablaze. She turned against the wall, all the fight knocked out of her, and buried her head in her hands. Her hands stretched up against the wall, encountered a metal frame, felt upwards. It was a fire-extinguisher. It would be as much use against that inferno as a glass of water. Perhaps she could smash open this door with it, though. She took it down from its stand, but at that moment she heard footsteps on the far side of the door, and then the key turned.

"Can't you smell smoke?" said the voice of Hargreaves Steele.

"Don't tell me that little bitch has—"

It all happened in a moment. Georgia had been crouching against the corner of the wall, hoping they would pass her in the dark. But, as Chilton came through the door behind Professor Steele, he switched on the light. In that instant, Georgia banged the knob of the extinguisher hard against the wall. Startled, the two men wheeled round on her, and she directed the stream of liquid full into Chilton Canteloe's eyes, then, as he fell back moaning, clawing at his face, she let Professor Steele have it.

She slipped between their tumbling bodies, locked the door on them, and ran lightly towards the main staircase, switching off lights as she passed. First to her bedroom where she hurried on her fur coat. No time to pack a bag. David Renton slept on the floor above, the servants high up in another part of the house. As for Chilton and Steele—let them burn, she thought coldly. But the rest ought to be warned. A plan formed itself in her head, its salient points miraculously emerging like a bold landscape out of mist.

Letting herself out of the front door, Georgia ran round the west wing of the house and down the gravelled drive to the garages. She pulled the chain of the great iron bell. Presently the head of Chilton Canteloe's chauffeur appeared at a window above.

"What the hell? Oh, beg pardon, Mrs. Strangeways."

"Quick! The house is on fire! The east wing. We can't get through to the fire brigade. Something's gone wrong with the telephone. Get a car out."

The man came clattering down the stairs. Georgia heard the scrape of the garage door being slid open.

"Shall I drive you, m'm? Best run in to Ashwell and call up the brigades from there."

"No, I'll manage alone. Now wake up every one else who sleeps here. Jump to it, man. One of you run over to the house, and make sure they're all roused up there. Tell the rest to make a relay of buckets."

"We've got an auxiliary fire-engine here, m'm."

"Good. Just start up the car for me first."

The self-starter whirred. Georgia leapt into the driver's seat of the big Rolls. Above the sound of the engine she could hear the chauffeur's shouts and the clanging of the alarm bell. All that din would drown for a while, at any rate, whatever noise Chilton and Steele might be making. Whether the fire or the rescuers reached them first was not of vital importance to her at the moment. She had had to allow them this chance of being rescued, in order to get hold of a car. It would give her a good start at least.

She spun the car out of the yard into the main drive. Fog steamed and streamed in front of her, blunting the beams of the headlights, but Georgia's eye for the country, that printed its vivid maps on her memory, enabled her to swing along the curving drive at nearly forty miles an hour. Nearing the park gates, she was seized with apprehension lest Chilton should have already escaped from the burning wing and telephoned the lodge-keeper to stop her.

Yes, the massive iron gates were locked. Well, of course, they always were at night. She kept her finger pressed on the bell till the lodge-keeper emerged.

"Quick! Where's the key? The house is on fire. I'm off to ring up the brigade. All our telephones are out of order."

The old man, stupid with sleep, peered at her fire-blackened face, scratched his head.

"What's to do, m'm?" he said.

"Chilton Ashwell is on fire," she yelled at him. "You're to go up to the house at once. His lordship's orders. Now fetch the key, for heaven's sake."

He fetched it. Georgia sighed with relief. It had not occurred to the old man that they might try ringing up the fire stations from the lodge telephone. She heard his feet clattering away into the fog. Opening the gates, she drove the car through. She locked them behind her and threw the key away into the bracken. There were two other exits from the park, but her pursuers would naturally come to this one which opened on to the main road.

Pushing the car to the very limit of safety along the Nottingham road, with the windscreen open so that she could see better through the fog, Georgia decided on her next move. On a clear morning, she might have risked driving straight to London. But this fog would slow her down too much. If Chilton was rescued, he would have the E.B. out after her in a twinkling, would probably inform the police too that his car had been stolen, and the car was so easily recognizable. Her first job must be to get rid of it, then.

She stopped at the public call-box in Ashwell to ring up the fire-brigades. They would at least add to the confusion, and possibly hamper Chilton a bit. Then she sped on towards Nottingham. She drove the car into the yard of the L.N.E.R. station. Luggage. She would be dreadfully conspicuous without any luggage at this time of the morning. Conspicuous! And her grimy face, too. For all she knew her eyebrows and half her hair might have been burnt off. Switching on the inside light a moment she found a mirror. Dear me, I look like the morning after the Witches' Sabbath. What a hag! She began to rub her face with a handkerchief. Before she was half clean, however, another idea struck her.

A hatless, rather grimy woman, arriving at a station at about four o'clock in the morning is bound to be pretty conspicuous anyway. Well, I must trade on that. If the eyes of the railway officials are going to come out on stalks, let them. I daren't bank on Chilton having been destroyed in the fire. Suppose he's survived it. He'll certainly expect me to make for London: he's thorough, so he'll have the trains watched as well as the roads. Therefore I dare not take a London train, unless there's a fast one leaving here very shortly. On the other hand, it'd be no harm for me to give the impression that I'm going to London.

Georgia got out of the car, opened the boot, and extracted from it one of the suitcases with which it was fitted. At the booking office she inquired about the next train to London. It did not run for nearly an hour. She bought a third-class ticket, and walked down towards the platform. The ticket-collector stared curiously at her face, as she complained how bad was the service to London: her car had broken down, and it was most urgent she should get up there quickly. Her dirty face and her lady-like voice made a contrast which impressed itself upon the ticket-collector. His private opinion was that she'd taken a drop too much and smashed her car up.

Georgia was indeed reeling a little from fatigue as she descended the steps, though her brain was still too keyed-up to feel it.

The long platform was deserted, its lights dismally marooned in the fog. Georgia cleaned herself up in the ladies' room, then strolled towards the far end of the platform. A fog-signal smacked dully from somewhere out in the gloom, and there was the distant clatter of a train. Glancing about her, Georgia hurried down the ramp, slipped like a wraith across the metals to an up platform. The train rumbled in and came to a halt, standing there with that derelict and lifeless look of trains in the small hours of the morning. It was a slow to Manchester, a yawning porter told her. As well Manchester as anywhere else: she could lose herself in a city that size, get a breathing-space, put through a call to Sir John; and the E.B. would not be looking for her yet in that direction. Wearily she got into the train. Sitting there, clanking slowly through the fog, she began to feel the smart of the burns on her forearms. It reminded her that tonight had been real, not the phantasmagoria of fear and violence it seemed. She was out in the open now against her enemies, England's enemies.

Georgia believed she was safe for the present, but it would never do to relax her vigilance. Alone in the compartment, she decided to keep awake by reading through Plan A and making a mental *précis* of it which she could transmit to Sir John Strangeways over the phone. She took the papers out of her dress and began to read. Her sensibilities dulled by exhaustion, she could feel no triumph in having the E.B.'s secret here under her hands as well as Chilton Canteloe's Plan B in her head. She might have been perusing the prospectus of a respectable company for all the thrill it gave her. Indeed, with its cold, impersonal setting-out of detail, its translation of flesh-and-blood hopes, greed, fears, idealism into an inhuman document, the plan did read rather like a company-prospectus.

At last the train drew into Manchester. Georgia had to pay for her ticket at the barrier. It reminded her how fallible she was. She ought to have got a ticket at the other end, as well as the one for London: this transaction would draw attention to her, and when the E.B. had discovered she was not on the London train, they would naturally start inquiries about other trains which had left Nottingham early this morning.

She was too tired to worry much about it now. Carrying the suitcase into the station hotel, she booked a room under the name of Anita Clay. Luckily the suitcase was a fitted one, heavy enough for the page who took it from her not to suspect that "Anita Clay" had no personal belongings in it at all. The initials stamped on it, C.A.C. — Chilton Anstruther Canteloe — were near enough the initials of Anita Clay to rouse no comment, she hoped.

Now that she was temporarily in refuge, the reaction of the night set in. The hotel's solid furniture swam before her eyes as if it were built of swirling fog: her whole body ached, and her feet felt like feather-stuffed bolsters. In the bedroom at last, the door locked, the betraying, empty suitcase tucked away under the bed, she reached out her hand for the telephone. Had she put through the long-distance call to Sir John at this moment, she might have been saved a great deal of trouble. But fatally she thought, it'll be a long conversation, I might as well do it in comfort; and undressed and washed, and got into bed in her underclothes. That nicely-sprung bed, the soft pillows, were too much for her. As her hand reached out for the telephone again, her eyelids would hold up no longer and sleep blacked out everything.

It was after midday when Georgia woke. Refreshed by sleep, she came awake with all her senses about her. She rang down for coffee, toast and the first edition of the evening papers. Yes, as she had expected, it was all there. Historic Mansion Gutted. Popular Millionaire Injured Fighting Flames. Injured. Only injured. That is bad. We have scotched the snake, not killed it. I'm getting soft. I ought to have finished him last night. I ought — oh, God, I ought to have rung up Uncle John. With Chilton still alive, and his plans stolen, not one of us is safe. But I was so sleepy. No excuses, my girl. You must make the best of it and get in touch with Uncle John now, before it's too late.

But it was too late. As she put the newspaper aside, her eye lit on another column. It reported that, walking to his office in Scotland Yard this morning, Sir John Strangeways, head of C. Department, had been knocked down by a car and was now in a critical condition. The car had not stopped. The police, however, were confident, etc.

Like hell the car didn't stop, she thought. I should have risked taking that train to London. I was thinking so hard about how to save my own skin, and now Uncle John . . . Oh, damn them all!

Georgia was so fond of Nigel's uncle, so horrified by the knowledge that she might have saved him from this lightning counter-stroke of the E.B. that she did not realize for a moment how much her own position was altered for the worse. Even supposing Sir John recovered, he would be *hors-de-combat* for at least a week, she imagined. And, during that time, what should she do? Sir

John had given her strict orders that, when she obtained any really vital information, she must convey it directly to him. She had no idea, so wide were the ramifications of the E.B. by now, which of his subordinates could be trusted: neither could she rely upon any protection from him for the present. She could not even walk into the nearest police-station and hand over the responsibility to them, for—though the majority of the police were no doubt still loyal—she could not be sure of any individual one.

"Georgia, my lass," she murmured to herself, sipping her luke-warm coffee, "you're on the run. They've got you going and coming. The fun is only just beginning."

The thought filled her with an absurd exhilaration. She'd got out of tight places before, and she might do it again if the luck ran her way.

# 16. The Episode of the Father Christmases

Georgia's first impulse was to ring up Nigel at Oxford and enlist his help. She desperately wanted him, even if it was only to hear the comfort of his voice for a few minutes. But she realized this would never do. In the first place, he had probably left Oxford to be with his uncle. Besides, it would only be bringing him into the danger-zone: whoever she attempted to communicate with might be marked down by the E.B. and attacked with the same ruthlessness that had been used on Sir John. She was like a person with a contagious disease: she must isolate herself from those she loved or they too would be struck down.

Alison Grove was another matter. Alison had been in this from the start, and she should be able to put her in touch with those who were carrying on Sir John Strangeways' work. Heartened by the thought of speaking with her friend, Georgia dressed and went to the hotel dining-room for lunch. She did not suppose that the E.B. could have caught up with her yet, but for all that it might be safer not to ring up Alison from the hotel. So after lunch, she strolled out into the station and entered a public call-box. Alison, fortunately, was at her flat when the call went through.

"Hello, Alison? This is Georgia."

"Hello! I see you've been indulging in arson, ducky."

"I'd have indulged in murder too if I'd had the sense — and a bit more time. Listen, darling, please don't chatter, we'll all have to move fast now. I've got hold of the doings. C.C. and the whole E.B. are out after me. You realize it was they who did that to Uncle John? How is he?"

"As well as you could expect. They say he has a fifty-fifty chance. Georgia, for heaven's sake, did you say you'd got hold of the —?"

"Yes. There are two plans. One's on paper and the other's in my head. I haven't time to explain. What's my next move?"

"Where are you? No! Wait a minute. You remember the Puce Goat?"

"Yes. But what on earth — ?" The Puce Goat was the long-suffering mistress who, some twenty years ago, had taught them both Latin — so called because of her complexion and incipient beard. It was soon explained. Alison broke into a rattle of dog-Latin.

"*Ubi es nunc, amice?*"

"*In urbe castra hominis.*" Georgia hoped this would convey Manchester.

"In *what*? Oh, I get you. *Mane ubi es. Curabo auxilium mittendum.*"

All very well to tell her to stay where she was, thought Georgia: the E.B. might find her before Alison's promised help arrived. She told Alison, in halting Latin, that—if she had to move away from here—she would try and get to Oxford.

*"Habesne satis pecunioi?"*

Georgia was reminded that she had very little money left. It was arranged that her friend should wire an order for £50, which she could pick up at the Manchester branch of her bank. They arranged a rendezvous in Manchester where Georgia could meet the escort Alison would be sending. Georgia had memorized the names of the E.B. organizers and the various centres of the conspiracy in England: she was about to pass these on to Alison when her eyes, straying through the glass partition of the telephone booth, lighted on David Renton.

Impeccably dressed in black overcoat and pin-stripe trousers, his white, fleshy face bland under the bowler-hat, Chilton Canteloe's secretary was earnestly conversing with the ticket-collector at the barrier. He looked the picture of respectability. So did the two young men in plus-fours and pork-pie hats lounging at the cigarette kiosk, to whom Renton, turning away now from the barrier, made an unobtrusive sign.

"Ring off, Alison. Some of the boys have arrived," said Georgia, and ducked down out of their sight behind the wooden door.

She thanked her stars she had brought the E.B. papers with her. There could be no going back to the hotel now. Renton would search there first, and that infernal suitcase would tell him all he needed to know. Georgia had to decide quickly between leaving Manchester at once with the little money she had, or staying till the bank opened again tomorrow morning. To stay was dangerous; but, without money, she would be helpless. It was not simply a matter of buying a ticket at Oxford.

She must have some disguise if she hoped to get there safely. Slipping out of the telephone booth, she jumped into a taxi and told the man to drive her to a small hotel in one of the suburbs. On the way she stopped and bought a cheap suitcase, a pair of pyjamas and a few necessaries. Her money now, when she had paid her bill for the night, would be nearly exhausted.

She spent the evening making a *précis* of Plan A and writing an account of Plan B. She would keep the original plan in her bag, so that, if the E.B. got her, they would have no difficulty in finding it. The copy and Plan B she decided to conceal on her own person: she might, after all, be able to escape from them again, though they would not be likely to leave loopholes. The problem of disposing of the copy now arose. It was all very well for people in books to talk so gaily about concealing papers on one's person. When the papers were as bulky as Plan A, even in *précis*, they were not so easily disposed of. Georgia could not sew them inside the lining of her fur coat, for instance, since she intended to disguise herself in men's clothing. After some thought she unpicked her corselette belt, slipped the sheets of paper between its satin panel and the lining, and sewed it up again. Her last action was to crop short her hair in readiness for tomorrow's change of clothing.

The next morning she paid her bill, packed her suitcase, took a taxi to the central branch of the bank, and received the money Alison had wired. She intended after this to find some small second-hand clothes shop where she could buy a man's rig-out with the least danger of the purchase being traced to her. But no sooner had she stepped outside the bank than she perceived, on the opposite side of the road, one of the young men who had been with David Renton yesterday at the station. He glanced at her, deliberately folded up the paper he had been affecting to read, and waved it at someone further down the street.

The E.B. certainly waste no time, she thought. This is where I get off. But surely they won't try to kidnap me here, in the middle of the shopping-centre, among these crowds? Let's hope they're all men—the ones who are shadowing me now: they'll need to be made of stern stuff if they're going to follow me in here. And she turned in at the door of a huge department store, already beginning to fill up with women shoppers.

The warm, scented air was a contrast with bleak Manchester outside. These hard-headed Mancunian housewives, obeying the advertisements which told them to Do Your Christmas Shopping Early, would have scoffed at the idea that every swing-door of the great building was now watched by a man who would stick at nothing to lay his hands on the small, fur-coated, Eton-cropped woman wandering dreamily from department to department. Georgia guessed they were there, though. She had only darted in here to give herself time to think, to invent a new plan, and because it was safer here than out in a street where cars could knock down pedestrians—as Uncle John had been knocked down—and drive on.

She thought of entering the men's department, buying suit, hat and overcoat, and changing somewhere on the premises. But this idea was soon rejected. Even if she were sufficiently well disguised to get past the watchers at the doors, her purchases could be too quickly traced and it would put them on her track again.

That shop-walker's eyes seemed to be fixed on her rather curiously, as she lingered among the Ladies' Underwear. She became aware of the suitcase in her hand.

It'd be darned funny if I was hauled up on suspicion of shop-lifting, she thought. It's darned funny how guilty the very idea makes me feel—considering I've already let myself in for charges of arson, attempted murder of a millionaire, and theft of a millionaire's Rolls-Royce, to say nothing of that unpaid bill at the station hotel. Georgia, you're in a spot.

She walked downstairs to the ladies' room and left her suitcase there. At the far end of the room was a door marked "Staff Only." It occurred to her that here might be an exit left unguarded by the E.B. men, and she determined to prospect it. Waiting till she was unobserved, she slipped through the door into a long passage. Like the behind-the-scenes of many other imposing façades, of theatres, restaurants or big shops, the passage was mean and ill-lighted. Georgia went down it till she heard voices in front of her. Employés, no doubt. She must pretend she'd lost herself, and ask them to show her the way out. She turned the corner to be confronted by no indignant supervisor or giggling employés. Sitting on a bench, desultorily chatting, smoking cigarette stubs and spitting on the stone floor, were half a dozen Father Christmases.

Georgia stopped dead in amazement. My recent experiences must have turned my brain. But no, there they are—one, two, three, four, five, six Father Christmases. Or should one say "Fathers Christmas"?

Then she saw the sandwich-boards piled up in a corner. Of course: it was a poster-parade. Do Your Christmas Shopping Early. Come To Hallam and Appleby's For Your Yule-Tide Gifts. Oh glory! thought Georgia; thank you, Santa Claus, for your nice present: the very thing I wanted. Now I can offer the E.B. the compliments of the season.

She picked out a man who seemed nearest to her own size, and led him round the angle of the passage. The other five Father Christmases paid no attention at all, as if ladies in expensive fur coats were quite the normal thing in this lobby. Maybe they hadn't even seen her. Maybe their eyes were still fixed on the gutter trailing beneath their broken shoes, on the sandwich-boarded back of the man in front.

"Here, Dad," said Georgia. "Be a sport. I want to borrow your robe and that beard."

The man unhooked his beard with great deliberation, revealing a pug-nosed, withered, sardonic old face.

"What's the idea, Mrs.?"

"It's a bet. A friend of mine bet me I wouldn't walk in the sandwich-board parade."

"A bit of fun, eh? You mean, you're out for a bit of fun, like?"

"That's it. I'll pay for it."

"I thought, when you asked me, you wur one of them Mass Observers they writes about in papers."

"No. I'm just one of the mass-observed. Particularly so at the moment. What do they give you a day for this job?"

"Half a crown, Mrs., and a snap at midday. You should see it. What they sweep oop from floor. Potage Maisong. And a ruddy sight more maisong than potage about it."

"I'll give you a quid for the loan of that fancy-dress for an hour. Change places with you, see?"

"Betcher life you will—and get me the sack too. I'll 'ave nowt to do with it, Mrs."

"You'll not get the sack. You hang about outside here. No, you'd better follow the parade. How far do they walk?"

217

"As far as the Green Man, if we gets a chance. But I'm having nowt to do with it."

"Well, you can keep up with us that far, walk along the pavement behind us to make sure I don't run off with your robe. And when we get there, we'll slip out of sight a moment and change clothes again."

"Seems to me you're daft, Mrs. Just like our Emmie. Always oop to soom daft notion." The old man stared at her lugubriously. Then his wizened face suddenly underwent a convulsion and rearranged itself into a sly smile. "Tickle our Mum, this would," he chuckled. "Aye, it would and all. Make it two quid."

"You're a sport, Dad."

Georgia handed him the money. She put on the red, white-fur-trimmed robe over her own coat, and adjusted the hood. It came down to her feet, made her look bulky and shapeless, but no harm in that. The old man punctiliously wiped the false beard on his sleeve before passing it to her. Spasms of chuckling shook him at intervals. Georgia tucked her bag inside the robe: it should be held up all right by the girdle, and its shape concealed under the sandwich-board.

"Am I quite covered up now? No skirt showing?"

"That's right, Mrs. Wouldn't know you apart from myself. It's a knock-out. Out you go, now. They're just off."

Georgia went into the lobby and hoisted the sandwich-boards over her shoulders. The procession moved apathetically through the door, along a cobbled passage with grimy buildings towering on either side, and shambled into the main street — as dispirited-looking a set of Santa Clauses as any one could hope to see. They certainly roused no interest in the pair of loafers who had been standing outside this alley for the last twenty-five minutes, on the look-out for a small, dark, hatless lady in a fur coat.

Turning left, the procession passed in front of the great display-windows of Hallam and Appleby's. Georgia could see at a glance that the store was in a state of siege: near every entrance a cluster of men had gathered: the E.B. was taking no chances. Her red sleeve, trimmed with fur that long usage had turned from snow- to slush-colour, brushed against the young man in the pork-pie hat and ginger moustache. She heard him mutter to one of his associates, "We've got her cold now."

The words brought a kind of delayed claustrophobia over Georgia. While she had been inside the shop, she was too busy to think of anything except how she could get out. Now she saw herself in there, like a rabbit in a warren, every hole watched by the implacable hunters. Shambling along in the gutter, she kept her head bent; but her eyes glanced sideways, registering the appearance of the E.B. agents. She would be able to recognize them again. A certain purposeful, attentive air distinguished them from the crowds that idled restlessly about the plate-glass windows.

The five Father Christmases walked slowly on, oblivious alike of the children who gaped at them and the man-hunt that was taking place under their noses. Georgia followed them, glad she had kept on her fur coat beneath the robe, for the leather straps of the sandwich-boards were already biting into her shoulders. They were far down the street now; out of the danger-zone, she thought. Her heart sighed with relief, and she began to plan the next move. The war of attrition was over. A period of mobile warfare had begun. Her safety depended on moving fast and keeping moving. Already she chafed at the slouching, tortoise-gait of the sandwichmen. Even a car drawn up by the kerb, round which the procession had to deviate, seemed a delaying obstacle. She walked past it, brushed against the front mudguard, fell into place again along the gutter. As she did so, the high heel of her left shoe caught in a grating and made her stumble badly. She recovered herself, moved on, unaware that a man had noticed the little accident and slipped out of the passenger's seat of the car.

It was one of the E.B. cars, its nose pointing away from the department store, ready to begin the chase in the event of Georgia getting through the cordon and trying to escape by taxi. The driver started his engine, kept it ticking over while his companion caught up with the tail of the sandwich-board procession.

Georgia knew nothing of this till, half a minute later, a man passed her, walking rapidly along the pavement edge, transferring cigarettes from a Player's carton to his silver case. When he was a couple of yards ahead of her, he fumbled with the case and several cigarettes fell into the gutter. The man bent down to retrieve them. It was all over in a few seconds. She perceived the tensing of his figure as he caught sight, bending down, of the high-heeled shoes that were the only part of her not disguised by the Father Christmas dress.

Damn, damn, damn! My Achilles heel. Why did it have to trip me up just then? Now I'm back at the start again. Worse, for they would scarcely have dared to start anything in the shop; but out here, out in the open . . .

She heard the car creeping up behind her, imagined the stunning impact, the hands lifting her solicitously into the car, the car driving away — but not to hospital. Why they did not employ upon her the same methods that had been used against Sir John, she never knew. Perhaps they wanted to make sure of searching her, without interference at the start. Policemen have a way of cropping up out of the ground as soon as an accident has happened.

At any rate, nothing happened for a while. The car had turned and gone back towards the shopping centre, the cigarette-dropping man strolled along a little distance behind the Father Christmases. They reached the Green Man. With a hurried glance round, the leader popped into the pub, followed by the others. Georgia knew her only hope now was to stick close to them: the car would be bringing up more of the E.B. agents and the pub would be surrounded.

The Father Christmases were having a quick one: a very quick one—already they were wiping their snowy moustaches and making for the door again. Through the glass partition between public bar and smoking-room, the old man whose clothes Georgia had borrowed was gesticulating to her violently but in vain. Soundless oaths took shape on that wizened old face behind the glass. Georgia pretended not to notice him, and followed the procession out into the street.

The walk back to the department store was her worst ordeal. It seemed as if their leader wished to display the posters through every street in Manchester before they returned. Georgia had managed to slip into a middle place in the parade when they left the pub, so that there was less danger of her being cut off: but every passer-by now looked like an enemy, and at any moment, in whatever unexpected form, the attack might take place.

If only they could get back safely to the store! A plan was forming in her head—a desperate last resort, but now her only hope. At last they approached the alley beside Hallam and Appleby's. Here, in this narrow, blind passage, she would be most vulnerable. Only five old men to protect her, and they without a glimmering of an idea that any protection would be needed. She could imagine the alley blocked at either end, the gleam of weapons, the deliberate hustling, the senile stupor of the Father Christmases. No, she was not going into that alley, not at any price.

As they passed the door of the toy department, Georgia suddenly unhitched her sandwich-boards, swung them hard against the shins of a man who tried to intercept her, dropped them, and whipped in through the door before either commissionaire or E.B. men could lay a finger on her. A shop-walker seized her arm and muttered angrily, his face still wreathed in an obsequious smile for the benefit of the customers, "Here, you. What the hell are you doing in here? Get back to—no, madam, leather fancies first floor up—I'll see you're fired for this, you old fool."

"Take your hands off me, you wax dummy," Georgia replied gruffly, "or I'll give you such a kick in the pants it'll send your spine out through the top of your head—if you have a spine, you invertebrate son of a misbegotten jellyfish."

The shop-walker's hand fell nervelessly from her arm. His mouth gobbled, and his eyes bulged after this outrageous Father Christmas who now proceeded leisurely through the toy department, pausing occasionally to pat a child on the head. "Did you hear what he said to me?" the shop-walker exclaimed when he had found his voice. "That's the thanks we get for picking an unemployed man off the street and giving him work. By gum, he'll find he can't treat Hallam and Appleby's like that. I'll—I'll report him to the manager."

"Report whom," said an assistant sweetly. "There's half a dozen of those Father Christmases. You'll have to use a divining-rod, Mr. Prendergast."

"None of your sauce, my girl. Ah t'cha."

Meanwhile Georgia had made her way into the passage that led to the staff-lobby. She took off her disguise, rolled it up, and flung it round the corner amongst the Father Christmases. Then, returning through the ladies' room, she began to perambulate slowly around the crowded departments again. The house-detective, who was shortly summoned to keep an eye on her, decided she was the most blatant and unskillful shop-lifter he had ever seen. Must be one of them kleptomaniacs, he said to himself as she stowed away two pairs of silk stockings, a bottle of expensive scent and a shopping-diary.

# 17. The Episode of the Pantechnicon's Progress

The house-detective placed his hand under Georgia's elbow. "The manager would like a word with you, madam," he said.

"The manager? I don't understand. Why, what—?"

"He would wish you to explain the presence of certain articles in your bag." The house-detective appeared to speak more in sorrow than in anger. He was constantly tripping up these loopy dames who couldn't keep their fingers off Hallam and Appleby's stuff. All in the day's work. You gave 'em a fright and pushed 'em out again: prosecutions didn't do the House any good. He was quite used, also, to the icy but brittle hauteur with which this woman replied:

"I'm afraid I don't understand you. Please leave go of my elbow. It's outrageous. Are you suggesting—?"

"Better wash the dirty linen in private, madam," he said paternally, indicating with a slight movement of the head the curious glances which other shoppers were beginning to give her. "This way, please." She followed

him like a lamb. They always did. Nothing these respectable dames dreaded so much as a scene. A queer
go, they were and all: afterwards, some of them even
tipped him for dealing with their little mistakes so
tactfully.

Outside the manager's door Georgia, still playing her
part, took out her compact and mirror and touched herself up a bit. All went well so far. The manager would
turn her over to the police. Unless she struck unlucky,
and these particular officers were in the pay of the E.B.,
she could count on a safe night in the cells, time to think
out her next move. That risk had to be taken, for it
would be sudden death to set a foot outside this shop
now without an escort.

The manager, sitting behind his desk as they entered,
gave her a surprise. She had expected some middle-aged,
pasty, self-important, wing-collared individual. Mr.
Dickon, however, turned out to be quite young, dressed
in a stylish tweed-suit which, with his horn-rimmed
glasses and bushy moustache, gave him more the appearance of a successful author.

"Sit down, won't you?" he said. "Mrs. er—?"

"Mrs. Smith. Mrs. *Percy* Smith. I demand to know
by what right—?"

"Would you mind opening your bag?" asked the
young man, his tone an odd blend of diffidence,
authority, and faintly bored amusement. Before she
could reply, the house-detective had lifted the bag neatly
off her lap and laid out the stolen articles on the desk.
Then he returned it to her, the papers of Plan A rustling
inside.

"You know, this is very naughty of you, Mrs.
Smith—Mrs. *Percy* Smith."

Georgia buried her head in her hands and broke down

225

—convincingly, she hoped. She heard the manager say, not unkindly, yet in a detached voice:

"Now you mustn't distress yourself. It was just a little mistake. Forget all about it. Hallam and Appleby's never prosecute first offenders."

Georgia sat up, gazing at him in consternation. Her whole scheme lay in ruins. He was not calling in the police: she still had to get away from this wretched shop of his unaided. She tried to stammer out thanks, her heart raging with disappointment. Mr. Dickon motioned the detective out of the room. Then he tilted his chair back at a dangerous angle, smiled at Georgia quizzically, and said:

"And now, Mrs. Strangeways, what can I do for you?"

Georgia had had quite a few shocks during the last forty-eight hours, but none that disconcerted her more than this. She stared at the young manager blankly.

"I heard you lecturing at the Travellers' Club a couple of years ago," he explained. "I used to do a bit myself—went on one of the Oxford University expeditions, to the Antarctic."

"But—"

"I know enough about you, Mrs. Strangeways, to be quite sure that—if you really wanted to pinch things out of this place—you'd have no difficulty in getting away with it. So, you see, I asked myself, why does the astute Mrs. Strangeways allow herself to be caught red-handed? And answer came there none. Perhaps you'll elucidate?"

Georgia, silent for a little, looked Mr. Dickon over. Everything now depended on her faculty, trained in strange places among strangers, for summing up character at a glance. If he were all right, as he looked, he could be her salvation: if, on the other hand, he were a member of the E.B., she might as well pack up straight away. The fact that, though she had been caught out shoplifting, he was for letting her go scot-free, told against him. But there was a candour, a humorousness in his eyes which persuaded her to trust him. She gestured towards the window of his office.

"That looks out on the front of the building, doesn't it? Just go over and glance down. See those groups of men hanging about by the entrances?"

"M'm!"

"They're there to get hold of me. I'm working for the Special Branch—counter-espionage. It's vital that I get to—get away from here this afternoon. This is something big, Mr. Dickon. So big that I daren't tell you more. I may have been mistaken in telling you so much, and in this game one isn't allowed to make more than one mistake. You follow?"

"What about the police?"

"They must not be brought into it."

"I see."

Mr. Dickon drew some geometrical diagrams on his blotter. He had that astonishing faculty for not showing astonishment, which Oxford imparts to her sons. Georgia's heart warmed to him: he was a traveller too; the most bizarre phenomena would be greeted by him with just that faint lifting of the eyebrows, that carefully concealed exultation. He asked for no explanations, intent upon the matter in hand.

"Where—roughly where do you want to get to? London?" he said at last.

"Farther west, shall we say."

Georgia grinned back at him. Mr. Dickon touched a button and spoke into the house-telephone.

"Furnishing department? What vans have we going out this afternoon? . . . Yes . . . No, he'll have to start earlier. Make it three o'clock. Who's the foreman? . . . Send him and the driver up here in five minutes." Mr. Dickon looked up at her. "How much can I tell them?"

"Are they absolutely trustworthy?"

"Yes. They're staunch Trades Unionists." His eyes studied her shrewdly. "I imagine that's the type you'd feel safest with in—er—the present circumstances."

"Mr. Dickon, I feel you perhaps suspect more than is healthy for you."

"What Manchester suspects today, madam, England will suspect tomorrow. By Jove, I wish I could come with you," he exclaimed boyishly. Then, the efficient manager again, he said, "We'd better have a diversion as well. Let me see . . . Are these people out to shoot at sight?"

"No. Kidnapping's what they're after."

The efficient Mr. Dickon pressed another button. "Tell Miss Jones I want to speak to her in quarter of an hour's time."

In a dream Georgia watched him organize the detail of her escape. She was to travel in the pantechnicon, scheduled to leave for Plymouth this afternoon. Trousers, coat, shoes, white overalls, cloth cap appeared as if by magic, and she retired into the manager's washplace to put them on. He opened the window, rubbed his hands on the sill outside, and artistically smeared Manchester grime over her face, neck and hands. "We supply all your needs," he said, fastening a black, toothbrush moustache on her upper lip with spirit gum. He was enjoying it all enormously in his quiet way. The driver and foreman, sworn to secrecy, had already been told what they must do.

Miss Jones, a head clerk in the accountancy department, a woman of Georgia's height and build, was to supply the diversion. Thirty seconds before the lorry left the yard, she would hurry out of a shop door dressed in a fur coat similar to Georgia's and a hat with an eye-veil. The E.B. watchers would intercept her, and shortly discover their mistake: but their attention would have been distracted for a minute from the outgoing van. Miss Jones, a leading light in amateur theatricals, could be relied on to make the most of the episode.

"And now," said Mr. Dickon, "I'll have lunch sent up. Just pop into the other room till they've brought it. You'll need a hearty meal if you're going to help load furniture. Let's see, now." He became absorbed in organizing the menu.

"Darling Mr. Dickon, I'll really have to take you with me on an expedition some day. What a comfort you'd be."

"That's a bargain . . ."

At four o'clock Georgia was sitting between driver and foreman in the wide cab of the pantechnicon. They were now twenty miles out of Manchester, roaring steadily south into the gathering darkness. Georgia had the papers of Plan A tucked away in a wallet in her coat pocket, and in the pocket of her baize apron lay a revolver supplied by the inexhaustible Mr. Dickon. She was feeling—of all unlikely emotions at this juncture—a dull boredom. The progress of a pantechnicon does not conduce to any lively excitement, for one thing: and besides, Georgia was no soccer enthusiast, and her two companions were already deeply involved in controversy about the respective merits of Manchester City and Manchester United. Statistics, reminiscences, judgments of form, dark hints of the machinations of managers, less guarded comments on the physical infirmities of referees, beat to and fro about the cab like bats' wings in a dark cave. Driver and foreman had replayed every move of the last three matches won by their respective teams when a sound of an electric horn stabbed the night and a mobile policeman, swerving past the pantechnicon, halted his motor-bike thirty yards ahead and raised his hand for them to stop.

Georgia was already slumped back in her seat, feigning sleep. She heard the driver slide back the side window and the policeman speaking through it. The police were stopping all cars and lorries, he said: they were looking for a woman, last seen in Manchester, wanted on a charge of car-stealing. Georgia's hand felt for the revolver in her pocket. She hoped she would not have to use it.

"Got no girls with us on this trip—worse luck," said the driver.

"My orders are to search the van."

"Search away, cock, I'm not stopping you. But you'll have to sign my road-book to show I've been delayed. I'm running to schedule."

"None of your lip, my lad. Come on, open up."

"You sign my road-book, cock, or I'm not opening this van. We haven't got all night to chat with fancy coppers on stink-bang machines."

After some blustering, the policeman signed. Then he stood his motor-bike in the road behind the pantechnicon so that its headlight shone into the interior which, with a good deal of passive obstruction from the growling foreman, he proceeded to search thoroughly. Georgia heard him stumbling about amongst the furniture, and suggestions from the foreman that he might

230

care to unload this wardrobe and take it home with him to examine at leisure.

"What say we lock oop t'bleeder inside and take him along with us?" the driver whispered to her.

"Better not, Joe. I don't want to get you into more trouble than I can help." Later, Georgia was to regret she had not accepted the driver's suggestion. At last the policeman declared himself satisfied. Poking his head into the cabin, he told the driver he could get on with it.

"What about your mate? He seen anything? Sleeping pretty sound, isn't he?"

"So'd you be, if you ever did any work."

"Wake him up," ordered the policeman brusquely.

"Here, cock, have a heart."

"Wake him up, I tell you."

"Ruddy pocket Hitler! Ain't this a free country? Can't even take a nap without you've got a licence from police," exclaimed the driver truculently. Georgia pressed her foot gently against his. He took the cue.

"Very well," he said, shaking her shoulder. "Come on, young Albert, wake oop."

Georgia answered the policeman's questions in a husky voice, sneezing frequently and wiping her nose with her sleeve. The man appeared satisfied, and shortly roared away in front of them on his motorbike.

"Has ter stolen a car really, Miss?" asked the foreman when they were on their way again.

"As a matter of fact I did. A Rolls-Royce."

"Well, fancy that now. To my mind, we ought to have knocked that copper on t'head."

"I'm not sure you're not right. I'm afraid we'll hear more of him tonight."

They did. Their route lay through Stoke and Stafford towards Birmingham. Mr. Dickon had decided on this, rather than the more westerly road by Shrewsbury, because there was more traffic on it and therefore less danger of interference. As they hummed on through the towns of the Potteries, the dark sky lit up intermittently with furnace-flares. Georgia pondered the recent episode. The policeman had evidently been an E.B. agent. His searching of the van suggested that perhaps Mr. Dickon had over-reached himself. When Miss Jones made her diversion, and the E.B. discovered she was not the woman they were after, they might well suspect the pantechnicon which had drawn out of Hallam and Appleby's yard just then.

They would assume she had contrived to hide herself somehow amid the furniture. But the mobile policeman, having found nobody there, had naturally become inquisitive about the third occupant of the driver's cab. She hoped, but without much conviction, that her husky voice had taken him in. The fact that he pursued the matter no further at the moment was not necessarily reassuring: he could not cut up rough when there were those two stalwarts in the cab to support her. But his search had held up the pantechnicon long enough for more thorough preparations to be made somewhere on the road ahead.

"Yes," said Georgia, "I think they'll try a holdup further along."

"Let 'em try," said the driver with relish. "We'll boomp 'em off t'road. They'll not stop this van, without they dig a hole in front."

After a while Georgia suggested they might turn off the main road: even the E.B. would scarcely dig pits in it, but they could strew nails on the surface. The driver nodded towards his reflecting-mirror. "No use doing that, Miss. We're being followed now. See those lights? I looked back at the curve just now. It's a small van. It could easily pass us if they wanted to. Reckon they're not starting owt yet. They're following oop to make sure you don't pop out of my van."

It was now seven o'clock, and in an hour's time they should have reached the outskirts of Birmingham. Georgia thought that, if she were to jump out of the pantechnicon somewhere in the city, the pursuers in the van would follow her, and she might slip them and rejoin the pantechnicon at a pre-arranged spot, thus throwing them off the scent. But she discarded the plan as quickly as she had made it. The risk of being cut off from her present comrades was too great. Instead, when they had reached the city, she told Joe to drive through the centre instead of taking the bypass. He navigated the one-way-street maze of Birmingham with all the skill of a veteran skipper sailing his ship amidst an archipelago. The following van was following no longer. They had shaken it off.

Their joy was short-lived, however. Emerging on to the Worcester road, on the far side of the city, they soon found the headlights had picked them up again. The van had come straight through on the bypass, or else another one had been waiting here to intercept them. There was nothing for it but to go on, and on they went along the broad, sweeping road through Warwickshire, drinking the coffee and eating the sandwiches which the provident Mr. Dickon had supplied so that they need not stop at any of the pull-ins for lorries.

Georgia was thinking how odd it was that the E.B. should content themselves with this waiting rôle, wondering what the object of these tactics might be, when the pantechnicon rounded a corner, entered a narrower stretch of road, and at that instant they saw a car drawn up across the road right in their path.

Joe had been driving fast and now he stamped the accelerator down to the floor. Whistling through his teeth, he drove the pantechnicon hard at the bonnet of the obstructing car, his own wheels bumping on the verge. "Duck!" cried Georgia, "they'll shoot!" Their huge conveyance struck the car, flipped it aside like a cigarette-card. Faces had appeared in the stream of the headlights, were tossed, bobbed away behind them to a rattle of shots, as if they had been drowning faces swept past into a liner's wake.

"Are we all here still?" asked Joe, chuckling. "Eh, but that was a warm bit of work."

"That's right," said the foreman stolidly. "Now as I was saying, ever since the City signed on Sproston at full-back—"

"Just a minute, boys, before you return to the business of the evening," Georgia interrupted. "I think it's time we got off the main road. We can't go on ramming obstructions all night without damaging this van. Can you find your way along secondary roads, Joe?"

"Can I find the mouth of a bottle of beer, Miss! But what about that van behind? It's still following us."

"I'll settle the van. I'll make 'em wish they had their feet up by the fireside at home. When you're round the next corner, brake hard: but don't stop; slow down, then speed up again."

Georgia, who now felt altogether in her element, opened the cab door, scrambled out over the bonnet and hoisted herself on to the roof. As they rounded the bend, she crawled along the roof to the back of the pantechnicon. She felt it checking under the brakes. The pursuing van swung into sight, overhauling them rapidly. It was less than thirty yards away. Georgia levelled her revolver and aimed at its headlights. It took five shots to knock them both out. Not so bad, she thought, considering I'm a bit out of practice and the way this pantechnicon's swaying. She fired the last shot deliberately into the windscreen of the yawing van, which at once slewed off the road and cocked itself up over the bank.

Feeling rather proud of herself, Georgia scrambled back into the cab. Her companions winked at her solemnly, in unison.

"Has ter been shooting goon?" inquired the foreman.

"Yes, I shot out their headlights. They're ditched."

"Ah. I thought I aird soomething," the foreman commented, sucking his teeth. "Now, as I was telling yer, Joe: Sproston brings him down in t'penalty area, and—"

"If it's O.K. by you, boys," said Georgia humbly, "we'll cut off cross-country now. Wake me up when you've won Coop-Final."

Many sleepy villages, far off the beaten track, heard the thundering vibration of the pantechnicon that December night. To Georgia, dozing in the cab, the drive had all the inconsequence of a dream. Trees, steeples, petrol-pumps, sign-posts, owls, rabbits were picked out by the headlights and streamed continuously through her consciousness. Every hour with forty horse-power I'm getting nearer to Nigel. So what does referee do then, the great gorm? You wanted an adventure, Georgia, my dear. Chilton. That charming smile, that ice-cold heart. The smiler with the knife. Where does that come? Chaucer. Good old Chaucer, he knew. Chaucer, thou shouldst be living at this hour. Chilton Canteloe. There saw I first the dark imagining of felony. Dark. Dark. Darker. . . .

"Wake up, Miss."

"What's—? Where am—where are we?"

"Evesham. Be in Gloucester soon. A chap on a motor-bike stopped us just now. Lost his way, he said. We didn't like the look of him."

The pantechnicon rolled on. Be in Gloucester soon. And then only fifty miles to Oxford. But Georgia felt anxious: it was incredible that the E.B. should have let her through so easily: it was, almost, an anti-climax. No doubt, at this ticklish time, they did not want to call attention to themselves more than was necessary, but—

"Look up there!" Georgia suddenly exclaimed.

At the top of a long rise which the pantechnicon was beginning to climb, against the skyline where the glimmering road surmounted the hill crest, lay a bulk of deeper blackness. The E.B. were making no mistake this time. They had blocked the road at a place where the lorry would be crawling so slowly that it would have no impetus to break through the obstruction.

"Drive straight on," said Georgia urgently. "Tell them you dropped me off at Evesham. Good luck."

The foreman held open the cab door, and she jumped out, landing with relaxed muscles in the ditch, where she rolled safely under cover behind the screen of the pantechnicon's blazing headlights.

# 18. The Episode of
# the Radiance Girls

Georgia's brain always seemed to work quickest in such emergencies. She knew she must get away from this place at once, find somewhere to lie low and change her disguise. But she must wait till the attention of the men in the E.B. ambush was distracted by the pantechnicon. She heard it whining up the hill in bottom gear, then a crash as it struck the obstacle, shouts, sounds of struggle. Driver and foreman were giving a good account of themselves, so that she might have a better chance of getting away. She slipped across the road, found a gate, ran across the field under cover of a hedge.

It was lucky for her that she had kept to this cover. Above the drumming of her heart, she began to hear another noise—an engine roaring. At first she thought her companions must, by some miracle, have repelled their assailants and started up the pantechnicon again. Then the whole night suddenly flowered into a livid light, in which every detail of the landscape for a mile all around could be picked out. What she had heard was the noise of an aeroplane, and it had dropped this flare to light up the scene for the E.B. men.

Georgia froze against the hedge—a pitifully inadequate protection without its summer foliage. Eyes in the aeroplane, she knew, were searching the landscape for her. She felt as big as a haystack. Before the light died out, however, she had got her bearings. In front of her lay an orchard of young trees, and a mile beyond them she had noticed—generously flood-lit by the E.B. aeroplane—a steeple. She must reach that steeple before the cordon was completed.

It was like a vast, mad game of Musical Chairs or General Post. Once inside the orchard, she sprinted from tree to tree, pausing at each, sprinting to the next, hoping not to be caught in the open by one of the flares which the aeroplane sent down at intervals. She did not know whether the men from the ambush had spread out after her, for the roar of the aeroplane drowned all sounds of pursuit. As she neared the village, she realized how lucky for her the flares had been. Not only had they shown her the steeple, but they had awoken all the dogs in the neighbourhood and set them barking. Her pursuers could not reckon on the barking to tell them in what direction she had gone.

At last she reached the church and dodged into its porch to regain her breath. Another flare illuminated the scene. A cock in the farmyard opposite, considerably rattled by this succession of false dawns, crowed peevishly. Georgia found herself giggling: poor cock, it would never quite get its nerve back again. In the light of the flare, she saw a graveyard, an iron gate, an ivy-covered house just beyond. The vicarage, no doubt. When in trouble, apply to the vicar. She went through the gate and paused for a few minutes under the shadow of the vicarage wall, her brain racing to devise a plausible story.

There were no more flares. The sound of the aeroplane died out of the sky, giving way to a well-modulated voice from a window just over her head:

"Winter lightning, my dear. A very remarkable phenomenon. Remind me to write to the *Times* about it tomorrow. Unexampled brilliance. Now I think we may go to bed again."

"But I'm sure it wasn't lightning, dear," said another voice, with a patient stubbornness that suggested the controversy had been raging for some time. "It was that aeroplane. It was trying to land, don't you see?"

"Nonsense, Aggie. There's no aerodrome round here, you know perfectly well. The phenomenon of lightning, unaccompanied by thunder, is, grant you, at this time of year, unusual. But not unprecedented. Not, I assure you, unprecedented. I well recollect—"

"But it wasn't lightning," said Georgia, standing out from the shadow of the wall. "Honestly it wasn't. It was me. My engine failed and I had to throw out flares. I managed to get down safely in a meadow just over there."

"God bless my soul!" exclaimed the vicar. "An aviatrix!"

In the dark, Georgia's white overalls might well have been a flying-suit. She had removed her moustache in the church porch, and the cloth cap was now concealed under her coat. The vicar's wife, a kindly, plain woman, insisted on supporting Georgia indoors and brewing her a cup of Ovaltine, while her husband fluttered in the background, glancing at Georgia half-incredulously, half-complacently, as though she had been no less than an angel alighted out of heaven on his doorstep.

I'm sitting pretty for the moment, she thought; but, unless Joe and the foreman convince them that I dropped off at Eversham, the E.B. will go over this district with a fine-tooth comb. That story about the aeroplane has got me into the vicarage all right, but it'd be the finish of me as soon as it reached the E.B.'s ears.

Georgia decided she must tell Mrs. Fortescue something of the real story. A certain amount of resistance had to be broken down, for the Fortescues had come to this village from a large town parish, and she was up to all the tricks of professional beggars: indeed, she had become adept at exposing people who tried to take advantage of her husband's unworldliness and generosity. At first, therefore, Mrs. Fortescue lent a by no means ready ear to Georgia's tale. But before long a gleam began to light her tired, kindly eyes: there was a romantic in her which had not been stifled by all these years of drudgery and good works. Romance, adventure had now landed out of the night on to her doorstep, disguised as a small, brown-eyed, magnetic woman in disreputable man's clothing, and Mrs. Fortescue was transfigured. She agreed to hide Georgia in the vicarage till they had worked out the best method of getting her away. In the meanwhile she would impress upon her husband the necessity of saying nothing about their midnight visitor.

"And I only hope nobody asks him," she added, smiling gently. "Poor Herbert is the most unconvincing liar I've ever known. I remember once when the bishop came to stay and our little dog ate the episcopal braces—but I mustn't waste time with that. Luckily our maid doesn't sleep in, so nobody but us could have heard you."

Georgia slept late next morning in the attic where Mrs. Fortescue had made her a bed. She slept through

the arrival of two men at breakfast-time and their discomfiture by the vicar's wife. They claimed to be plain-
clothes police inquiring about a young woman wanted
on a charge of car-stealing and last seen in this vicinity.

"No," said Mrs. Fortescue, firmly entrenched on
her doorstep, "No one came here last night, I can assure you."

"This woman might have got in while you were
asleep. I suppose you have no objection to our searching the house?"

"Of course not. Provided you have a search warrant."

"Well, as a matter of fact, madam—"

"You haven't? I'm afraid, in that case—"

The men began to bluster. Mrs. Fortescue was not
in the least alarmed by them, but she was on tenterhooks
lest their voices should fetch her husband out from the
dining-room, where he was deeply engaged with a boiled
egg and the *Church Times*.

"I'm sorry," she said. "We get so many beggars and
undesirable characters at the vicarage, I couldn't possibly let you in until you've established your bona fides.
Good day to you."

She related the episode to Georgia when she brought
up her breakfast tray. Evidently the village of Nether
Cheype was in a state of siege. Not only would it be
difficult for Georgia to be smuggled out, but there was
great danger even in getting a message through to London or Oxford. Mrs. Fortescue dared not leave Georgia alone in the house, and at the same time she had
to keep a watchful eye on her husband lest his lips
should become unsealed or his conscience, already irked
by the duplicity in which she had involved him, should
get the better of him.

They remained silent for a while. Glancing at the

paper Mrs. Fortescue had brought up, Georgia noticed a bulletin about Sir John Strangeways: he was still in a critical condition, but hopes of ultimate recovery were now entertained. Well, thank God for that, she thought, and fell to wondering about the fate of her two companions last night. Her thoughts were interrupted at last by Mrs. Fortescue who asked, with apparent irrelevance:

"Do you know anything about eurhythmics, dear?"

"Eurhythmics? I used to do them at school. I should think my kind must be out of date by now. Why?"

"I'm just wondering if the Radiance Girls wouldn't be our solution," said Mrs. Fortescue, tapping her teeth with a pencil and frowning down at the shopping-list in her hand.

"The Radiance Girls?" asked Georgia meekly. Nothing had any power to surprise her now.

"Herbert thinks it's all rather pagan. But, as I tell him, if the morals of our village can't stand up to a few strapping young ladies in magenta knickers, they're past praying for. Besides, we get them free. And it's such a pity we don't make more use of that stage Lady Cheype presented to the village hall. Though it would be terrible if they broke it—they do jump about rather, don't they?"

Nothing to the way *you* jump about, thought Georgia. But she let Mrs. Fortescue run on. The vicar's wife was expanding almost visibly under the influence of Georgia and the extraordinary situation into which she had been plunged. Her flow of inconsequential talk made it difficult for one to remember that they were ringed round by danger and that every way out was probably blocked by desperate men, who would hardly allow even a black-beetle to leave the district without subjecting it to their scrutiny.

Mrs. Fortescue might try one's patience with her amiable ramblings, but she certainly got somewhere in the end. Georgia realized that, for the second time in two days, her safety was being catered for by a born organizer. Mrs. Fortescue's plan was that Georgia should change places with one of the Radiance Girls when they visited Nether Cheype tomorrow night to give an exhibition of eurhythmics—or, as the leader of the Sisterhood of Radiance preferred to term it, "Psycho-physical Irradiation." The Sisterhood, which throve in places where there was a superfluity of women with more time than sex-appeal on their hands, had a centre in Cheltenham whence they sent out parties round the countryside to propagate their particular blend of theosophy and physical jerks. They would be arriving at Nether Cheype in a small private bus and departing as soon as their show had finished.

Manifesting the wisdom of the serpent, Mrs. Fortescue informed Georgia that the Sisterhood laid great importance upon the mystical number, seven: they always performed in teams of seven, led by the indefatigable Miss Lobelia Agg-Thoresby. What could be simpler than for one of the Radiance Girls to become indisposed on arriving at the vicarage, and for Georgia to volunteer to make up the mystical number? Miss Agg-Thoresby, the vicar's wife opined, would stretch a point over Georgia's doubtless not altogether satisfactory aura if thereby she could be assured of keeping the seven intact.

The idea of eluding the E.B., disguised as a ray of sunshine, tickled Georgia's fancy immensely. She feared at first that Mrs. Fortescue intended to poison one of the Radiance Girls in order to make a gap for herself: but Mrs. Fortescue assured her that she knew personally one of the visiting team, a woman not too dissimilar to Georgia in build and appearance, and could work the transposition quite easily. The main difficulty would be to keep this girl tucked out of sight till Georgia had got well away from Nether Cheype.

For the next thirty hours or so, Georgia had to possess her soul in patience. She dared not leave the attic or even move about in it much during the daytime, lest she should betray her presence to the Fortescues' maid. The vicar made his sole appearance on the Thursday afternoon, bringing her a book of sermons, a bound volume of *Punch* and a brochure of his own authorship on the antiquities of Tewkesbury Abbey. At intervals Mrs. Fortescue darted in with food and gossip: there was plenty of gossip in the village just now, what with last night's aeroplane, the collision between a car and a pantechnicon on Rootley Hill, and the presence of so many inquisitive strangers in the district.

At last Friday night came, and the Radiance Girls with it. Their leader, Lobelia Agg-Thoresby, was the flattest woman Georgia had ever seen: "willowy" was the word Lobelia applied to herself; Georgia, regarding the flat figure in its drooping poses, nicknamed her "the Curve to end all Curves." Her only salient features were a thin, jutting nose and a pair of rather protuberant eyes, both of which came into play when, quarter of an hour after their arrival, Miss Blande announced that she felt ill and could not take part in the exhibition tonight.

Miss Agg-Thoresby's eyes registered suffering and spiritual resignation, her nose twitched with less refined emotions.

"Nonsense, Mabel," she said. "We don't understand the word 'illness.' It's not in our vocabulary. Your soul is a little out of tune, dear, that's all. Breathe deeply

244

and plunge yourself into the Infinite."

Mabel Blande followed her leader's instructions, but to no purpose.

"I'm sorry," she said obstinately. "It doesn't seem to—I mean, I must have eaten something that disagreed with me."

Miss Agg-Thoresby winced. Mrs. Fortescue, who had been watching the scene with an expressionless face, now remarked,

"I'm afraid she does look rather unw—rather out of tune. I think you'll have to—er—perform without her."

"We don't *perform*, Mrs. Fortescue," said Lobelia gently. "We *interpret*. We are vessels. We receive, and we pour out. But it's quite out of the question," she went on more sharply. "We must have seven. The seven-pointed star, you see. But I'm afraid you wouldn't understand."

"Perhaps my friend, Miss Lestrange, could help you," replied the vicar's wife, pointing to Georgia.

Miss Agg-Thoresby's pale eyes turned slowly towards Georgia, focussed on her as though she were an object infinitely remote, to whom distance lent only a dubious enchantment.

"Are you initiated, Miss Lestrange? Are you of us?"

"Oh, yes, indeed," answered Georgia boldly. "In my own circle I am known as the seventh pillar of light."

Miss Agg-Thoresby expressed her satisfaction, and they all retired to change for the rehearsal. Georgia put on Miss Blande's garments. The seven wore flowing orange draperies which, in their less statuesque movements, were discarded to reveal magenta knickers and brassière—the latter being for Miss Agg-Thoresby rather in the position of a sinecure, Georgia imagined. The rehearsal went off fairly well, and Georgia had little difficulty in picking up the hang of the thing. She was not sorry, however, when Lobelia approached her afterwards, cooing:

"Yes, dear. I can see you have the" — her hands wove a misty gesture out of thin air — "the *tone*, the *vibrations*. But perhaps you'd better remain rather in the background this time."

"Of course." The background is just where I want to remain, Georgia reflected. Still, Mrs. Fortescue was quite right that I must take part in the performance in order to establish myself as one of the Radiance Girls and get away with them afterwards. Let's hope the village hall is not too well lighted.

Miss Agg-Thoresby had seen to that, it transpired. She had had the flood-lights swathed in red, so that the Radiance Girls posed and moved in a dim, pink glow which gave them, when the draperies were discarded, the appearance of being lightly coated with Euthymol toothpaste.

The village audience was somewhat overawed by Miss Agg-Thoresby's opening remarks, which urged them to relax, breathe deeply, and render their souls plastic to the influence of Psycho-physical Irradiation as about to be let loose by the seven. It remained impervious to the orange-draperied evolutions, too. But when the Radiance Girls put off their outer coverings and began to prance in all the glory of magenta knickers and toothpaste-pink flesh, psycho-physical irradiation really seemed to set in on the audience. A gasp went up. Some hardier spirits at the back, whistling, cat-calling and stamping their feet on the boards, began to evince a plasticity of soul which the vicar found it necessary to quell rather soon. While a very old man by the gangway remarked audibly that that were a tidy bit a goods in the front row, dang his eyes if her weren't.

It's lucky, thought Georgia as she wove about on the stage, that this gang goes in for free interpretation, or I'd be shown up properly. Remaining well in the background, she let her eyes rove over the audience. They were mostly village women, with a sprinkling of youths. She noticed one man, leaning against the side wall, who looked rather out of place here: he wore riding-breeches and a check coat, he had a heavy, lowering face; and his eyes were scrutinizing the audience covertly, intently, as though taking a silent roll-call.

After the first interpretation was over, Miss Agg-Thoresby delivered some poems of her own composition in front of the closed curtain. Georgia drew aside Mrs. Fortescue, who was helping behind the scenes, led her on to the stage, and asked her to peep through the curtain.

"Who's that young man standing up at the side — the one in riding-breeches?"

"Let's see now. Oh, that's Mr. Raynham."

"A local?"

"Yes. He came here about five years ago. He's a gentleman farmer. I mean, that's what he calls himself. If you ask me, he never was a gentleman and never will be a farmer," Mrs. Fortescue giggled: then looked rather ashamed at her own malice. "My dear, I'm afraid you lead me on. I'm sure he's quite a worthy young man in his way."

And *I'm* quite sure, thought Georgia, that he's one of the E.B. I must keep my weather eye lifting for him. When the Radiance Girls took the stage again, Georgia noticed Mr. Raynham observing them attentively. After a few moments he walked out, making no attempt to soften the clump of his boots on the wooden floor.

A mannerless young man, thought Georgia: but that's scarcely the point just now. Is he quick-witted, too? Did he spot me? Has he gone out to make preparations?

Twenty minutes more, and the show was over. The vicar, bemused but still courteous, made a speech of thanks. The team retired to change. This was going to be the awkward passage. Mrs. Fortescue took Lobelia Agg-Thoresby aside, told her that Miss Blande was too ill to travel tonight, asked if "Miss Lestrange" could go back in the bus with them instead. She and Georgia had previously decided that this, though risky, would be a safer course than for Georgia to try and pass herself off as Miss Blande to the team in general when they embarked on the bus. On receiving Miss Agg-Thoresby's assent, the vicar's wife sat down beside Georgia and whispered:

"Someone's been in the vicarage while we were out. We left it locked: but I found a window opened when I went back just now."

"What about Miss Blande?"

"She's all right. I took her across to a neighbour just before the show started, as we arranged. I'm sure no one could have seen us—it was pitch dark: and the neighbour won't talk. We'll smuggle her out of the village in a couple of days' time. Will that give you long enough?"

"Mrs. Fortescue, you've been an angel. I don't know how to thank you," said Georgia, pressing her hand.

"Don't be silly, my dear. It's I who should thank you. I don't get so much excitement that—well, never mind—I hope everything will go well with you. Let us know, won't you?"

Lobelia Agg-Thoresby marshalled the Radiance Girls and hooshed them outside. A few villagers, standing by the roadside, watched them phlegmatically. There was no sign of the young man in the riding-breeches. Carrying the suitcase Mrs. Fortescue had lent her, wearing the vicar's-wifely clothes which Mrs. Fortescue had altered for her yesterday, Georgia darted into the small private bus. The seats faced each other along the sides of the vehicle. Georgia took up her position at the far end from the driver, next to the emergency-door. It was vaguely comforting to be there, though she did not suppose any emergency-door would be adequate to the kind of emergency the E.B. might contrive.

Miss Agg-Thoresby clambered in last, throwing over her shoulder a parting remark to the vicar, whom she had been attempting to proselytize:

"But it's not religious, Mr. Fortescue. It's just cosmic."

The bus started . . .

# 19. The Episode of the Station Barrow

In the rackety bus, Georgia weighed up her chances. She had little doubt that they would be stopped by the E.B. before they left the district. If she managed to get past them unrecognized then, she would be out of the danger zone — or the worst part of it, and could take a train from Cheltenham to Oxford. The very thought made her almost crazy with relief and happiness, but she thrust it firmly from her. Time enough for that, if and when . . . The question was, had she been recognized by the "gentleman farmer," Mr. Raynham, in the village hall? If not, the scrutiny of the bus would be more perfunctory and she might get through. If she had been recognized, her number was up. She put the odds against herself at three to one, therefore. Had she known who was awaiting the bus a mile ahead, in a car drawn up by the roadside, she would have made a very different bet.

The bus clattered through the night. The Radiance Sisters chatted desultorily. Presently the driver, perceiving the bull's-eye of a torch waving at him from the middle of the road ahead, slowed down and came to a halt.

Now for it, thought Georgia. She pulled Mrs. Fortescue's hat closer down upon her head, adjusted the old pair of pince-nez Mrs. Fortescue had lent her. A pitiful disguise, she thought: "there's more enterprise in walking naked."

A man opened the sliding door in front and held a brief, muttered conversation with the driver. It was Mr. Raynham. He glanced up and down the aisle of the bus, his eyes pausing on Georgia a moment. Then he said to Miss Agg-Thoresby:

"Sorry to hold you up and all that. Was driving a friend of mine into Cheltenham—car broke down. He's in rather a hurry—he's got to catch a train. D'you mind taking him along with you?"

The leader of the Radiance Girls fluttered, blushed, said, "Why, of course. Certainly." Georgia was edging her hands towards the bar of the emergency-door: but then she saw a couple of men standing in the roadway behind. She couldn't understand the tactics of the E.B. patrol. Nor was she given any leisure to contemplate them. A little stir and mutter went up from the Radiance Girls—a kind of stir created by an invalid or a blind man when he comes into a room full of people. The man whom Mr. Raynham was helping into the bus was, indeed, blind. At least, he wore a shade over his eyes and held a walking-stick out in front of him like an antenna. There were sympathetic murmurs, in which the word "blind" vaguely recurred.

"Blind," Georgia wanted to shriek: "that's not the point, you fools! It's you who are blind! Can't you see? Don't you know who this is? Don't you know it's Chilton Canteloe?"

251

In a flash, while Mr. Raynham solicitously escorted Chilton down the gangway towards the vacant seat beside Georgia, she realized the whole truth. On hearing of her escape from the ambushed pantechnicon, Chilton must have hurried to the district to direct operations himself, preferring that he should lose his anonymity as leader of the E.B. rather than that she should slip through their hands again. The local E.B. no doubt had no more than a photograph and verbal description of Georgia to go on. Mr. Raynham thought he had recognized her on the village-hall stage, but he could not be sure. Chilton was here to make sure. He did not need the sight of his eyes to recognize her.

All he had to do was to sit down beside her, as he was sitting down now, and whisper, "Good evening, Georgia."

She knew that any attempt to disguise her voice would be futile. She might waste a little time that way; but what was the use?

"Good evening, Chilton," she said. "Fancy meeting you here."

"I thought so," he remarked, loud enough for Mr. Raynham to hear, who at once moved back along the gangway to sit next to the driver. Chilton, leaning towards her, began whispering again.

"Are you going to come quietly, as they say?"

"And if I don't?"

"My friend has a revolver. He will compel the driver to turn up a side road. There'll be a car following, and everybody will be taken out of this bus and shot. I can't leave any loose ends just now."

Georgia knew he was not bluffing. There was an edge to his voice, cold as steel, utterly merciless.

"Very well," she said.

The bus rattled on. The Radiance Girls chattered, yawned, threw curious glances at the handsome, blind man sitting so quietly there. A motor-bike and sidecar, travelling fast, roared past them and ahead. Presently Chilton's stick fell with a clatter to the floor. It must have been a pre-arranged signal. Mr. Raynham looked round, then spoke to the driver. The bus ground to a halt, a car stopping just behind it.

"They seem to have got our car to go," Mr. Raynham said. "Here it is. We'd better change back into it. Thanks for the lift."

"Would you care to come with us?" Chilton asked Georgia. "The chauffeur can drop you at your destination after he's left me at the station."

"Thanks very much." Georgia would have liked to add, "Lord Canteloe," but she knew it would seal the fate of every one in the bus. Mr. Raynham helped Chilton through the emergency-door, then politely lifted out Georgia's suitcase. She felt quite numb as they escorted her to the waiting car: helpless as a cork on a stormy sea. Is this what people feel like when they walk out to their execution, she dimly wondered—to the blindfold drop, the bloodstained wall?

They put her into the back of the car. Fatalistically, as one who greets a death grown familiar by suffering and long expectation, she breathed in without a struggle the chloroform of the pad that was held over her face. She thought, why bother with all this? The last thing she heard was Chilton saying, "Don't be rough with her. I want to deal with her myself, later. . . ."

She awoke in utter darkness. Her head ached, and the fumes of chloroform were in her throat, mingled with a faint smell of mildew. The darkness appalled her. For a moment she was seized by an absolute terror, believing that Chilton had already taken his revenge and put out her eyes. Then, coming right out of the anaesthetic, she realized how absurd this was: there was no pain in her eyes — yet.

Her bag, containing the papers of Plan A, and her revolver, had been taken away. Automatically she felt inside her clothes, to see if they had found the copy which she had stitched up in her corselette. No, it was still there. Not that it made any difference. They'd never let her get out of this place alive. Where was she, anyway?

With a dull curiosity, she began to feel her way through the darkness. Smooth stone floor, damp walls, a window boarded up with wood: a room about twelve foot square, smelling of mildew. The living-room of some derelict cottage, she imagined: on the land of Mr. Raynham, perhaps — Mr. Raynham who had never been a gentleman and never would be a farmer. She tried to find a crack in the boarded window: it seemed suddenly important to know whether it was still night outside: but there were not cracks big enough to see through. The emptiness of the room, like some figure in a nightmare which advances step by step from immeasurable distance to reveal its sinister intent, gradually forced its full meaning upon her.

It was to be the arena of her last struggle with Chilton Canteloe. Nor did he intend to give her the least chance. Every scrap of wood or old metal, which she might have used for a weapon, had been removed. For an instant, panic got the better of her. She ran at the door, beat her fists against the panel. As if it had been a signal, footsteps were heard outside. Georgia ran back and crouched in a far corner. Chilton Canteloe was saying to someone:

"All right. I'll go in now. You can lock the door behind me."

The door opened and closed, revealing a faint false dawn that disappeared at once and made the darkness more intense. Georgia could hear his unhurried breathing twelve feet away. She imagined the smile on his face.

"Well, Georgia, pipped on the post, aren't you?"

She said nothing.

"I've been looking forward to our reunion. You nearly blinded me that night. They say I may recover my sight, however. Won't you congratulate me? I'm afraid you'll not recover yours, my dear. I shall make quite certain of that."

Georgia remained silent, immobile, though she felt that her heart, lurching inside her body so sickeningly, must betray her.

"Wouldn't you like to scream, or something?" he asked politely. "No one will hear you, of course, but they say it brings relief. No? Well, I hope you'll enjoy our little game of Blind Man's Bluff in your own quiet way, then."

He began to advance upon her through the darkness. Her only instinct was to keep away from those outstretched fingers as long as she could. Or perhaps his arms were swinging loosely before him in that bear-like gait she recollected too well. She slipped aside from his first rush, vaguely surprised that her feet made no sound on the stone floor, realizing for the first time that they had taken her shoes away. Of course they had. A shoe's heel would serve at a pinch for a weapon. Chilton was thorough.

For a few minutes she continued to elude him. But her efforts made her breathe hard, and she knew her breathing must give her away. Round and across the room he lumbered after her, his fingers feeling at the darkness like antennae, taking his time about it. There was a remorselessness, a horror about the blind pursuit which made her want to shriek for help, though no help could ever come; but she was determined not to let Chilton have this triumph over her weakness too. At last, almost distraught, she decided to end it. Standing still against the wall, breathing hard, she awaited his leisurely approach. When she heard him close in front, she hurled herself forward knee-high in the darkness, hoping that she might knock him off his feet, perhaps crack his head against the stone floor in falling, anything to stop this cruel, deadly game he was playing with her.

Her body struck his legs just above the knee. He fell forward, but in doing so grabbed her dress. Now she was aware of his strength. She struggled like a wildcat, but soon he had her down, his knees pressing into her body, his fingers feeling delicately towards her eyes. Suddenly she went limp. She knew that this ice-cold, chuckling maniac would defer his revenge if he believed she had fainted. He wanted her to feel it all.

"Oh, no, Georgia, it won't do. Don't pretend you've passed out," said Chilton and, lifting her limp hand, deliberately broke the little finger. Georgia bit her lip to repress a cry, but a shudder of agony went through her body, and now she fainted in real earnest . . .

At this moment, two men appeared outside the derelict cottage, gave a pass-word to the guard at the door, and were directed towards the little room where Chilton and Georgia had struggled.

"A message for the Chief. Urgent," said one of the men to the guard outside the room.

"He's busy," said the man, jerking his head towards the door.

An E.B. badge was flashed before his eyes. "Open up, blast you, or he'll take it out of you."

The guard turned to unlock the door. . . .

Coming out of her swoon, Georgia moaned. She was being carried like a sack, slung over a man's shoulders. They were emerging into cold air and the beginnings of dawn. She heard the man who carried her say to someone:

"It's O.K., boys. The Chief told us to take this dame away — what's left of her — and dig a nice deep hole. He's busy over the message we brought him, and doesn't want to be disturbed for half an hour. So long."

Georgia's brain began to work quickly. Chilton could only have meant to frighten her, then. Well, he'd done that all right. But it was these men who were to be the executioners. Better them, a thousand times, than — and she might even escape them, now she was out into the open, out of that devilish, mildew-smelling room.

The men bundled her into a car. They set off, bumping fast down a grassy track. Georgia pretended to be unconscious still, hoarding her strength for a last effort. The two men remained silent. After about ten minutes the car slowed down. She was lifted out, hoisted on a shoulder again, carried quickly towards a high bank which she was seeing upside down. They were scrambling up the bank. Suddenly, with a dreadful stab of fear, Georgia recognized that it was a railway embankment. They were not going to "dig a nice deep hole" for her: they were going to put her across the line in front of a train: neater, in a way. She stayed relaxed, waiting till they put her down before springing to life.

But they were carrying her across the metals, towards a small shed at the side — a plate-layer's hut. The door was opened. A man in greasy clothes, neckerchief and cloth cap was sitting inside, his back turned to them, warming his hands over an oil-stove. As they entered and she was put gently down, he turned round, sprang forward, held out his hands. With a gasp of pure astonishment, Georgia stumbled forward into Sir John Strangeways' arms. . . .

A few minutes later, revivified with brandy, she was saying shakily:

"But I thought you were—the papers said—"

"I'm tougher than they give me credit for. Actually, I left the nursing-home a couple of days ago, but we thought it best for the E.B. to imagine I was still there."

Sir John's eyes twinkled in his dirty face.

"You do look ruffianly, Uncle John. I never supposed a man in your exalted position would descend to these low disguises. How did you find me? Is Nigel all right? Where is he?"

"He's very well. Awaiting you in Oxford. I've had some trouble keeping him out of this, especially when we heard you were on the run. We found you by keeping tabs on Canteloe in the first place: we knew he would come out in the open after you'd got away with the plans. He followed you, and we followed him. The two chaps who drove you in that pantechnicon turned up trumps too. They had a bit of a towsing from the E.B. men, but they got away in the end and turned in a report at the nearest police-station. Luckily the Inspector there was a sound chap. He phoned through to me, and that's how we knew you were in this district. It was the first we'd heard of you since you rang up Alison Grove from Manchester. Even then, you'd concealed yourself so well that we couldn't find another trace of you for a bit. I was getting a little worried."

"I was getting a little worried myself," Georgia replied sardonically.

"At any rate," said Sir John, vigorously rubbing his moustache, "my men who were tailing Canteloe saw him stop that bus you were in last night. Queer company you do keep nowadays, Georgia. The Radiance Girls! Oh my aunt! Well, they followed you up to that cottage. Couldn't do any more. Too strongly guarded. Afraid there was a bit of a delay there. Had to call up two of my chaps who are in the E.B. and send them to hoick you out. A ticklish business, my dear. I didn't dare attack the place in force—I knew they'd kill you the instant the alarm was given."

"He didn't need any alarm to do that—or try his hardest to," Georgia said. She still found it difficult to mention Chilton Canteloe by name. Sir John leant forward and stroked her hand, noticing the way she winced when accidentally he touched the little finger he had reset and bandaged in a make-shift splint. A look came into Sir John's blue eyes—a look Georgia had seen once or twice on Nigel's face, and was never likely to forget: a smouldering anger that would not be extinguished till somebody had paid up in full.

"Canteloe will not be allowed any more rope," said Sir John, "you can be sure of that. Let me see the plans."

"I shall have to undress a bit. I've been using them to pad out my meagre figure."

"You've done very well, my dear. We're all proud of you. I don't think anybody else could have pulled it off."

Sir John's brisk, kindly voice brought tears to her eyes. She felt suddenly weak, ready to indulge in one of her very rare moments of self-pity.

"He—he was trying to put out my eyes, Uncle John," she said in a wavering voice.

"He was, was he? Well, I don't expect he's feeling too good himself at the moment. Here, take another swig at the brandy, my dear. That's right. The man who rescued you knocked the guard over the head as he was unlocking the door. Then they did the same for Canteloe. They left the two of them locked up in the room. The cottage is surrounded. It's all over now, bar the shooting," said Sir John grimly.

"Here's what he called Plan A. And this is his double-cross, Plan B."

"Yes," said Sir John, after he had glanced through the second document. "I never suspected this. He was bigger, in his damnable way, than I reckoned. Shall I thank you all over again?"

"Don't be a goose." Georgia rubbed his oily sleeve affectionately. "You know, you look rather impressive as a plate-layer. Is it a plate-layer you're meant to be? Do you know how to lay plates? I'm sure you do—you know everything. I—oh hell!—"

Georgia surprised them both by bursting suddenly and comprehensively into a flood of tears.

"There, darling, it's all right, it's all over and done with," said Sir John, taking her into his arms. . . .

Later that morning she was travelling in a train through the Cotswolds. Her compartment was locked. One of Sir John's men was sitting with her, another stood in the corridor outside. As she looked out of the window, it seemed to her that never in all her travels had she seen anything as beautiful as this country, the stone-built walls and villages, the hills modest in their brown-green winter dress. At one point the London road ran close beside the railway. Along this road, a few hours ago, had travelled a convoy of armoured cars—a common enough sight on the roads today, only that the guns of these cars were loaded and their crews alert in the turrets. Sir John Strangeways was taking no chances. Nothing short of an earthquake or an army brigade would stop him getting to London with the E.B. plans.

Georgia's eyes returned to the countryside sweeping past. The little train puffed importantly along, hurrying to catch the express at Kingham. The hills unfolded, as if they were taking the train into their gentle arms. Hurry, train, hurry, thought Georgia. Nigel is waiting for me at Oxford. We mustn't keep him waiting. Nearly a whole year now—that's a long time out of one's life. Will he look just the same? I'm safe, I'm safe, I'm safe! I'd forgotten what the word "safety" meant. We're all safe, all the decent, ordinary, hard-working people, the people who make England . . .

In the station yard at Oxford, ten minutes before the train was due, stood a sports-car, its engine ticking over. There were two men in it, men with thick necks and small, stupid, arrogant eyes. One of them played with the safety-catch of a revolver. They had driven up to the station after a telephone call had come through ordering them to get Georgia Strangeways at all costs.

One man had slipped through the cordon Sir John had thrown round the derelict cottage. Chilton Canteloe, on recovering consciousness and finding Georgia gone, knew that he was finished. The whole rancour of his defeat concentrated itself upon Georgia, who had turned all his plans and ambitions to dust. She, at least, should not live to enjoy her triumph. His last order to the E.B. was that Georgia Strangeways must be killed. He did not tell them the killing would be as pointless as a boy crushing an ant under his foot, though the manner of Georgia's rescue left no doubt in his own mind that by now she must have passed the plans into other hands.

The man with the revolver glanced at his wrist-watch. "Due in any moment now," he said. "Suppose we can get away O.K.? Seem to be a lot of people waiting about."

"You plug this woman and I'll do the rest. Getting cold feet or what? They'll not be expecting any one to start anything here . . ."

The train slowed down along the platform. Standing at the window, Georgia could not see Nigel at all: there was such a crowd of undergraduates milling about. It must be a rag, she thought. Then a tall figure came thrusting down the platform. It was Nigel. For a moment they stood there, holding hands, beaming all over their faces, unable to say a word.

"Well, you got here all right," Nigel got out at last. It was not one of the world's most memorable sayings, but Georgia would never forget it.

"Yes. I got here. You're looking very well. Oh, darling, I just can't kiss you in front of all these young men. Why are they staring at me so? Is my hat on upside down?"

"Well, as a matter of fact they're a kind of reception. For you. Just a little tribute to—"

"Nigel, I flatly refuse—"

"Come on, boys."

A flat luggage-barrow, something like a coster's cart, emerged from the crowd. Before Georgia could begin to protest, she was hoisted up by three pairs of arms and seated firmly in the barrow. Nigel pushed it towards the exit.

"Nigel, you devil. I'll never forgive you for this," she yelled at him; but her voice was drowned by the laughing, cheering mob of undergraduates, who formed a phalanx all round the barrow and marched out thus into the station yard, showering platform-tickets all over the bemused ticket-collector as they passed.

"What the devil's all this?" exclaimed the man with the revolver to his companion in the red sports-car.

"There she is!" said the other. "That's her. Make it snappy now!"

"Christ, I can't shoot through that mob. They'd lynch us." His revolver wavered in his hand, trying to find an opening amid the crowd that hemmed the barrow round.

Wheeling the barrow, regardless of his wife's black looks, Nigel thought of the phone message he had received from his uncle early this morning. "They may try something on at Oxford," Sir John had said. "One of them got away from my men, and Canteloe's quite cross with Georgia. I can't spare more than two men for a bodyguard, so you'd better see to it. If possible, she mustn't know. She's rather near the edge."

Nigel had seen to it. He didn't want Georgia to be alarmed. She'd been through enough already. So he had hit on the idea of an undergraduate rag and told his young cousin to organize it.

Georgia, fuming at this dreadful publicity, yet beginning to be infected by the wild hilarity of her escort and the ludicrousness of the whole situation, was wheeled out through the station yard, quite oblivious of the killer whose gun poked ineffectively at the crowd, only ten yards away from her body as they passed the red sports-car. Nor was she in a position to see Sir John's two men, who had escorted her in the train and were now walking rather sheepishly at the tail of the procession, suddenly grow tense as they observed the cold glint of metal half concealed by the E.B. man's gauntlet—grow tense, give each other one glance, swerve aside a little from the procession, and pounce on the occupants of the sports-car.

None of this did Georgia see. Down the station road they went, over the canal, across the Cornmarket into the Broad, the crowd swelling every minute, windows opening in the staid college walls—a shouting, cheering, singing crowd, with the small, brown-eyed woman on the station-barrow quite lost in their midst. But Georgia was now enjoying herself. Yes, she was really enjoying her triumph. Bless you, Nigel, you crazy darling idiot. Bless you all.

# 20. The Episode of the Last Laugh

Georgia and Nigel were driving home to Devonshire. It was a week after her triumphal procession through the streets of Oxford. During this week, she had received communications from several Important Personages; they wished her to come to London and receive the thanks of the Nation from them, but she pleaded ill-health, preferring to stay with Nigel in the peace of Oxford. As a matter of fact, with her extraordinary resilience she had quickly overcome the effects of those last desperate days: the whole of this year now seemed to her a nightmare interlude in a normal life, and she did not wish to be reminded of it by the fulsome compliments of politicians whose own pusillanimity or self-interest were responsible for its having happened at all. She had performed her task, and wanted no thanks for something which should never have been necessary.

During this week Sir John Strangeways, with the speed of attack, the economy and decisiveness of a great general, broke the E.B. for good and all. There were a few sporadic outbreaks of violence up and down the country; but the E.B., leaderless and bewildered, forced prematurely into a rising that had already lost its heart, caved in quickly. Chilton Canteloe had made a fatal mistake in not launching the rebellion a week ago, when Georgia first escaped from his burning house. But, with Sir John out of action and Georgia's recapture, as he believed, only a matter of hours, he had decided to keep his men in check. The arrangements for foreign intervention had not been wholly completed; and, like other dictators and would-be dictators, he was misled by vainglory and the flattery of subordinates into underestimating the opposition.

During his first period of imprisonment, Chilton had leisure to meditate these mistakes. His thoughts were sufficiently disagreeable to break down the thin partition that had stood between him and madness. When the other leaders of the E.B. came up to stand their trial, Chilton was already tucked away in an asylum, where he spent much of his time playing with a mechanical race-horse and a rocking-horse . . .

Georgia leant her head against Nigel's shoulder. The little car bumped and swayed up the lane towards their cottage, brambles scraping against its side. A plume of smoke rose out of their chimney, that appeared above the top of the unkempt hedge. Georgia felt weak with happiness: this home-coming was almost worth their year of separation and everything she had endured. Suddenly she put her hand to her mouth.

"Heavens, darling!" she exclaimed. "We forgot—"

She couldn't go on. She gestured weakly towards the hedge, neatly pared on the far side, but rank and luxuriant all along the border of their own property.

"But Coombes was told to keep the garden tidy for me," said Nigel.

"Poor old Coombes has a very literal mind. If you didn't mention the hedge, he wouldn't do the hedge."

They garaged the car and went indoors. There were a few bills and letters lying on the table. Georgia began opening them.

"Nigel, come here. The worst has happened," she cried tragically.

"What's that?"

"Look, a notice from the Council. It starts off, 'Inasmuch as . . .' There's a nasty ring about that phrase. Yes, we've failed to cut our hedge, we have to appear before a Justice of the Peace, we are to be prosecuted. D'you think they'll put us in prison?"

"I'm afraid so," said Nigel solemnly. "We have broken the law. We must pay."

Georgia waved the official notice in the air. "The Thanks of a Grateful Country," she declaimed. "I shall wear it next my heart for ever."

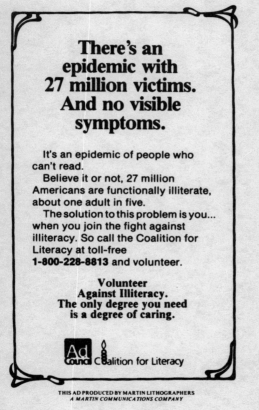

# There's an epidemic with 27 million victims. And no visible symptoms.

It's an epidemic of people who can't read.

Believe it or not, 27 million Americans are functionally illiterate, about one adult in five.

The solution to this problem is you... when you join the fight against illiteracy. So call the Coalition for Literacy at toll-free **1-800-228-8813** and volunteer.

**Volunteer
Against Illiteracy.
The only degree you need
is a degree of caring.**

Ad Council    Coalition for Literacy

THIS AD PRODUCED BY MARTIN LITHOGRAPHERS
*A MARTIN COMMUNICATIONS COMPANY*